S0-DFK-207

The POWER

The POWER

STANLEY BRZYCKI

THE POWER

This is a work of fiction. All of the characters, names, incidents, organizations, and dialogue in this novel are either the products of the author's imagination or are used fictitiously.

iUniverse books may be ordered through booksellers or by contacting:

iUniverse
1663 Liberty Drive
Bloomington, IN 47403
www.iuniverse.com
1-800-Authors (1-800-288-4677)

ISBN: 978-1-4917-6891-4 (sc)
ISBN: 978-1-4917-6893-8 (hc)
ISBN: 978-1-4917-6892-1 (e)

Print information available on the last page.

iUniverse rev. date: 06/17/2015

To Cathy 9-11-15
When you're alone and
you hear a noise that
is un-natural... know
that a monster from

To two very special furry friends, Zoey and Tinkerbelle, for being there through good and bad and for helping me with your wet noses and wagging tails—thank you. To my parents, who gave me the determination to go after my goals no matter *what the challenge*! To Peter Shoff, because his love of superheroes with special powers inspired me to write this book and model the character Peter after him. You taught me what it means to be a real dad; you are already a superhero to me. To Deborah Smith, my favorite alien, whose advice on this book kept me focused and thinking outside the box!

To my sister Frances Brzycki for editing my book. And to the special lady in my life, Beverly Frank, who is one of the many people I know who is willing to give me a kick in the behind when I get stalled. I would also like to thank my fans, who enjoy my stories of horror, and iUniverse, who has helped me publish both of my books.

And finally, to the man whose books challenged me to write books of horror of my own—Stephen King, here is the second book of this amazing adventure you have started me on. I hope to one day meet you in person and shake your hand!

my mind is on the lose!
Hope you enjoy!
Stanley J. Brzycki

The Power I
The Beginning

Lightning flashed and thunder crashed louder than ever before, it seemed, as Paula Bristol screamed. Paula was in labor with her and her husband's first child. The baby was a week overdue; now, however, Paula was in terrible pain and terrified that her child had decided to come into this world during one of the worst rainstorms they had seen in a while. The downpour turned the muddy, potholed excuse of a road into a quagmire, causing their car to get stuck on the way to the hospital. Paula's husband, Samuel, tried to comfort his wife while trying to recall his Lamaze training.

Sam laid Paula into the backseat of the car to make her more comfortable. With one arm across the back of the backseat and the other against the back of the driver's seat, sweat glistened on Paula's forehead as Sam patted it away. It seemed that every labor pain was punctuated with lightning and thunder.

"Sam, I've never seen lightning that was so colorful," Paula yelled.

Paula's screams of pain grew louder as the labor progressed; suddenly, her hand came off the driver's seat as an especially sharp pain engulfed her. She jammed that hand against the car door window over her head, palm down. Paula screamed long and hard. The baby was on the way, and Sam was sweating heavily, soaking his clothes like he had just walked through a shower. All of a sudden, a lightning bolt struck the window where Paula had her hand; the thunder clap was deafening, and the inside of the car lit up. Sam could see Paula's body shaking from the electricity going through it, and Paula's mouth was frozen in a scream. When Sam recovered from the shock of seeing Paula like that, he realized his hands were full with his newborn son. As Paula started breathing normally, Sam looked up where Paula's hand had been, and his mouth fell open. The outline of Paula's hand was etched into the window in electric neon blue.

By the time they reached the hospital, two hours had passed. The nurse announced that their son seemed to be fine, but they would need a doctor to give him an exam.

"What is his name, Mr. Bristol?" the nurse questioned.

"Peter is his name," Sam exclaimed.

Doppelganger

At the same time that Peter was being born during a violent storm, across the Atlantic Ocean and during an equally violent storm, another son was being born. Although the birth was especially painful, the family gathered around reveled in the mother's pain and cherished it.

"Attention, everyone," the head of the family announced. "Here is a new missionary for our family's purpose; he will likely be an excellent missionary to wipe out the plague on mankind that we are committed to, and his name is Newel!"

The family that Newel had been born into was unique, to say the least, because all the members of the family were dedicated to one purpose—to wipe out the world's prostitutes like their great grandfather taught them centuries ago!

Peter's Problems

By the age of two, Peter hadn't started walking and talking at all, and Paula was becoming very worried about her son. Whenever Paula questioned the doctors about Peter's seemly slow development, they just dismissed her as an overly concerned new mother. Finally, Paula had a discussion with her husband about how the doctors were treating her concerns.

Sam agreed. "Okay, Paula, let's take Peter to a specialist and see what he has to say."

As Paula and Peter entered the doctor's office, they noticed how the office looked with the standardized chairs all the same and the pale wall color. However, there was one thing in the doctor's office that some might say was a bit off; down one hallway hung framed posters from movies based on Stephen King's books—the doctor was a big fan.

The doctor did a whole series of tests on Peter and told Peter's parents he would have the results within a few days. When Peter's parents returned to the doctor, he had them sit before discussing the test results. This put Peter's parents on the verge of panic. The doctor explained that Peter was suffering from several types of ailments, including ADHD, Asperger syndrome, and mild retardation. As he grew, the doctor explained, he might experience violent mood swings and some speech problems, but all these could be dealt with using therapists and medicine. Sam and Paula were in shock and remained silent all the way home. When they arrived at their house, they just held each other as Paula cried on Sam's shoulder.

"How could this happen to our son, Sam? He looks so normal and healthy," Paula said.

"I don't know, Paula; maybe it has something to do with the lightning. All I know is that I love both of you, and we will get through this together," Sam said.

As Peter grew and learned to walk and talk, he roamed all over the house exploring. One day things got very quiet, and Paula figured she better go check on Peter to see what he was up to. When Paula found Peter, he was standing in the far corner of the family room; he had his hand outstretched toward a butterfly on the opposite side of the room.

"Come here, pretty." Peter motioned with his hand.

Paula thought that was so cute of Peter, to try to call a butterfly over to play with him, but Paula's expression changed from a smile to awe as the butterfly glided straight to Peter's arm and landed, walking along Peter's arm and fingers.

"Go away, pretty," Peter said.

The butterfly flew past Paula as she held the door open so the butterfly could go outside.

"Peter, do you play with any other bugs or animals like that?" Paula asked.

"Sure, Mom, I play with all sorts of bugs, bunnies, squirrels, cats, and dogs," Peter answered.

"Well, aren't you special, my little animal trainer," Paula said with a smile.

Newel

One day Newel and the rest of his family went on a little outing in London; because they lived in the town of Dover, it was a short trip. They visited all the normal touristy spots, but then Newel's father took him to an area called the White Chapel district. Newel couldn't see anything really spectacular except the huge chapel it was named for.

"Father, why have we come to this part of town?" Newel asked as he and his father sat on some nearby benches.

"Newel, this area is very famous for our family; this is where your great-grandfather started our families' missionary work and went down in history as a famous person," Newel's father explained.

Just as Newel's father was talking, a scantily clad woman came up to Newel's father and bent low, whispering in his ear.

"Hello there, sir; when you're done entertaining your tot there, maybe you would like to come and entertain my pussy," the prostitute said to Newel's father as she rubbed against him.

"Listen to me, you nasty bitch. If I come back and play with you, you might not like the way I play," Newel's father said.

The look on the prostitute's face changed from seductress to something like she had just swallowed a bug or dodged a bullet. It was a look of fear. Newel couldn't hear what was being said, but he saw his father's teeth as he spoke. They were all shiny and glistening with saliva just like the big jungle cats before they pounced on their prey, drool running down their fangs before they tore their prey apart. Those were Newel's favorite shows, when they showed lots of blood.

"Newel, you're smiling. Are you having a good thought?" Newel's father asked.

"Oh yes, Father, a very good thought," Newel replied.

With that, Newel and his father returned to the family and started home.

After the family had their dinner, Newel saw his father kissing his mother good-bye very passionately. He was all dressed in black and carrying a small black bag that Newel didn't remember seeing before.

"Mother, where is Father going this late at night?" Newel asked.

"Newel, your father has a late business appointment," Newel's mother said with a smile.

Newel's mother knew what these business appointments resulted in. Another prostitute would not be plaguing men anymore, and Newel's father would be sexually supercharged when he got home, so much so that Newel's mother would barely be able to get him into their bedroom before they started having sex. They would experience all the pleasures of their bodies and revel in each other's total surrender, one to the other, for pure sex any way they desired. Newel's mother looked forward to all the business meetings her husband went on, because she loved what came afterward.

Newel's father drove back to London and back to the White Chapel district; he was looking for someone special, someone who had dared to proposition him as his son sat only a few feet away. Newel's father parked in an alleyway and then walked to the chapel where he waited. He didn't have to wait long before he saw the lady who had spoken to him earlier that day, Newel's father walked up to her and smiled.

"Well, look who is back to play with Roxy. Did you come to give Roxy's pussy a good workout, sir?" Roxy asked with a sly smile.

Newel's father only nodded yes and smiled, his teeth glistening with saliva.

"Sir, where would you like to entertain Roxy this evening?" Roxy asked.

Newel's father escorted Roxy to a nearby alley that was cool, dark, and damp and turned her so her palms were flat against the brick wall. As Newel's father stood behind her, Roxy rubbed her round behind up against his crotch.

"Sir, how did you know that I enjoy being fucked this way the best?" Roxy giggled.

Just as Roxy hiked her skirt up so Newel's father could plunge his manhood into her, she got the surprise of her soon-to-be-short life. Roxy didn't see the long, stainless-steel blade in Newel's father's hand as she raised her skirt. Suddenly, Roxy felt two sharp stabbing pains, one over each of her lungs. She tried to scream, but no sound would come out because her lungs had been punctured. Roxy felt herself being turned around and laid down on the damp alleyway; the only slim bit of light came from a distant street lamp. As Roxy looked up into the dark silhouette of her customer, he leaned close enough so the small amount of light temporarily showed his face. Roxy remembered him.

"Lady, I told you if I came back to play with you, you might not like how I played, but now the real fun begins, dear," Newel's father said, smiling.

As Roxy lay there, her eyes bulging and wide with terror, she watched as a razor-sharp knife was inserted at her waist and opened her right up the middle. Roxy's last thoughts were that she couldn't feel any pain, and then everything went black. Newel's father walked out of the alley as if nothing had happened, a smile on his face like a predator after a big meal. He walked slowly back to his car with no one the wiser as to what had happened. He was like a shadow. Once back to his car, Newel's father stripped naked and changed into clean clothes that he kept in a spare suitcase in the trunk. He then tossed his blood-stained clothes into a bag, which he tossed into a river on the way home.

Once Newel's father got home, Newel's mother's heart jumped with excitement. As her husband entered their home, he hugged and kissed her lustfully, pressing his hardness into her thigh. Newel's mother had already made sure all the children were in bed before their father got home. She dragged her overly passionate husband to their bedroom, making it with only her blouse being torn open and the sound of her laughter.

Peter's Abilities Show Up

As Peter grew, his parents began to realize some of the future problems that the doctors had warned them about. Peter had a small speech problem that was being dealt with in school, but the worst problem was Peter's mood swings, which were always explosive and violent. Now, with the help of Prozac, Peter was no longer putting holes in the doors with his elbows or feet by pounding on them when he got mad.

Things were fairly normal for Peter until he turned twelve. It was at that time when some changes started occurring with Peter, and not just the normal ones for a boy Peter's age. One day in class Peter had finished his work sooner than others, so he was sitting at his desk daydreaming. Suddenly, the image of a pencil in his desk flashed in his mind, and Peter felt a push or surge go from the back of his head to the front. At the same instant, Peter heard something in his desk bounce around. Peter, not knowing that not everything is possible, thought about his pencil again and pushed with his mind. This time, the pencil in his desk made a loud enough noise for the teacher to hear it. The teacher made Peter open his desk to make sure he hadn't brought a pet from home to school. Seeing that the desk was empty, the teacher walked on.

Peter took his pencil out of his desk. Shielding it with one arm so no one could see what he was doing, Peter positioned his index finger above the pencil. As he concentrated, he moved his finger a little one way, and the pencil moved in the same direction. When Peter left school that day, he almost ran all the way home, eager to see what else he might be able to do. Once he was home, he ran in and slammed doors shut as he went upstairs to his room.

"Hey, young man, what's the big hurry?" Peter's mom asked.

"I have lots of homework, Mom. I need to get started right away," Peter replied.

Peter closed the door to his room to try his new abilities. First he tried to make his pillow rise, but no matter how hard he concentrated, all the pillow did was form a deep crease. He thought that maybe the pillow was too heavy for him and his new skill. What Peter didn't realize was that it didn't have anything to do with the weight of the object but instead with the concentration and discipline of the mind. The more the mind practiced, the stronger and more disciplined it would become.

Peter started concentrating on moving smaller objects back and forth and making them fly through the air by imagining the object and then pushing it with his mind. He realized that if he pushed and felt the surge in his brain moving forward, then it was working and suddenly whatever he was concentrating on would fly across his room.

Peter tried the pillow again. He concentrated very hard, envisioned it rising off the floor, and then pushed hard. The pillow flew across the room and landed against the door. Peter was so pleased with figuring this out that he was almost giddy—until his mom walked in.

"So this is how you study, young man, by tearing apart your room? I want this cleaned up right now," Peter's mom said in a stern voice.

Peter did as he was told, but when he went to pick up his pillow, something happened. It was like a movie he'd already seen playing in his head, only it was a replay of a dream he'd had last week. The dream was the type that a lot of boys Peter's age were having about girls, but it was like it was real and not just a dream. When Peter came out of his dream state, he was hot and sweaty, and he quickly realized he needed to change his underwear. Peter got cleaned up, changed clothes, and went downstairs.

"Mom, do you know where Dad is?" Peter asked.

"He's in the shed, Peter," she answered.

Peter walked out to the shed and saw his dad.

"Dad, could I talk to you a minute?" Peter asked.

"Sure, Peter. What's on your mind?" Sam asked.

"Dad, some things have been happening to me that I don't really understand."

"What kind of things, Peter?" Sam asked.

Peter told his dad about the pencil in school and the pillow and the dream he'd had when he grabbed it. These were not the normal things that Sam expected to be questioned about by his twelve-year-old son. He was a bit shocked but then smiled at Peter.

"Peter, as far as the type of dream you had, it's normal for a boy your age to start having dreams like that. Everybody has them, including girls," Sam said. "As for the other thing with the pencil, Peter, I need to show you something. Come over here and help me with this box."

Sam and Peter moved a narrow rectangular box out into the open. It was marked *fragile*, and when Sam opened the box, a brilliant electric-blue light lit up the interior of the shed.

Peter stared into the box as Sam pulled the car door window out enough to show Peter the outline of his mom's handprint etched into the glass in neon blue light.

"Peter, when you were born, your mom had her hand against this window. A bolt of lightning struck her hand just as you were born, Son," Sam told Peter.

Peter stood there awestruck as he touched the glass.

"I think, Peter, that when the lightning bolt struck your mom as you were born, it imparted some energy or power to you that is only now coming out because of the regular changes your body is going through," Sam explained. "I think we better talk with your mom tonight to bring her up to date and let her know just how special you are."

"Dad, I think I'm going to check the library at school to see if I can find any information to shed some light on what happened," Peter said.

At dinner Peter's dad told his wife about the talk he'd had with Peter, including the fact that he had told Peter all about when he was born and showed him the car window.

"Why did you do that, Sam? I thought we would wait till he was older and could understand better," Paula said.

"Paula, some things have happened recently that make this the right time to tell Peter the truth," Sam said.

"Peter, why don't you show your mom a bit of what you can do," Sam suggested.

Peter smiled at his dad and then concentrated on the lazy Susan in the middle of the table; slowly, the lazy Susan started to spin gently. Paula's mouth fell open just like the day she saw Peter playing with the butterfly. Then Peter concentrated on his plate. He raised it about a foot off the table and made it travel all the way down to where his mom sat before setting it down gently.

"Peter, after dinner, we are going to have to talk about the right time and the wrong time to use these abilities," Peter's mom said. Sam agreed.

"Peter, with these new skills, you must be very careful not to use them in front of anyone," Sam warned. "Don't even show off for your friends."

"But what good are these abilities if I can't use them?" Peter asked.

"Peter, someone who sees your abilities may decide to use you for criminal activities and then blame you. Do you understand?" Peter's dad asked.

"And you must never harm a living thing with your abilities, not a person or an insect," Peter's mom said.

"But what if I discover new things I can do?" Peter asked.

"Show them to your dad or me first, Peter. Okay?" Peter's mom said.

After the family meeting, Peter was so excited he could hardly sleep. He couldn't wait to go to the library and see what else he might be able to do. When Peter got to school the next day and recess rolled around, it was a normal rainy day in Portland, Oregon, which meant as a choice they would be able to go to the library instead of outside. Once in the library, Peter looked through the card catalog for books on the brain, but all he found were books explaining the medical functions of the brain relative to the human body. He couldn't find anything about what he was experiencing. As Peter sat in front of about six books he had looked through, a familiar voice spoke to him.

"Hello, Peter. Having trouble finding something in our library?" Mrs. Burke said.

Peter really liked Mrs. Burke. She had taught him how to use the library and had helped him several times to locate books he was having trouble finding.

"Hi, Mrs. Burke. Yes, I'm having trouble finding information about brainpower. All I can find are these medical-type books on the brain."

"Peter, why on earth are you looking up that subject?" Mrs. Burke asked.

"Well, I was watching a science fiction movie yesterday about a mad scientist who took over a city with his brainpower, and I got curious," Peter said.

Mrs. Burke smiled when she heard his explanation and motioned Peter to follow her to a row of books right on the opposite side of the medical books he had been looking at.

"Peter, I think what you're looking for is books on the power of the *mind*. We only have about a dozen books, but I hope you find what you need," Mrs. Burke said with a smile.

Peter picked six of the books to start, and as he read, he started making notes. It seemed that people with his type of abilities were said to have the Power. Some of the abilities he found discussed included levitation, ESP, receiving impressions from objects, astral projection, mind control, and receiving mental communications from others with the same abilities from long distances. There were other words that Peter didn't know, but he wrote them down and would show his parents the list. As Peter was getting ready to leave the library, Mrs. Burke stopped him.

"Peter, if you are really interested in the powers of the mind, there is a TV program on tonight. If it's okay with your parents to watch it, you might find it interesting," Mrs. Burke said as she handed Peter a slip of paper with the time and channel of the program.

"Thanks, Mrs. Burke!" Peter said as he left for his homeroom.

As school ended for the day, Peter saw Mrs. Moyer dumping the contents of the bag she carried out on her desk and searching through things frantically.

"Mrs. Moyer, is something wrong? Did you lose something?" Peter asked, concerned.

"Yes, Peter. I can't seem to be able to find my car keys, and I know I brought them in and put them on my desk when I got here this morning. Have you seen them?" Mrs. Moyer asked.

"Not since this morning when you laid them on your desk. They're the ones with the butterfly on the key ring, right?" Peter asked.

"Yes, Peter, those are the ones," Mrs. Moyer responded.

Peter got an idea about how he might be able help Mrs. Moyer. First he concentrated on the butterfly key ring and then pushed with his mind. Peter felt the surge and got an impression of the keys lying in the lining of the leather bag after going through a hole in the corner.

"Mrs. Moyer, have you checked the corners of your bag for holes? If there is one, the keys might have gone through it," Peter said.

Mrs. Moyer started checking. All at once she grabbed at something and was pulling her keys out of her bag with a big grin. "Peter, how did you know where to look for my keys?" she asked.

"Mrs. Moyer, I'm just good at finding stuff. I'm always losing stuff at home, and then I have to figure out where I left things," Peter said with a smile.

Mrs. Moyer gave Peter a big hug and sent him on his way home. Peter was feeling terrific after all that had happened, but his fine mood was disrupted by a commotion coming from a park he was passing. When Peter snuck up and peeked around one of the large fir trees to see what was going on, he saw the biggest bully in his school—a kid named Jenkins.

Jenkins was throwing things at a squirrel and terrifying it so it didn't know which way to go. He had the little animal trapped. Jenkins was throwing anything he could at the squirrel and yelling and cursing. Jenkins was a number one asshole and bully. As twelve-year-olds went, he was the biggest kid in school and was even taller than some of the teachers.

Jenkins was always bothering Peter and his friends. Peter wondered if he might be able to help the squirrel by teaching Jenkins a little lesson. Peter peeked around the tree just enough to see Jenkins as he was getting ready to throw something again. Peter visualized Jenkins and gave a hard push with his mind. Jenkins's feet flew up in the air like he had just hit a patch of ice and then came down hard on his ass, yelling.

"Who the hell did that, you son of a bitch?" Jenkins yelled, seeing nobody.

As Peter watched Jenkins pick himself up, he saw the squirrel look right at him as he peeked around the tree. The squirrel then quickly took off. Peter was still trying to stifle his laughter as Jenkins left the park. Peter felt so great that he ran right home and told his mom all about what had happened. But his mom was not very excited about everything that Peter was telling her.

"Peter, it's good that you helped your teacher and that you helped the squirrel escape, but what if when you made this bully fall, he fell and hit his head on a rock or seriously hurt himself. How would you feel?" Peter's mom said in a stern tone.

"Okay, Mom. I understand, but the other stuff I did was good. Wasn't it?" Peter asked.

"Yes, Peter," his mom said.

Peter went outside and sat on the porch steps. How did a great day go to crap so fast? Peter got angry. He saw a stone near his foot and pushed it hard with his mind. The rock took off like it was a bullet, hitting the corner of the shed with a loud crack. *That could have really hurt someone if it had hit them,* Peter thought. In that moment, Peter had his first reality check of his young life and of the power he wielded.

Suddenly, Peter noticed movement out of the corner of his left eye. It was a squirrel creeping cautiously toward Peter.

The squirrel came right up to Peter's shoe, curled up on it, and seemed to be sleeping.

"Mom, could you come out here quietly?" Peter whispered through the screen door.

"What is it, Peter?" she said quietly as she saw Peter pointing to the squirrel.

Peter leaned down slowly and with one finger stroked the head of the squirrel. The animal didn't seem to mind at all.

"Do you think that's the same squirrel you helped earlier today, Peter?" Peter's mom asked.

Peter let his finger lay on the squirrel's head and concentrated. He saw what had happened that day through the squirrel's eyes, being trapped by Jenkins while looking for food, seeing himself peek around the tree to look at Jenkins and the squirrel, and finally Jenkins landing hard again on his ass, which made Peter laugh again. The squirrel just looked up at Peter and slowly walked away, unafraid.

"It is the same squirrel, Mom," Peter told her.

"And how do you know, Peter?" she asked.

"Because I saw the whole thing happen from the squirrel's point of view as I stroked its head. Mom, I can get impressions from things," Peter said.

Peter's mom went into their home and told Peter to wait in the living room. Paula had been in her and Sam's bedroom. She wanted to test her amazingly gifted son and came out with an antique ring. A cameo about the size of a dime was mounted in the center of the piece of jewelry. Peter had never seen the piece before.

"Peter, what can you tell me about this ring?" Paula asked.

Peter held the ring for about a minute and smiled. "Mom, this is a ring that dad bought during World War II in Italy and sent to his mother. She gave it to you to pass on to your first daughter," Peter said with a smile.

"Peter, you seem to be always amazing me. We are going to have to show your dad this one when he comes home," Paula said.

When Peter's dad got home, Paula told him about Peter's new ability. He shook his head and went to get something of his to test Peter again. When he came out of the bedroom, he was holding an amethyst necklace.

"Peter, what can you tell me about this necklace?" Sam asked.

Peter held the necklace for an even shorter time than the ring. "Dad, you bought this necklace during the war at the same time you bought the cameo ring. Grandma wanted you to take care of it when she passed away," Peter said.

Both Peter's parents were blown away and wondered what else he might be able to do in the future. And then Peter remembered his library list.

"Dad and Mom, I did that research I told you I would do and wrote down a list of possible abilities I might be able to do as I get older."

Peter's parents looked the list over and were amazed by the items on the list and their son's ability to use the library.

"Actually, Mom and Dad, I was looking in the wrong area. It's not called brainpower but power of the mind. Mrs. Burke helped me look in the right place, and she also gave me something," Peter said. "Mom and Dad, Mrs. Burke said if I was really curious about this stuff, there was going to be a program on TV tonight to watch if it was okay with the both of you," Peter said as he handed the slip of paper with the time and channel to his parents.

"Considering how fast things are developing for Peter, I think it would be a good idea for all of us to watch the program," Sam said.

As Peter and his parents watched the program, they realized that the future for Peter could be quite an adventure. In the meantime, in the town of Dover, just outside of London, another family was making a discovery.

Newel Gets Caught

Newel's brothers and sister were not like regular children. After they went to their regular studies and got home, instead of being allowed to go out and play with their friends, they had more studies related to preparing them for the mission of exterminating prostitutes worldwide. These classes included anatomy, the use of weapons in the most deadly and quietest ways, and strategy for evasion of the authorities. Both of Newel's parents realized that some of their children did not excel at those later classes and might only get away with two or three murders before they were caught, while others, like Newel, seemed to be naturals at the art of killing and absorbed their classes with ease. Newel's parents were happy to sacrifice some of their children so the children who excelled would bring fame to their family as wolves in sheep's clothing, wiping out prostitutes.

One day Newel's parents heard slight noises coming from the den of Newel's father, a place where the children weren't permitted. As Newel's parents went to investigate, they saw the door to the den open halfway. Newel's father peeked in, and before he could get angry, he was shocked by what he saw. There was Newel with some of his father's razor-sharp knives. He was balancing them in the air as he stacked them tip to handle. Newel's father smiled and cleared his throat.

"Newel, what are you doing in here?" he asked.

"I'm sorry, Father, but I was so bored I just wanted to come in here and play," Newel replied.

"Newel, do you see those darts lying on the table there?" Newel's father asked.

"Yes, Father," he replied.

"Newel, can you throw the darts at the dartboard without touching them?"

Within seconds of asking, all the darts went sailing through the air by themselves. Newel smiled at his father as his father picked up an ornate box with a key lock on it. As Newel's father opened the box, he took out a razor-sharp knife with a polished wooden handle.

"Newel, what can you tell me about this knife?" his father asked.

"Father, this was my great-great-grandfather's knife that he used when he first started his missionary work in London. He sent many prostitutes to their graves in London and in America!" Newel marveled.

Newel's father smiled at his wife.

"Newel has the same abilities as my great-grandfather, Wife. This is very rare and could mean that our son is destined for greatness as a missionary for our family and possibly historically," Newel's father said.

Peter Makes a Friend

As Peter was walking home from school one day, he noticed a girl from his school was walking behind him.

"Are you following me?" Peter asked.

"No, but you and I live very close to each other. Can I walk with you?" she said.

"My name is Peter."

"I'm Amy," she said.

As they walked, they found out that they liked some of the same things, like biology, science fiction, and horror movies. As they talked about school, Amy told Peter that she only lived one block up and over from his house.

Peter was silent for a while when he shyly asked Amy if she would like to go to the movies on Saturday to see the latest sci-fi movie.

"If my parents say it's okay, then yes, Peter, I would like that very much. I'll let you know in school tomorrow," Amy said.

When Peter got home, he was so excited. He told his mom about meeting Amy and inviting her to the movies Saturday if it was okay with Amy's parents and the both of them.

"Peter, what are you going to use for money?" Peter's mom asked.

"I thought I would ask dad for an advance on my allowance, Mom," Peter said.

"Well, talk to your dad when he gets home," Peter's mom said.

When Peter's dad got home, he came into the living room after talking to Peter's mom.

"Your mom says you have something to ask me, Peter."

"Yes, Dad. I met a girl named Amy, and I invited her to the movies this Saturday if it's okay with you and Mom. But I would like to get an advance on my allowance so that I can take her. Would that be all right?" Peter asked.

Peter's dad smiled. "I think that would be fine, Peter, on two conditions—that you get her back home by whatever time her parents want her home by, and you make sure you keep her safe," Sam said to Peter.

Peter agreed, and his dad put some cash in his hand. As Peter looked at it, his mouth fell open. It was forty dollars. Peter's dad just smiled and nodded in Peter's direction. The next day in school Peter found out from Amy that it was okay with her parents to go to the movies.

That night as Peter tried to sleep, he started to have a dream that he was flying over a large body of water, and then he circled over a town and hovered. In his dream, he felt a darkness closing in around him and sensed foreboding. He had an urgency to leave, as if his very life depended on it.

As he drew away from the darkness, he heard a voice that said: "I am Newel, and I can feel you!"

Peter suddenly became aware that he was being shaken violently by his dad.

"Peter, are you okay?" Sam yelled to his son.

"Yes, Dad. I am not quite sure what happened." Peter then relayed what had happened.

"Peter, if that person ever contacts you again, don't let him get any personal information from you, not your name or where you live. I think it's likely that this person has similar powers to yours, Peter. What you experienced is called astral projection. Right now we can't be sure if this Newel person has good or bad intentions," Peter's father said.

What Peter couldn't know at that moment was that Newel was lying in his bed reaching out with his mind, and when he contacted Peter's mind and introduced himself, he smiled a predator's grin.

Saturday arrived, and Peter could hardly sit still because he was so excited about going to the movies with Amy. When it was time to leave for the movies, Peter wondered if he would meet Amy's parents. He got his answer as he knocked on Amy's door. Amy's dad answered the door. He was a tall man and smiled at Peter.

"Is Amy ready to go to the movies?" Peter asked.

"Come in. You must be Peter. Amy has been telling us about you," Amy's dad said as he shook Peter's hand.

Peter's hand almost disappeared in the large hand of Amy's dad. As Amy came down the stairs to meet her date, Peter noticed she looked different from when he'd seen her in school, more like a tomboy and dressed in jeans. Peter and Amy took off for the movies, wondering about what the movie would be like and talking about their favorite movies.

The movie was terrific, and Amy was surprised when Peter offered to pay for everything. She asked Peter how he could do that, and he told Amy he had gotten an advance on his allowance. It impressed Amy that he wanted to take her out enough to get an advance on his allowance, but Peter didn't know Amy was impressed because all she did was smile at him.

Peter and Amy were walking home and just talking about the movie when they heard Peter's name being called.

"Hey, Peter, you dumbass, did you and your girlfriend like the movie?" Jenkins yelled at them.

"Leave us alone, Jenkins!" Peter yelled back.

With that, Peter and Amy changed directions to avoid Jenkins, but Peter caught a glimpse of Jenkins out of the corner of his eye. It appeared he was starting to wind up like a pitcher would right before throwing something. As Peter turned, he saw Jenkins throw a rock at them, and he immediately realized it would miss him and hit Amy. Peter remembered what his dad had said about keeping Amy safe. He focused on the rock as it made a beeline for Amy and then pushed with his mind. All of a sudden the rock that was flying so straight and on target went off to the left like it had been yanked out of the air and bounced harmlessly on the ground. Jenkins, who had been smiling after he threw the rock, was standing with his mouth open in disbelief because of what he had just seen the rock do. Peter and Amy went home, and Amy asked Peter if he had anything to do with what had happened when Jenkins threw the rock. Peter just smiled.

"Maybe one day I will share a special secret with you, Amy, if you are good at keeping secrets," Peter said.

"Peter, I am good at keeping secrets, and if you want it to be something just between you and me, that would be no problem," Amy said.

After dropping Amy off at her house, Peter went home feeling good. As he went in his house, he announced to his parents that he had made a decision as to what he wanted to do as a career.

"I want to be a police officer like you, Dad," Peter said.

Sam got a woeful look on his face that Peter didn't understand.

"Dad, what's wrong? I thought you would be happy that I want to help people in trouble," Peter exclaimed.

"Peter, I'm afraid the police force wouldn't let you be a policeman. It has to do with your mood swings and the medicine you take," Sam said.

You could see the different emotions play over Peter's face, shock, confusion, and finally intense anger. Peter kicked at one of the hallway doors and put a hole in it.

"What good are these abilities? I can't show them to anyone. I can't use them as a cop, which would give me an edge over criminals, because the police won't let me be a cop because of my other problems. Dad, it's like being in heaven and hell all at the same time. *Damn it!*" Peter yelled.

"Peter, try to calm down. Things will work out; they usually do," Sam said.

"Dad, I need to be able to show my abilities and share my experiences with someone outside of this family so I can keep myself on an even plane," Peter told his dad.

"Do you have someone in mind, Peter?" Sam asked with a smile.

"Yes, Dad. Amy already told me she could keep a secret, and I trust her," Peter said firmly.

The Field Trip

One day Newel's father called him into the den.

"Newel, how would you like to go with me one evening on one of my appointments to see how I work my magic as a missionary? It would be a sort of field trip," Newel's father said.

"Father, that would be great. When will we leave?" Newel asked.

"In a couple of days, but first you must get everything on this list ready and stored so we can leave at a moment's notice. If you can't find something, ask your mother to help you," Newel's father said.

It was a unique list that included dark clothes to wear going out, a set of clean clothes to change into, and six razor-sharp daggers six inches long with very narrow blades.

"Father, what are the daggers for?" Newel asked.

"It's just in case something gets out of hand while we are out together, Newel," his father explained.

As the day grew near, Newel could hardly contain himself. He was so excited to be going out with his father. On the night of their departure, Newel's mother watched her two men leave all dressed in black, each with his own black bag. She was so proud of them. As they traveled to London, Newel's father gave him some tips for the evening.

"Newel, if for any reason things get out of hand, I will call out your name. If I do that, I will need you to silence the lady we host tonight by using your mind to throw the daggers you brought with you. Can you do that, Newel?" his father asked.

"Father, I won't let you down."

As they arrived in the White Chapel district, they parked in a dark alleyway where they could watch the street.

"Newel, which lady do you think we should host tonight?" his father asked.

It took Newel only minutes to decide on a gaudily dressed whore who was boasting about what she could do for a man or a woman and prancing around and talking down to other people on the street.

"Father, the loud whore over there," Newel said as he pointed in her direction.

"Good, Newel. You have your father's eye. You stay in the car but be ready if I need you," his father said.

Newel's father stepped into the light and motioned for the whore to cross the street. She smiled and crossed the street eagerly.

"Well, hello, sir. Aren't you a dandy. Are you looking to give my pussy a good workout? Or some other location?" she said.

"Miss, that sounds fine with me. Could we step over to the alleyway?" he asked.

"That would be fine, sir, and my name is Connie," she replied.

Newel's father turned Connie around to face the wall, her palms flat against the moist brick. She rubbed her behind against Newel's father's hardness, waiting for the usual penetration, but to her surprise she didn't feel anything and started to turn.

"Come on, dear. I haven't got all night," Connie said out loud.

Just then, Connie felt the searing pain of a knife through one of her lungs. She tried to turn and run, twisting away from her attacker.

Newel's father knew he had to do something quickly, so he called Newel's name just loud enough for Newel to hear it. Connie took one, maybe two steps deeper into the alley before she sank down against the wall, three of the thin daggers that Newel had brought dead center in her throat.

Newel's father told him to change into clean clothes while he finished with Connie. After Newel's father finished and changed clothes, he climbed in next to his son. Something seemed different about the body than before. Newel watched as they left and realized that Connie's head was sitting on her chest. Newel's father had decapitated her.

"Father, why did you do that to the whore?" Newel asked.

"Newel, it's like a predator marking his territory," Newel's father replied with a smile.

Newel could understand this because he realized his father was a predator. On their way home, his father noticed that Newel was fidgeting a lot and saw by accident the bulge in Newel's pants.

"Newel, you can take care of that when you get home. Don't worry about it. It's a trait of the members of our family that after a kill we are sexually supercharged," Newel's father said.

"I know of this a bit, Father. I have seen you and Mother after you've come back from a few of your appointments," Newel confessed.

Newel's father smiled. "Well, it seems we've been teaching you about sex without knowing it, Newel. Your mother, I think, is going to like that idea," his father said, smiling.

When they got home, Newel witnessed his mother and father fondling each other lustfully as Newel's father whispered in his wife's ear. Suddenly, she smiled broadly at Newel, and as his parents left to go to their bedroom, Newel's father encouraged him to go to his bedroom.

Newel could hardly contain himself long enough to get out of his clothes. When he put his palm against the wall that was between his room and his parents' room, what he saw filled him with excitement. His parents were already having sex but in ways that Newel had never seen and with much more enthusiasm than before. Newel sensed that something was different, and then Newel wondered if his parents were positioning themselves so that Newel had the best vantage point. Newel was so exhausted from the evening's activities of his parents and his own that he wondered if his parents had put on a show especially for him since they had found out he was watching. He got his answer just before he fell asleep as his parents stood facing the wall that Newel shared with their bedroom and each took a bow, smiles on their faces.

The next morning Newel's mother greeted him. "Newel, you must have been tired. You slept so late," she said.

"I was, Mother, once I could get to sleep," Newel replied smiling.

"Did you enjoy the show we put on for you, Newel?" Newel's mother asked.

"Yes, I did very much, Mother."

The Secret

One day after school when Peter and Amy were walking home, Peter invited Amy to come to his place so he could share with her the secret he had mentioned.

"Peter, I can be over in half an hour. Okay?" Amy replied.

"Sure, Amy," Peter said.

When Amy came over, they went into the backyard where no one could see them.

"Amy, you have to promise me that this secret will stay between you and me. You can't tell anybody—not even your parents," Peter said.

"Okay, Peter, but is this secret that big?" Amy asked.

"Let me tell you and show you. Then you can decide how big it is," Peter said.

Peter saw some squirrels playing on a tree near where they were. He concentrated on the squirrels, and the squirrels came over to Amy, crawled on her lap, and jumped around. The look on Amy's face was bewilderment and pleasant joy. Peter smiled, and the squirrels laid down by them and dozed off.

"What do you think?" Peter asked Amy.

"How did you make the squirrels do that, Peter?" Amy asked.

Peter told Amy about his birth and the lightning striking his mom's hand when he was born.

"Can you do anything else, Peter?" Amy asked.

"Yes, I can levitate things, get impressions from things, and move objects. There are other abilities I'm finding out about as I get older. In the books I've read, it's called having the Power," Peter told Amy.

"Peter, can you show me some more?" Amy asked.

Peter smiled as he floated a plastic ball across the yard over to Amy, who was obviously amazed.

"Amy, do you have something special with you?" Peter asked.

"Will this do, Peter?" Amy asked as she took off a small necklace she was wearing.

Peter smiled and held the medallion on the necklace. Peter pushed with his mind, concentrating, and he got an image of Amy's dad giving the necklace to her the previous Christmas.

"Amy, this necklace was given to you by your dad last Christmas," Peter said, smiling.

"How did you do that?" Amy asked.

"I can get impressions from people or things, Amy," Peter said.

After that first day, Peter told Amy he needed someone to talk with and show his abilities to so he could keep his head on straight. If it was okay with Amy, he wanted her to be the one person he confided in outside his family.

"Peter, that would be great!" Amy said.

After that, Peter and Amy became best friends, and Amy became a fixture around the Bristol home. Both of Peter's parents liked her very much. Peter and Amy were getting ready to go into high school the following fall. As Peter walked Amy home one day, she was unusually quiet.

"Amy, is something wrong?" Peter asked.

"Yes, Peter. I am going to be moving away soon. My dad got a new job," Amy said quietly with tears in her eyes.

Peter's mouth fell open with shock. When they reached Amy's home, Amy gave Peter a kiss on his lips and ran inside. Peter couldn't figure this out. Amy was moving away. He was losing his best friend, and then she kisses him right on the lips. Peter was very confused as he walked through the door of his own home. He told his mom and dad about Amy and the kiss he didn't understand.

"Peter, Amy was just showing you how much she was going to miss you," Paula said, smiling.

Peter thought about that as he rested in his room. He decided he needed to do something the next morning. He got up early and dressed in clean jeans and a nice shirt and walked over to Amy's house so he wouldn't get all sweaty by running.

As Peter stood at the front door of Amy's home, he rang the doorbell. Amy's father opened it.

"Hello, Peter. Can I help you?" Amy's dad said.

"Yes, please. Could I talk to Amy for a minute?" Peter asked.

Amy's dad smiled and called for Amy. When Amy saw it was Peter, a big smile brightened her face.

"Can I see you for a moment outside, Amy?" Peter asked.

Once they were outside on the porch, Peter spoke again. "Amy, you will always be my best friend. I wasn't sure why you kissed me yesterday, but my mom explained it to me. Can I show you how much I'll miss you, Amy?" Peter asked.

Amy smiled and nodded. Peter gave Amy a very heartfelt kiss, trying to show her how much he would miss her. What they didn't know was that Amy's parents were watching. Amy's mom saw the concern on her husband's face and told him not to worry, as they were just saying good-bye.

When Peter started back home, he was on autopilot until he saw the police car in front of their house. He ran the rest of the way. He burst through the front door and saw his mom crying, while his dad tried to comfort her. The officer with them was his dad's friend Bob from down at the station.

"Peter," Bob said, "your Uncle Pete was murdered as they tried to rob his cab today."

Peter sank into a chair, and tears welled up in his eyes. His namesake and favorite uncle was dead. Peter was quiet and just shook his head.

Slowly, Peter grew quiet as he heard his dad and Bob talking. There were no suspects in the case, and it was one of many robberies with similar characteristics.

Peter stood. "I've changed my mind about what I want to do for a career," he announced. "I just want to be a cabdriver to honor my uncle, and I'll be the best in Portland!" With that, Peter slowly walked out of the room.

Liz Moves In

Newel had noticed that a new family was moving in next door to them. He didn't pay much attention until he saw a young lady his age helping to carry things into the house. The next day Newel was in his own backyard when he spotted someone next door. He peeked over the fence and saw the young lady from the day before.

"Hello, miss. My name is Newel."

The young lady smiled. "Hello, Newel, and I already know your name because I asked one of your sisters. My name is Liz," she said.

They talked for a while until they noticed the prostitutes along their street.

"Damn, I wish they would round up all those vermin and ship them to a deserted island," Liz said with venom in her voice.

"I agree, Liz, or maybe some solution more permanent," Newel said with a low laugh.

Newel was surprised that Liz felt the same way as his family did about the whores. She even laughed at his small joke about a permanent solution.

"Would you like to walk with me to school tomorrow, Liz?" Newel asked.

"I can't tomorrow. My father always takes us on the first day of a new school year, but maybe you could walk me home if you'd like," Liz said to Newel.

"I'll see you in school, Liz," Newel said, smiling.

The next day at school Newel saw Liz only briefly until their basic biology class, which they had together. The class was supposed to dissect large cockroaches, which some of the students found to be disgusting. A couple of the students, Liz being one, just couldn't do it, and a local bully named Dirk decided the first day of school was a good time to tease someone.

Liz was almost in tears from the teasing, and Newel had had enough of Dirk abusing Liz.

"Why don't you just leave her alone, Dirk? You asshole!" Newel told Dirk.

"And what are you going to do if I don't stop, Newel?" Dirk asked.

Newel stepped to within six feet of Dirk. "If you don't stop, I will put you in such pain, Dirk," Newel whispered.

"Are you going to punch me out, Newel?" Dirk responded. He leered at Newel as he dropped his cockroach down the back of Liz's blouse.

Liz felt the insect and fainted as Dirk laughed out loud. Then, all at once, Dirk was silent, his face a mask of shock. In the middle of Dirk's palm was a dissecting needle buried and pushing out through the other side. Suddenly, Dirk began to howl like a wounded animal, not making any sense as the teacher took him to the infirmary. Newel helped calm Liz, but as he touched her arm, he got an impression of a nude Liz writhing on her bed in ecstasy. The vision took Newel's breath away for a moment until Liz called his name as he helped her to get up.

"Are you all right, Liz?" Newel asked.

"Yes, I think so, Newel," she said.

With that, the class was dismissed, and Newel didn't see Liz until the end of the day in their last class.

"Liz, can I still walk you home today?" Newel asked.

"Yes, Newel, I would enjoy having you walk me home," Liz said with a smile.

As Newel and Liz walked home, they made small talk and didn't mention anything about what had happened earlier until they were almost at Liz's house.

"Newel, thank you for standing up for me today, of all the people in the class, you were the only person who had the guts to speak up for me and try to stop Dirk," Liz said quietly.

"Liz, it was my pleasure. That *ass* Dirk has had that coming for a while," Newel said, smiling.

"But, Newel, I don't understand how Dirk got a wound like that. One minute there was nothing in his palm, and the next minute he had a dissecting needle going through it. You were the closest to him, but you were still six feet away," Liz pondered.

"Liz, maybe one day I will explain it to you," Newel said with a smile as they parted company.

The next day in school Newel was called to the principal's office.

"Newel, Dirk here has made a serious accusation against you. He says that you stabbed him in the hand with a dissecting needle," Principal Darrens said.

"Honest, Principal Darrens, I had nothing to do with Dirk's accident," Newel said with a sly smile on his face.

"You lying bastard. It had to be you!" Dirk yelled.

"Dirk, shut up. Newel, how close were you to Dirk?" the principal asked.

"I was about six feet away. You can ask any of the people in class," Newel said.

The principal looked in Dirk's direction before dismissing Newel. "Dirk and I are going to have a talk about accusing people falsely and wasting my time," Principal Darrens said.

Newel noticed as he left that Dirk's expression had soured a lot, and Newel let Dirk see his face smiling slightly like a predator, just like his father.

High School for Peter

Peter left for his first day of high school. He wasn't sure how it was going to go. Amy was gone, but his parents had volunteered to be Peter's sounding board and to let Peter show them any new abilities that he became aware of. Peter's first few classes were okay, but the day took a downward turn when he heard a familiar voice.

"Hey, Peter, heard your girlfriend moved away," Jenkins said.

Peter turned toward Jenkins, who was tossing a baseball in the air. Of all the places in this school he could have his locker, it had to be in the same hallway as Jenkins.

"Jenkins, you had better leave me alone. You don't know what you're messing with," Peter said.

"Really, Peter? You know, I never could figure out how that rock I threw at you and Amy could have missed, especially since when I throw at something, that's where it goes. That's why they let me be on the varsity baseball team as a pitcher," Jenkins yelled at Peter.

Peter tried to avoid any further confrontation, but Jenkins wasn't going to be ignored. Out of the corner of his eye, Peter saw Jenkins start a pitcher's windup. Peter turned and faced Jenkins just as the ball left his hand. Peter concentrated on the ball, which was a blur, and pushed with his mind. The ball went from being a blur to stopping dead in space halfway between Peter and Jenkins. Jenkins's mouth fell open from shock, and then Peter shot the ball back to Jenkins at crotch level, stopping two feet away.

"Leave me and my friends the *hell* alone!" Peter yelled. With that, he pushed Jenkins up against his locker with his mind, the baseball following Jenkins's movements. When Peter released Jenkins and the ball, Jenkins had fainted, and the ball rolled harmlessly away from him.

Peter went on to lunch, and as he was sitting with a couple of friends, one of them started asking him if he had heard about any thefts in school.

"Damn, Jimmy, it's only the first day. How much could have been stolen?" Peter asked.

"I heard one of the freshman girls had a gold ring stolen from her gym locker. It was from her parents for a high school gift," Jimmy said.

"Has the school notified the police, Jim?" Peter asked.

"Why don't you ask your dad, Peter? He might know," Jim said.

"Okay, but in the meantime, let's keep our ears open for anybody else getting stuff stolen," Peter said.

Peter arrived home, and when his dad got home, he asked him if the police had any knowledge of thefts at his high school.

"I don't know, Peter, but I can ask the burglary division to see if they heard anything. Is anything valuable missing?" Sam asked.

"A gold ring from a freshman girl's locker," Peter said.

In the next few days, Peter learned from his friends that about a dozen high-end items had been stolen from students' lockers. Peter's father checked with the burglary division and was told that they were instructed to go through the principal, a Mr. Andrew Hardy. Principal Hardy had suggested that the thefts had been the usual petty stuff and had delegated any further inquiries to go through Assistant Principal Drew Manning.

"Peter, what kinds of things are being stolen?" Sam asked.

"Smartphones, jewelry—all expensive items," Peter said.

Sam started to wonder if maybe there was more to these school thefts than met the eye. He decided to talk to his friend Bob, who he had already been talking to about Peter's unique abilities. Bob believed in all that psychic stuff and had been educating Sam about his son's possible abilities for months. What Sam learned was that after they had talked to Assistant Principal Manning, no further communication about thefts had occurred. The burglary unit was surprised to learn that the thefts were still happening and that such expensive items were missing.

"Peter, can you and your friends keep an ear open for any more thefts of expensive items in your school and try to get some idea of how many items have been taken?" Sam asked.

"Sure, Dad. I kind of asked my friends to do that already in case you needed to know," Peter said with a smile.

After a couple of weeks, Peter talked with his friends again at lunch about the thefts and relayed what he had learned from his father.

"Peter, it doesn't sound like the principal or assistant principal think the police should be involved," Peter's friend Mike said.

"Yeah, they're both pretty useless," Peter said.

"Well, they better get the cops involved with what I just learned," Jimmy said. "I just found out that there have been dozens of thefts since school started, and every item was expensive."

Peter and his friends couldn't believe their ears. If the thefts were that widespread, why weren't the police involved?

"I think I had better make my dad aware of this," Peter said.

As Peter went home, he saw something that just didn't make sense. Peter saw Jenkins and a group of his buddies going into the local movie theater, and Jenkins was paying for all of them with a wad of cash. Peter wondered if Jenkins had gotten a job. Or was he getting money from some other source? Peter felt he had to find out. As Jenkins noticed Peter, he waved to him. Peter walked over out of curiosity.

"Jenkins, what do you want?" Peter asked.

"I just wondered if you wanted to see the movies with my friends and me. It's on me," Jenkins said, smiling.

Suddenly, Peter got an idea. "I can't go to the movies, but could I have a dollar for a candy bar? I can pay you back tomorrow," Peter said.

"Sure, Peter, here you go," Jenkins said as he smiled and went into the theater.

As Peter walked away, he noticed that the dollar Jenkins had given him had a strange gray glow to it. Peter held the bill and pushed a little with his mind. He got an image of Jenkins getting money from one of the school janitors for spotting expensive items that belonged to other students. That was why Jenkins had so much extra cash. Peter got home before his dad and decided to take a nap while he waited. As Peter slept, he felt himself being enveloped by a cloud, and out of the cloud came a voice.

"Hello, I'm in London, and I would very much like to meet you one day. Hopefully, we can have some fun together."

Suddenly, Peter realized his dad was waking him from his sleep.

"Peter, are you awake, Son?" Sam asked.

"Yes, Dad, but right before you woke me up, someone spoke to me in a very creepy and guttural voice."

"What did the voice say, Peter?" Sam asked.

"The voice said he was in London and that he hoped we could meet one day."

Sam's face had become a mask of concern for Peter because of this other mind that was communicating with him. Peter and his dad went downstairs and relayed the whole story to Peter's mom, who also voiced her concern.

"So, Peter, your mom tells me you have some information about the school thefts," Peter's dad said.

Peter told his dad how he had found out that Jenkins was getting extra money for spotting expensive items to be stolen and was being paid by one of the janitors in school.

"Peter, did you get any impression of who the janitor was selling the items through?" Peter's dad asked.

"No, Dad, but it must be someone with a lot of know-how, because I'll bet thirty items have been stolen since school started, all of them expensive," Peter said.

Peter's dad was on the phone to his friend Bob, and they talked for almost an hour. At the end of the conversation, Sam looked at his son.

"Peter, how would you like to help us trap the thieves at your school?" Sam asked.

"That would be great, Dad!" Peter exclaimed.

The next morning the plan was going into effect.

"Peter, what I would like you to do is wear my watch to school. It's very expensive, and any thief could spot it a mile away as being worth a lot of money," Peter's dad told him.

"Dad, is this what they call baiting a thief?" Peter asked.

"Yes, Peter. Make sure everyone sees you wearing it and take it off at times you don't want it damaged, like in PE and shop or if you go outside," Peter's dad cautioned.

Peter smiled. He liked helping his dad catch the thieves at his high school. Peter went to his homeroom class first thing in the morning. He showed his new watch to a few of his friends and glanced up once and saw Jenkins eyeing the watch. Peter smiled to himself. *Yeah, come to the bait, fishy, fishy,* he thought.

Peter's dad had told him it might take a few days to finally get the thieves to make their move, but when they did, some special friends of Sam's from the police department would be there. Peter went to all his classes just like normal. His dad's watch had been locked away twice in his locker, but it was still there each time he returned to claim it. It wasn't until the end of the day that the thieves made their move.

Peter had gone out to PE and locked the watch in his locker. When he returned to change back into his school clothes, he discovered the watch was gone, but the locker wasn't busted or broken into. Peter called a phone number his dad had given him, and within minutes, police arrived at the school. Sam and Bob had come too.

"Peter, do you know where the janitor is who's been dealing with Jenkins?" Peter's dad asked.

"Yes, I do. He's on the second floor," Peter said.

Some members of Bob's special squad of police went upstairs as Bob, Sam, and Peter followed. When they got near the janitor's room, the door was open, and Jenkins was talking to the janitor. As the police surrounded the two individuals, Peter's dad whispered to Peter, "Peter, do you sense anything?"

Peter concentrated and saw one of Jenkins's pants' pockets glowing gray.

"Check out Jenkins's right pocket," Peter whispered to his dad.

When they searched Jenkins, they found the watch.

"Hey, that's my watch, mister," Jenkins protested.

"No, this is my watch. I gave it to Peter to wear today to trap the thieves in this school who have been ripping everyone off," Peter's dad said as he showed Jenkins his initials on the back of the watch.

Peter walked past Jenkins and the janitor and looked into the janitor's closet. Inside were many cabinets with drawers, and they all glowed gray. Peter told his dad what he saw, and the police started opening all the drawers after presenting a search warrant to the janitor. The police found many stolen items tagged and ready to be sent to the seller. Bob was questioning the janitor to reveal who the seller was, and when he learned who it was, he just shook his head. Bob, Sam, and a couple of the police, along with Peter, went to the main office. Bob and Sam knocked on Assistant Principal Manning's door.

"Just a moment," Manning said as he slipped a gold ring he had been looking at onto his little finger. He intended it for his little girl.

Bob, Sam, and Peter walked in. "Hello, Mr. Manning. Can we talk to you for a moment?" Sam said.

"Sure, what can I do for you?" Manning asked.

"It seems there has been a theft ring operating in this school since the start of the school year, and we wanted to let you know we caught the persons responsible. They also gave up their seller," Sam said.

"And who did that turn out to be, Officer?" Manning asked.

"It's you, Mr. Manning," Bob said calmly.

Manning's face smiled, and he seemed very confident. "That's ridiculous," he replied.

Both Bob and Sam were temporarily stuck to implicate Manning. Then Peter spotted the gold ring on his finger. Peter pushed with his mind and realized that that ring was from the freshman girl who had it stolen on the first day of school. He sensed her name and birthday were engraved inside the band. Peter got his dad's attention and signaled to him about the ring on Mr. Manning's finger.

"Mr. Manning, that's a nice gold ring you have," Sam said.

"Oh, that's something I bought for my daughter. I didn't want to lose it, so I put it on my little finger till I got home," Manning said nervously.

"What's your daughter's name, Mr. Manning?" Sam asked.

Manning knew he was caught, and his guilt was showing in the form of a heavy sweat forming on his forehead.

"Do you mind if we take a look at that ring, Mr. Manning?" Bob asked.

Manning surrendered the ring begrudgingly. Bob looked inside the band. It was inscribed with the name *Katey* and a date.

"What is your daughter's name, Manning?" Sam asked.

"Cindy," he whispered.

They later found out that the thieves had been sending out a shipment of stolen items every week, all high-end stuff.

When Peter helped break the theft ring in school, he became a little bit of a celebrity, especially when the stolen items were returned a couple of weeks later. Peter was very happy with how he had been a part of the whole thing. One day as he turned the corner to his house, he saw a police car sitting in front again. He could only imagine the worst. Had something happened to his dad? As he rushed in the door out of breath, he saw his parents and Bob. Everyone looked at him and smiled.

"Peter, come on in. We've been waiting for you," Bob said.

Now Peter was really wondering what was going on.

"Peter, we really appreciated your help and your willingness to use your special abilities to help nail that theft ring in your school," Bob said, smiling. "Don't worry, Peter. Your dad has been talking to me about you since your abilities started showing up. It's kind of a hobby with me. Peter, I would like to make you an offer to be on a list of people with special abilities who help us solve difficult crimes or cold cases that we just can't make any headway on."

"What would I have to do?" Peter asked.

"Well, you would be on call day and night, whenever we needed you. Usually when we ask people to do this, they end up helping us for a minimum of two years. You'll almost be out of high school at that time," Bob said. "And, Peter, we would pay you a monthly salary because of your availability."

Peter thought about it a long time without saying anything. Finally, he spoke up. "I would need some conditions before I agree to help. My family now or in the future comes first, and I pick the cases I want to work. And when I help catch someone, if there's a reward, who gets that?" Peter asked.

Bob smiled at Peter. "Sam, he is definitely his father's son."

They all laughed.

"As for rewards, Peter, that's the other reason I had to stop by. Any rewards are yours totally, and it just so happens I have a check for you. It seems the janitor had warrants out for his arrest," Bob said as he handed Peter an envelope.

Peter opened the envelope and took out a check for a thousand dollars. His mouth fell open with shock.

"I agree to your conditions, Peter, and I will make sure to keep your special abilities between us. Okay?" Bob asked.

"I think that would be a good idea," Peter's dad said in agreement. He was thinking about what a media circus it would be if the public found out about all the abilities Peter possessed.

Although they couldn't have realized it then, Peter would get a phone call from Bob by the time he was sixteen. He was officially the youngest person on the police department's special list.

Liz Sees Newel's Ability

As the high school years went by, Newel and Liz became closer. At one point, Newel's parents were watching as Newel walked Liz to her home, and they kissed passionately.

"It seems that the young lady next door has caught our son's eye, Husband," Newel's mother said.

"I wonder if she is deserving of Newel's attention," Newel's father said.

"From what I understand from our son, she shares a violent distaste for prostitutes," Newel's mother said.

As Newel was kissing Liz, he got an impression in his mind of Liz writhing with lust in her bed. Her arms outstretched, her body was sweaty with passion as she called out to Newel by name to make love to her. When Newel got home, he barely acknowledged his parents when they suggested he might like to invite Liz to dinner one night.

Newel responded. "Sure, I'll ask her." He then headed to his room, the image of Liz burning in his thoughts.

The next day as Liz and Newel walked home, they passed a secluded park. Newel asked Liz to follow him. When they got to a private location, they sat.

"Liz, remember when I said one day I would show you how Dirk had his accident with the dissecting needles in biology?" Newel asked.

"Yes, Newel, I remember," Liz said.

Newel took out his pocketknife, opened it, and laid it in front of himself. Then, by concentrating, he made the knife quickly fly through the air and embed itself into a nearby tree trunk. Liz's mouth flew open with surprise as Newel smiled.

"I thought you had something to do with it, Newel. I just didn't understand how? Can you do anything else?" Liz asked.

Newel nodded and smiled. He picked a rosebud from a rose bush with his mind and made it float through the air to his hand. Then Newel made the rosebud open and bloom, revealing the reddest rose Liz had ever seen. It was bloodred. He handed it to Liz, kissing her as he did.

"Newel, I want you to make love to me—right here, right now," Liz told Newel.

Newel didn't need any extra encouraging, and for the rest of the afternoon, Liz and Newel were at each other in full-out lust. Newel felt that his parents would have been proud of him and Liz. After dropping Liz off, Newel walked along, his mind completely open. All of a sudden, he became extremely dizzy to the point that he slumped against a fence. Newel felt a surge on his mind like a large wave, and it carried a message with it: "I am Peter, and I feel you out there!"

Newel was so surprised that he talked to his parents about everything, including telling Liz about his abilities.

"Newel, are you sure she can be trusted?" Newel's father asked.

"I'm sure, Father," Newel replied.

"Well, we need to meet this special lady at dinner, Newel," Newel's mother said with a smile.

"I'll ask her tomorrow," Newel said.

The next day Newel asked Liz to dinner with his family, and she enthusiastically said yes. The dinner went very well, and afterward, Newel's parents asked Newel how serious he was about Liz.

"Newel, is Liz someone you just need to fuck once in a while, or does she mean more to you than that?" Newel's father asked.

"Father, I think that Liz will be the one I eventually marry," Newel said.

"Well then, Newel, Liz will have to know our family secrets and be okay with them. Before you can marry her, you must have a job that pays well enough to support you and your family by the time you go to do your missionary work," Newel's father said.

That same evening Newel's father excused himself for a late-night business appointment. As he left all dressed in black, Newel's mother knew she would be having a fun time when he returned afterward! Newel's father decided to go to a different area this time, because the White Chapel district had begun crawling with police. He settled for the Somersby district and parked his car in an alley. He watched for several hours before he saw a lady of the evening, all dressed in red but only five feet tall. Newel's father came out into the light at the end of the alley and motioned the prostitute over.

"Hello, sir. Would you like to entertain Carla tonight?" the woman asked.

Newel's father nodded, leering at her. As they turned and went into the alley, Newel's father put his arms around her from behind and squeezed her breasts. He forced her to lean against the moist brick wall of the alley.

"Mm, sir, I enjoy a nasty fuck from a man like you," Carla said with a giggle.

Something about Carla, intuition or impatience, made her turn around just in time to see Newel's father with the long, thin, razor-sharp knife poised above her back, ready to strike. Carla reacted fast, as living on the streets and being in her line of work had taught her to be quick. She turned away from Newel's father and was suddenly brandishing a police billy club. Carla struck at Newel's father as hard as she could. She had heard about the murders in White Chapel and carried the club lashed to her wrist for protection.

Newel's father didn't see the club until it was too late. It struck him so hard he almost went unconscious as he fell against the car. He had blood flowing freely down one side of his face, and his last image of Carla was of her hauling her ass up the street and screaming for help. Newel's father barely managed to get in his car and off the street before the police came. He knew he was in trouble. His head throbbed, and he kept wanting to fall asleep. When he finally pulled up to his home, he just sat there and eventually slumped forward against the horn on the car.

Newel and his mother came running out and found him. They managed to quickly get him inside. Newel's mother saw that her husband would need a few stitches, which she could take care of, but the car would need to be cleaned up spotless of the blood. Newel knew how to do that and got to that particular chore. By the time he finished, his father was resting comfortably in bed and recounting what had happened.

Later, Newel spoke to his mother. "Mother, the whore is a danger to our family. Father was probably recognized, and that would bring the police down on our whole family unless that whore is taken care of!" Newel said.

"But, Newel, do you think you can do it to protect the family?" his mother asked.

"Yes, Mother. In a couple of days when the hooker ventures out again, I'll be waiting for her, and then there will be one less whore in this world," Newel said with a smile.

Newel started preparing his bag with great diligence, and as his mother watched, she found that she was very proud of her son. On the day of Newel's adventure to the Somersby area, he had dinner with his family, which included Liz. Newel's mother had invited Liz to stay till Newel got back, and she eagerly agreed. Liz was excited to find out about the attitude of Newel's family toward whores and how it was very much like hers!

When Newel got to the Somersby area, he parked and waited a very long time. Just when he thought he wouldn't see the little tart, he heard footsteps echoing across the wet brick sidewalk. Then he spied her. Newel stood against a wall as Carla passed; that was the little whore his father had described to him.

"Hello. Are you in a hurry to get home, miss?" Newel asked in his kindest voice.

At first, Carla just stopped and looked, making sure it wasn't the same nut who had tried to kill her earlier in the week. When she saw it was a young man, she smiled and walked over to Newel.

"Well, a young man ready for some pussy, are you?" Carla asked with a smile.

"Yes, and I'd like to try yours first," Newel said, smiling.

Newel led Carla into an alleyway and pulled her close to him, his hands on her ass. As she wiggled and giggled, Newel's mind took over. Suddenly, all six knife darts pierced Carla's lungs, and she gasped quietly.

"What's that, dear? Can't catch your breath? Well, you won't need to be able to breathe anyway, because you'll be dead. The man you struck last week was my father," Newel said.

Then he put Carla into an open field behind one of the local buildings and marked his territory. When the police found Carla, the whole area was closed down. Carla had been laid out on her back, and all her skin was filleted off the front of her torso. Every cop who saw the scene lost his lunch, violently.

When Newel arrived home, he changed to clean clothes and disposed of the ones he had been wearing before walking in. "Mother, it's done. She won't threaten us anymore," Newel said.

With that, Newel took Liz to his bedroom. Liz was amazed at Newel's energy, and for the next few hours, Liz and Newel ravaged each other.

Liz got up when she heard someone stirring in the kitchen. It was Newel's mother.

"Can I ask you something personal?" Liz asked Newel's mother.

"Sure, Liz," Newel's mother replied.

"Are all men in this family as sexually charged as Newel?"

Newel's mother smiled. "Yes, they are, especially after their evening appointments. So are the women," Newel's mother said, smiling at her. "Does that bother you, Liz?"

"No. As a matter of fact, I enjoy letting myself go with someone I care for like Newel," Liz said, smiling.

* * * * *

Liz stopped in often to Newel's home and became a regular fixture around the house and with all the family. Most of the time, she would help take care of Newel's father as he continued recovering from the attack or help Newel's mother with basic housework.

Then one day Newel came home with some news so exciting he couldn't sit still.

"Mother and Father, I've been offered a job, and you'll never guess where," Newel said with a smile. "I've got a job at a cutlery store, and part of my job will be sharpening knives and cutting utensils."

Everyone laughed but for different reasons. Liz was laughing with everyone and for joy, because she knew Newel needed to have a job before he could get married, and somehow she knew he would be asking her to be his wife soon. Everyone else in the family was laughing because of their family secret and where he now would be working. With his knowledge of knives, he would be requested by everyone to sharpen their items.

Amy Returns

For Peter, the next few years seemed to be normal for any teenager, and so he didn't think his first day as a senior would be special. That changed when the teacher announced that they were getting a new student. The teacher started to introduce her, but when the girl saw Peter's face, she smiled. Peter recognized her instantly. It was Amy; she had returned to town. Peter could hardly keep in his seat, and his heart rate had just taken a big jump.

Amy went and sat in a desk next to Peter. At the end of class, she passed him a note. It read: "Peter, meet me for lunch today."

Peter smiled and nodded slightly toward Amy as she left the room. At lunch, Peter saw Amy looking for him, and she came right over when she spotted him.

"Peter, how have you been?" Amy asked.

"I've been good, Amy. What brought you back to town?" Peter asked.

"My dad got a promotion, and we had to move back," Amy said.

"I'm glad your dad got the promotion, Amy. I've really missed you!" Peter said.

"I missed you too, Peter. Can I ask you a question?" Amy asked.

"Sure, Amy. What is it?" Peter said.

In a hushed whisper, Amy leaned toward Peter and asked, "Can you still do the stuff with your mind, Peter?"

Peter smiled a bit and then looked at the banana in front of Amy and started concentrating. Slowly, the banana started spinning clockwise, and then Peter made the banana stop and spin counterclockwise.

"My parents decided to help me practice when you left, Amy," Peter said.

"That's great, Peter. Would you mind walking me home today, so we can catch up on things? I just live one block farther over from you now," Amy said.

"I would really like that," Peter said with a smile that threatened to break his face.

As Peter and Amy were walking home, they were talking and laughing constantly. As they turned down a street with a long picket fence and large groups of flowers poking through and over the fence, Peter asked Amy, "Amy, how would you like to do something fun with butterflies?"

"You're not going to hurt them, are you?" Amy asked him.

"No, Amy, don't worry," Peter said.

They walked slowly to the flowers and could see hundreds of colorful butterflies among the flowers. Then Peter took Amy's hand and rubbed some flowers along her hand and fingers.

"Amy, put your hand or finger under a butterfly so they can taste it," Peter said.

Amy did as Peter said, and soon she had butterflies clinging to her hand and finger.

"Peter, you're not using any of your mind stuff to do this, are you?" Amy asked.

"No, Amy. I learned about this in biology class. Butterflies taste with their feet, so if they land on something sweet, like pollen, they start feeding." The whole time they played with the butterflies Amy was smiling at Peter. As they got to Amy's house, Peter thought he would show Amy just how glad he was to see her, so he gave her a quick kiss on the lips. Amy smiled and then kissed Peter a second time, very passionately. Peter had never experienced this type of kiss, but now that he had, he wanted more. What Amy and Peter didn't know was that Amy's parents were watching them with great interest, especially Amy's dad. When Amy entered the house, she was greeted by her parents.

"Was that Peter, Amy?" Amy's dad asked.

"Yes, Dad. He was just welcoming me back and wanted to show how much he missed me with a kiss," Amy said.

"Amy, what was the longer second kiss for?" Amy's mom asked with a smile.

"That was for teaching me how to feed butterflies on the way home," Amy said with a big smile.

Amy's dad looked at Amy's mom. "Feeding butterflies rates a kiss like that from my daughter?" he questioned.

Amy's mom burst into laughter. "As I remember when you were Peter's age, you were pretty imaginative as to how you impressed me," she said, her laughter barely down to a giggle.

* * * * *

Amy became a fixture around Peter's parents' home, helping Peter work on his talents as they developed. Peter's parents really liked Amy. Peter had started to study for his driving test and started studying some city maps that his dad's friend Bob had given him when he learned he was going to be a taxi driver. One afternoon Bob showed up at Peter's parents' home.

"Hi, Sam. Could I talk with Peter if he's here?" Bob asked.

Sam let Bob in, but Sam's face was grim. He thought he had a good idea why Bob wanted to talk to Peter. The police hadn't had any luck nailing down who was committing the taxi driver robberies/murders. Some of the drivers had been beaten so badly they had died before they got to the hospital.

"Peter, Bob's here. He wants to talk to you," Sam called up to Peter.

Peter came down slowly. Bob looked up at Peter; he felt as if Peter already knew why he was there, but he thought he should do Peter the courtesy of letting him refuse if he wanted.

"Peter, we need your help on a case that's been hounding us for a few years now. It's the taxicab robberies case," Bob said.

Peter flew down the steps to get his coat, and Amy joined him at the bottom of the stairs.

"Peter, are you sure you really want to take on this case?" Amy asked.

"Yes, Amy, it might make it possible for me to save some lives!" Peter said.

"Then promise me, Peter, to protect yourself in every way you can whenever you go out on one of these cases, including using your special abilities," Amy whispered as she kissed him.

Peter and Bob left for the police station. Peter was very quiet, almost to the point of brooding. He wondered if he was actually going to be able to make a difference like a real cop and catch the bastard who murdered his uncle. Before Peter realized it, they were at the police station; many people were staring at Peter because of his young age but also because they knew why Bob had gone to pick up this newest member of the special squad. This was the person Bob wouldn't talk about with other cops except to say that he was special in so many ways there were too many to list. Bob had radioed in ahead of their arrival for all the evidence from the last taxi robbery to be displayed in the evidence room. As they started looking through all the evidence, Peter paused here and there, picking up an evidence bag and then replacing it.

"Peter, if you need to take something out of one of the evidence bags, just let me know first. Okay?" Bob said.

Peter nodded without saying a word and kept walking around the table of evidence. He could feel something was there, but it wouldn't come through.

"Bob, were there any small personal items found in the cab?" Peter asked.

Bob brought a small half-gallon plastic bag out with the loose items in it.

"Can I handle these," he asked.

"Sure, Peter. Go ahead," Bob encouraged.

As Peter handled the individual items, he gently pushed with his mind. Suddenly, he saw something that he hadn't seen before, a lapel button that was glowing gray. Peter picked the button up and turned it right-side up to read it. The slogan on the button read: "Police Are Pigs!"

"Bob, this button was put there by the robber. Were there buttons at any of the other robberies?" Peter asked.

"Peter, I don't know, but let me check the evidence log and find out," Bob said as he hurried off.

When Bob came back, he was a bit winded from running. "Peter, every robbery had a button at the scene, each with something degrading about cops," Bob said. "Peter, can you get a handle on the person who's doing this?" Bob asked.

But before Peter could answer, they were informed that another cabdriver had been robbed. Bob told Peter to come with him to the fresh crime scene. As they arrived, Peter recognized the driver. He was a driver who had agreed to take Peter under his wing and teach him how to be a great taxi driver. His name was Big John. Big John's cab was standing partially on the curb with the doors on the driver's side wide open.

"Is Big John okay?" Peter asked.

"He was beaten very badly, but they think he will be fine after a long hospital stay," Bob said.

Beaten badly was an understatement. Big John was sporting two black eyes, wearing a neck brace, and probably suffering from some broken ribs.

"Did you find a button or anything else?" Peter asked.

Bob smiled. "Yeah, Peter, I found the button and a bonus. I think that Big John got hold of the robber's coat and wouldn't let go, so the robber left it behind," Bob said as he handed the coat to Peter.

Peter's mind was at full power. Someone had hurt his friend, and they would pay. As Peter concentrated, he saw an address. He was shocked to discover he knew the address. But when he got hold of the button, he got an even bigger shock. Bob could see it on Peter's face.

"Peter, what's wrong?" Bob asked.

"When I held the button from the cab, I saw my uncle's old hack license number, and I know the address of the person doing the taxi robberies!" Peter exclaimed.

Peter told Bob the address and cautioned everyone that this should be a silent arrest, because in his mind's eye Peter saw many weapons in the home. Slowly, the police approached the home and broke the door in. The person living there was handcuffed and on the floor in minutes. They had just arrested Jenkins's father, who was claiming he was innocent.

It became clear he was lying once they searched his home. Jenkins's father had stolen one item to keep as a trophy from every taxi he robbed—the driver's hack license. Peter went right to the cabinet drawer that held them and opened it. As he looked through the licenses, he held one up; it was his uncle's. Peter felt his anger boiling like a volcano getting ready to erupt.

Peter was well aware that he could kill his uncle's murderer with his mind, but he'd made a promise to his parents. So instead of killing the man, Peter just nudged him backward, and as the man's back met the wall, it cracked loudly. The man fell unconscious against the wall, leaving his broken silhouette in the plasterboard. While Bob waited with Peter for the man to be booked, Bob shook his head.

"Two bad apples from the same tree, Peter, and you ran into them both and caught them both," Bob said.

"I gather there is a nice reward for this guy?" Peter asked.

"Yes, Peter, but why do you ask?" Bob said.

"I've been thinking of buying a house after graduation and giving my parents some space to enjoy life," Peter said.

"Well, I think that's a great idea, Peter. Plus, it would give you space if you wanted to have a girlfriend come over," Bob said with a smile.

Peter just smiled back. With the life he was leading on the special list with the police, it would take someone very special to share his life. When they arrived at Peter's home, Bob gave everyone his account of the events. Peter's parents were very proud, but Peter walked to the backyard and sat down with Amy by his side and cried quietly as she held him without explanation. The one thing that Peter had to resign himself to was that he enjoyed helping people who were in trouble just like his dad, Bob, and other cops on the force. It was very satisfying.

* * * * *

The rest of the school year went by normally for Amy and Peter through graduation. Peter and Amy were talking about what the future held.

"Peter, is a cabdriver all you want to be? After all, they don't make much money for a family," Amy said with concern in her voice.

Peter looked Amy in the eyes. "I'm not like regular taxi drivers. I get my salaried check from the police every month whether I work a case or not, and if I help solve a case, I get the reward too. I've saved everything I have made with the police, and I now have enough for a house to live in, Amy," Peter said.

"Peter, are you kidding me? Really?" Amy exclaimed. "Peter, you know that I'm planning on going to city college, don't you?"

Peter had a little smirk on his face. "Amy, do you know how much I care about you?" he said.

"I think I do, Peter. Why?" Amy said.

"Because I was thinking that if you could put up with my being a bit of a slob that you might consider living with me. And if things go well, something more permanent in the future," Peter said, smiling.

Amy's mouth fell open, and she had to take in some air. She suddenly burst into laughter and tackled Peter into the grass as she kissed him. Peter and Amy went to both their parents together to give them the news. Surprisingly, both sets of parents thought it was a great idea.

Once Peter turned eighteen, he was eligible to be a taxi driver, and after studying all the city maps Bob had given him, he seemed like a natural. He became so good his first year as a cabbie that he won the annual top cabbie award. Peter started to get requests for VIP service, which meant big tips. Peter always seemed to have a knack for getting through the thickest traffic any time, day or night. Of course, some help from his highly tuned mind abilities helped.

* * * * *

One evening as Peter and Amy were sleeping, Peter became violently restless and woke Amy. Amy tried shaking Peter awake, but he just kept shaking, sleeping, and sweating like he was running a marathon. Amy called Peter's parents, and they recognized the problem. It had happened once before.

"Amy, just hold Peter close. Talk to him using his name and tell him where he is," Peter's mom said.

"Okay," she told Peter's mom and went back to Peter, carrying her cell phone.

Peter was dreaming a dark, sinister dream. It felt like fingers of wet fog were wrapping around his mind, trying to enter and retrieve information. But Peter's concentration was broken by Amy's voice full of worry and her shaking his body. Peter heard the voice speak to him from the fog.

"Hello, Peter. I now know where you live. I will be coming to your city soon, but you may not like how we meet!"

Then as the fingers of fog pulled back into the dark recesses of Peter's mind, he heard the laughter again, but it was somehow different. It was dark, evil, and seemed to spread through Peter's mind the way black ink mixes with water.

Peter finally woke with a start and stared at Amy. "We have to get to your parents and my parents to tell them about the dream and to warn them," Peter said after telling Amy what had happened.

Talking to Peter's parents was the easy part, because they were used to Peter's special abilities. But Amy's parents had no idea about Peter's abilities or that he helped the police from time to time.

When they arrived at Amy's parents' home, Amy and Peter asked them sit down for the bombshell they were about to drop.

"Mom and Dad, what I have to tell you may be hard to believe, so let me finish before you say anything," Amy said. "Peter works with the police on a special team of people who help solve desperate cases or cold cases."

"How does a taxi driver help the cops?" Amy's dad asked.

"Peter is on a list of people with special abilities whom the police find useful, and the people on the list are salaried to be available 24/7," Amy said.

Amy's dad's face grew skeptical. "Amy, are these people psychics?"

"Some are, Dad, but Peter's abilities are much wider in variety," Amy said, smiling. "Peter, why don't you show my parents some of what you can do."

Peter smiled and focused, and suddenly, several items in the room levitated and moved toward Amy's parents. They couldn't believe their eyes.

"I can also receive impressions from objects and people. Give me your hand," Peter said to Amy's mom. As Peter held her hand, he smiled. Leaning close to Amy's mom's ear, he whispered. "I know you found the cruise tickets for your upcoming anniversary that your husband was planning to surprise you with. I also know you bought a special sexy nightie that has hardly anything to it to surprise him. It's purple, just like the one Amy has," Peter said as Amy's mom blushed.

"What did he say to you? Was he right? I want to know," Amy's dad said.

Peter smiled at Amy's dad. "You'll find out next month," he said.

Amy's dad was about to argue but stopped when it dawned on him what next month was.

"Your wife has something special for you too, but you won't get to see it till you're on the cruise ship," Peter whispered to Amy's dad.

"Okay, we believe you, Amy, but what's made you tell us now?" Amy's mom asked.

"Let's all get together at Peter's parents' house, so it only has to be explained once," Amy said.

As they went to Peter's parents' place, both Amy and her mom were talking, and Amy found out about what Peter had said to her. When she found out Amy had a nightie just like the one she bought for her anniversary, they both broke into gales of laughter. Peter and Amy's dad followed and just shook their heads. When they arrived at Peter's parents' place, coffee was on, and they all sat to talk.

"I didn't realize just how special a person my daughter was with until today," Amy's dad said to Peter's parents.

"Peter was special before he had these abilities, but now he's more so. And the work with the police can be dangerous," Peter's dad said before turning to his son. "Peter, what happened to get you so alarmed for all of us?"

"Well, I had a dream. There's another person out there with abilities like mine, and we can communicate with each other mentally," Peter said. "The person calls himself Newel. He lives in London and says he's coming to this city to visit me but that I might not like how we meet."

"That sounds like a definite threat," Peter's dad said as everyone nodded in agreement.

"I just want you all to be aware of your surroundings and anyone who has even a hint of abilities like mine," Peter said.

"How do you know he isn't already here, Peter?" Amy's mom asked.

"Because I would sense his presence, like an irritation I couldn't scratch," Peter said.

* * * * *

Across the Atlantic Ocean, as Newel rested, he suddenly started to smile broadly. How ironic that he had found out that the city Peter lived in was also where Peter was using his abilities to help the police with hard-to-solve crimes. As Newel lay there on his bed, an idea bloomed in his head like a large black rose. He would introduce himself to Peter by becoming one of the cases they called on Peter to help solve!

Newel's First

If Newel were to become as great as his legendary great-great-grandfather, he must take a wife, and only one woman would be right for Newel—Liz. Newel invited Liz over to have a very special dinner with his parents and him, but before he could invite Liz, Newel's father had a hard talk with him.

"Newel, you know that if Liz can't accept the secret ways of our family, I will have to kill her before she leaves our home to keep our family safe. Can you deal with that?" Newel's father asked.

"Father, Liz is the one, I'm sure; we talked about what a disease whores are to society," Newel said.

"How can you be that sure, Newel?" Newel's father asked.

"One time when I was holding Liz, I saw an image in my mind of no more prostitutes on any of the streets, and Liz was celebrating with our family at their extermination," Newel said.

"Well, then by all means, bring your lady to dinner with us," Newel's father said with a smile.

On the day Newel was bringing Liz to dinner, he arrived early and walked a bit with her first. If she couldn't accept his family and their secrets, it might be the last time he saw her. Dinner went very well. It was just Newel's parents, Liz, and Newel. After dinner, Newel's father asked Liz what she really felt about the whores who roamed the streets.

"I wish there was a permanent solution to that vermin spreading all that disease," Liz said with disdain.

"Liz, has Newel told you about his great-great-grandfather? He was a bit famous," Newel's father said.

"No, he hasn't," Liz said.

"Newel's great-great-grandfather became famous in London and in America for what he did. He was the first missionary of our family for our great cause, which is to wipe out all prostitutes," Newel's father said.

The whole family was watching for Liz's response to the new information. Suddenly, Liz smiled broadly and kissed Newel passionately, as Newels parents smiled on.

"I think your family's mission is a great effort. Who was Newel's legendary great-great-grandfather?" Liz asked.

Newel's father smiled. "He gained a nickname back in the 1800s. He was known as Jack the Ripper," Newel's father said, watching Liz's expression closely.

"*Wow*, that's fantastic!" Liz exclaimed.

With that, everyone started celebrating the new arrival into the family, Liz. Later, when Liz and Newel where alone, Liz had some things on her mind.

"Newel, when will you have to go on your missionary work?" Liz asked.

"Not till I'm twenty-one," Newel replied quietly.

"When you leave, Newel, I'm going to miss you horribly, especially having you physically next to me," Liz said.

"Well, Liz, we best make good use of every minute we have together," Newel said with a smile as he pulled her toward a deserted home and into an empty backyard.

There, Newel and Liz took pleasure in each other's bodies till the sun came up, waking in each other's arms and gathering their clothes. Newel slept till noon and then started planning where he would go to make his first kill as a missionary for his family. He knew just where he would do it. Newel's mother had been talking with Liz about what it was like being away while their men were doing missionary work for the family.

"Liz, it can be very difficult to stay faithful during such times because of the length of time the missionary work can take. It may be six months or a couple of years. Just remember that once you marry Newel, he must be the only man you sleep with," his mother said. "But the wives of these men, we learn to be resourceful to get our needs met."

Liz smiled back. She knew exactly what Newel's mother meant and had no problem with finding ways to meet her needs without men or women.

"Newel, have you decided where you will do your missionary work?" Newel's mother asked.

"Yes, Mother, I have decided. I'm going to Portland, Oregon, in the Pacific Northwest," Newel said.

"Why would you choose to go there, so far away from us?" Newel's mother asked with concern in her voice.

"For two reasons, Mother. First, it's virgin territory, and I will open it for our family's mission. Second, I found out that the person I've been communicating with lives in that city, and I want to meet him," Newel said with a smile. "Liz, does it bother you that I'm going so far away to do my missionary work?"

"No, Newel, but promise me you will do your best to be legendary like your great-great-grandfather and that you will use your special skills so that you come home to me safely," Liz said.

Newel smiled broadly but devilishly at Liz. "I will, Liz. You can count on it!"

Next, Newel needed to make preparations for when the time came for him to go out and make his first kill, all by himself. Newel spent time preparing for his special day, but he also spent time with his father, talking about methods and tactics for not getting caught and about his great-great-grandfather Jack and what he had done in London to become famous.

"You see, Newel, few people realize that when the police presence became too intense in London, he got out of town and flourished in another location—the East Coast of America, New York, Philadelphia, Baltimore, and that general area. Some of the newspapers of the time even suggested that Jack the Ripper had arrived in America because the murdered prostitutes were killed in your great-great-grandfather's special way," Newel's father said.

"But why didn't that stir up a hornets' nest in America if the newspapers were suggesting it?" Newel asked.

"Sometimes people read things and just can't believe what they're seeing, so the accusations of the reporters just died out," Newel's father said. "After all, Newel, how many people would believe in your special abilities if they couldn't see them? Even then, they might think it was a magic trick of some kind."

"I see what you're saying, Father," Newel said.

"Newel, when you meet the person you have been communicating with, be sure not to underestimate him. After all, he has the same abilities as you," his father said.

With that, Newel left to go to bed. Liz was waiting for him. In the morning, Liz and Newel announced that they would marry when Newel returned from his work in America and that he was giving himself a time limit of six months to be back home. They had a huge party to celebrate the announcement, and Newel's mother showed Liz the antique diamond wedding ring that had been passed down to the males in the family to give to their brides. It was beautiful. Liz tried it on, and it fit like it was made for her.

* * * * *

While celebrations carried on in England for Newel and Liz, across the ocean in Portland, Oregon, Peter was getting a phone call in the middle of the day from Bob. Up until then, life had been everyday, normal life with Peter and Amy talking about getting married when Amy graduated from City College. But now the phone rang, and Peter sensed it was for him and his talents.

"Peter, we need you. It's something urgent. I'll come by in fifteen minutes," Bob said.

Peter could hear the stress in Bob's voice and knew this was something out of the ordinary. When Bob picked Peter up, he clued him in on what had happened. It seemed that someone had decided to kidnap the mayor's daughter-in-law, which the mayor took as a personal insult and threat.

As Peter and Bob pulled up in front of the mayor's home, they were greeted by personal security and the police who had been looking over the area for clues. The scene inside was chaos. Peter saw crying individuals, a worried husband, and a father-in-law who happened to be the mayor. He wielded a large amount of power, which at that moment was directed right at the police to solve this crime.

"What exactly happened?" Bob asked of the mayor.

"My son's wife, Abby, was outside talking with the lawn man when all of a sudden we heard a scream, and a car screeched away down our street. All we found was her shoe on the lawn," the mayor said.

All the evidence had already been bagged so that it could be gone over back at the police headquarters.

"Did your wife have any enemies, Mr. Dorne?" Bob asked the mayor's son.

"Not that I know of. Not anyone who would do something like this," Mr. Ken Dorne said.

* * * * *

After spending a few hours at the mayor's home, Peter and Bob headed straight back to police headquarters so Peter might be able to solve this sooner using his abilities.

Once at headquarters, all the evidence was spread out on a table so it could be processed by Peter and Bob and a few trusted technicians. It was strange. Peter walked around the table several times but kept stopping at the shoe that the wife had left behind.

"Bob, is it okay to handle this shoe?" Peter asked.

"Sure, Peter. Everything's been printed and photographed," Bob said.

Peter removed the shoe, but as he pushed with his mind, all he got was a replay of Mrs. Dorne's daily routine. As Peter was putting the shoes back into the bag, the bottom of the shoe was scraped by the bag, knocking clumps of cut grass off near

Peter's hand. On a hunch, Peter picked up the grass and pushed with his mind. All at once, a license plate number swam to the surface of his mind as clear as a bell, and he wrote it down, to check it against the Mayors' home employees.

"Bob, I think this is the gardener's license number. Could you run it and get an address?" Peter asked urgently.

"Sure, Peter. Right away!" Bob said as he hurried off.

Soon Bob came running back a bit winded. It turned out that the gardener had a rap sheet, which was bad enough if he were involved, but what was worse is that he had a houseboat on the Willamette River. If he murdered Mrs. Dorne, he could just dump her into the river, and they would never find her body. Bob and Peter made a beeline for the car, and along with several police cars, they headed to the gardener's address. Bob had passed the word that this was to be a silent bust with no lights or sirens.

As they arrived near the houseboat, they quietly approached on foot. Under a cold evening sky, the moon shone bright like a harvest moon. When they got close, they heard voices.

"You are such a stupid bitch. They told me when they paid me that they would prefer you be dead and disappear for good," the gardener was saying.

When the police heard that, Bob gave the go sign, and the police caved in the doors. The gardener started to raise his gun, but Peter saw this and pushed his mind at the gardener hard, slamming him backward and bending his gun in half so nobody would get hurt. When they got the gardener to the police station, they had Mrs. Dorne taken to the hospital but kept away from the media until they knew who was behind the kidnapping. When Bob and Peter got to the interrogation room, the district attorney was already there recording the gardener's statement. When he was done, he came out shaking his head.

"Bob, this case is going to shake things up a bit," the DA said.

"What do you mean?" Bob asked.

"I'll let you read the transcript and do the arrest. Okay, Bob?" the DA said.

When Bob read the transcript and the arrest warrant, he only had one thing to say. "Holy fuck! What an asshole!" Bob exclaimed.

Bob told Peter where they were going as Peter read the arrest warrant. Peter just shook his head. Bob and Peter pulled into the long driveway behind the police car to bring Mrs. Dorne home from the hospital. They all walked in together.

"Officers, there was no need to give a personal escort to Mrs. Dorne," the mayor said.

"Well, Mayor, we are here on another matter. The man we caught told us who paid to have this lady kidnapped and eventually killed," Bob said. "Mr. Dorne, we have a warrant for your arrest for the kidnapping and attempted murder of your wife."

Two cops immediately cuffed Mr. Dorne.

"But why would you do this to me, Ken?" Mrs. Dorne asked of her husband.

"Because I'm bored with you. Why would I want to stay with you when there are so many young, sexually adventurous ladies out there for the taking? And believe me, I've sampled a few," Mr. Dorne said as he started laughing wildly while being led to a waiting police car.

Both Bob and Peter made their apologies to the family, and the family thanked them both for everything they had done. On the way back, both Bob and Peter were quiet, but then Bob spoke up.

"Peter, you really did great, and although there wasn't any reward, it might help the funding for the police next budget time," Bob said. "And maybe an especially nice wedding gift from the police department and the mayor when you and Amy get married," Bob said.

Peter smiled broadly. "Thanks, Bob!"

Police Mystery

The police in the London area were amazed at the crime rate, particularly violent murders, which had taken a noticeable jump over the past six months—in particular, the murders of prostitutes. A Detective Marsh was appointed to lead a task force to catch the mad man or men doing the murders. At a meeting of the task force members, Detective Marsh was bringing everyone up to speed when the silence of the group was broken.

"Maybe we should be looking for Jack the Ripper or his relatives," one young officer quipped, which brought laughter from the group.

"Do you think this is funny, gentlemen?" Marsh said violently.

"Maybe you should take a look at these slides of the crime scenes," Marsh announced.

As the slides came up, the room grew silent. They were in color and showed every gory detail, from severed heads and filleted torsos to the removal of organs. Some of the group retched out loud.

"Now it's not such a laughing matter. You can see that the person or persons responsible do have a Jack the Ripper mentality, but we are not looking for some feeble old murderer from the eighteen hundreds. These individuals are present day, and we will find them!" Marsh thundered.

Detective Marsh could not have known just how close he had come to hitting the nail on the head for this case. The murders were, indeed, being committed by the relatives of Jack the Ripper, and they intended on continuing to commit murders in England and any other country until the prostitutes were wiped out.

As the task force was working on the murders, something kept bothering Marsh. There seemed to be an interruption of a week to ten days between the last murder and a hooker who had been attacked in the Somersby area. She was going to come in and talk to the police sketch artist, but she never showed up.

"Michaels, could you check with the area residents and local working girls in the Somersby area and see if the girl who was murdered was the same one who was attacked the week before?" Marsh directed.

"Sure, Chief. I'll take a few people with me to try to cover the area quicker," Michaels said.

Michaels and his team searched until night came, which improved their chances of running into the working girls. They explained what they were doing to everyone they met and actually knocked on several doors that had lights on. Most of the people were more than willing to talk to them just to get that butcher off the streets.

It wasn't until late in the evening that luck finally struck. They knocked at the door of a home, and a small lady peeked out but relaxed once she saw the police badges. When they asked her if she knew the lady who was attacked the week before, her eyes teared up.

"She was my sister. Just when she thought it was safe to go out again, she ended up getting killed by some fucking beast of a man," she said.

Michaels reported everything they had found out, including a general description from one of the working girls who had seen Carla, the victim, talking with a young man all dressed in black. Marsh wondered if these two attacks were related or if it was just a damn copycat crime.

Several of the detectives on the task force had begun to realize something as they searched cases of murdered prostitutes with mutilations. There were many of them stretching over the years but with small differences. Some were more brutal, while others had a touch of finesse or class to the crime, if that was possible. It was becoming clear that they may have a bigger case then they originally thought, which kicked the task force into high gear to catch the person or persons responsible!

Newel's First

The time had come, and Newel was ready. Newel didn't think of the killing of the whore who had struck his father as his first. That had been more an act of preservation of the family way. This adventure was entirely his own for making the world know of his presence. All his tools were in his bag, and his suitcase was filled with clean clothes and waiting in the back of his father's car. Tonight Newel would make himself known to the police and claim his territory as a predator by ridding the world of one of those whores.

"Newel, where will your appointment be this evening?" Newel's mother asked.

Mothers are always mothers to their children. No matter how old they are and what they do, they worry about them.

"Mother, tonight my appointment is in the White Chapel district where my great-great-grandfather started our mission," Newel said with a smile that reminded Newel's father of a shark's grin just before it attacked!

"Newel, remember what we talked about regarding not getting caught. Use all your abilities," Newel's father said.

"Don't worry. I won't be caught. After all, I have a trip to America coming up," Newel said. As he passed through the front door of the home, it looked like he just left the front door open, but suddenly the door closed shut all by itself in front of his parents' eyes.

Newel's mother's mouth was agape, but Newel's father just smiled.

"I think that was just our son's way of showing off a little, dear. Don't worry. He's going to make our family proud tonight and in America," Newel's father said.

Newel was all excited about going into London for two reasons. He was anxious to start his family's work, and it also meant he was that much closer to getting out on his own to Oregon, to the city where the person he had been communicating with mentally lived. Once there, he would start a bloody reign of terror among the whores of that city like they had never seen before.

The drive to London was relaxing to Newel in a more sinister way. It had been raining off and on, and it was very dark. Newel imagined himself as a big jungle cat coming out to feed like in the TV shows he liked to watch. *Look out, prey,* he thought to himself. *There's a new predator around who is even more dangerous than the others!* Newel drove to the White Chapel district and found an alleyway that suited his needs. It had a great view of the street that was noted for the whores who patrolled it.

As Newel sat waiting for the right person to walk by, he was toying with an obscure good-luck charm. It was a carved ivory dragon rearing up. It had appealed to Newel because of the savage appearance of the figure, even though it was only two inches tall. But the way Newel played with it was not normal.

Newel slowly spun the charm midair as he thought about which woman was going to be his first. Suddenly, the figure dropped to the seat of the car. Newel saw the woman he wanted; she would be perfect for his first kill. She had bright natural red hair and wore a light red dress with a slit up the front to her waist. She was what men might call voluptuous, but Newel just thought of her as tonight's fodder. She sauntered toward where Newel was standing near a street lamp and smiled as Newel rubbed his crotch brazenly while looking at her. She walked right up to him.

"Hi there. My name is Coleen. Do you have something in there that you would like to share with me?" she asked as she rubbed Newel's crotch.

"Yes I do, Coleen, but not out here in the street. Will the alley be okay with you?" Newel said with a broad smile showing lots of teeth and glistening with saliva.

If Newel could have seen how much he looked like his father right then, he would have been ecstatic.

"That would be fine, but why would a good-looking young man need my services?" Coleen asked.

"Because, Coleen, I want the nastiest sex I can have. No love, just animal lust!"

"Well, come with me deeper into the alley so our moaning won't be so easily heard," Coleen said with a smile.

Newel turned Coleen so she faced the wet brick wall of the alley.

"Oh, aren't you the nasty one. You want me doggie style first?" Coleen said with a giggle.

"Do you really want to see just how charming I can be?" Newel asked in his best sugar-sweet voice right in her ear.

"Sure I do," Coleen said.

Newel turned Coleen around and kissed the cleavage of her ample breasts. Then smiling, Newel made Coleen's throat spasm so she couldn't scream. Coleen's eyes bulged out even though she could still breathe; fear and shock were taking over her mind. Newel lifted Coleen's body six feet off the ground. She could feel the wetness of the wall seeping through the clothes on her back.

"Coleen, you don't know it yet, but you're very special, because you're my official first lady of my mission. I guess it's fair to say you sort of captured my heart for this evening," Newel said, smiling.

Coleen was bucking against the wall, suspended, trying to get free with no results.

Then Coleen saw Newel take out a long, thin knife that looked razor sharp. She saw Newel slide it slowly into her where her belly button would be. She couldn't understand why she felt very little pain. Then Newel smiled and slowly released his hold on Coleen's body, allowing it to slide along the knife, which seemed to be staying in place all by itself. Coleen's torso below her rib cage was opened, and as Newel laid her back down, she was taking a few last breaths as Newel bent closer.

"Coleen, since you have stolen my heart, it seems only fair that I return the kindness."

Newel proceeded to surgically cut out Coleen's heart and then laid it next to her lifeless body. He had placed an index card in Coleen's pocket where it would be noticed easily.

When her body was discovered, everyone, including the older veterans of the police force, retched. Some even lost their lunch completely. When the index card was found and examined, it had no fingerprints at all and only a few words: I'M BACK!

It was ironic that Detective Marsh was the person who first found the card. Reading it made him boil with anger. He didn't just want to capture this maniac. He wanted him dead and not waiting out a death sentence or life sentence. What he didn't realize was that he may not get his chance unless he captured Newel before he left London for America.

When Newel arrived home, Liz and his mother were waiting for him.

"Newel, how did your appointment go this evening?" Liz and Newel's mother asked at the same time.

Newel smiled as he stood there in his fresh, clean clothes, looking very much like a younger version of his father. "It was delicious!" he said as he took Liz's hand. They made for his bedroom in haste.

Newel and Liz didn't reappear till noon the next day.

"Newel, when do you think you might be leaving for America?" Newel's father asked.

"Father, I think that I should be leaving sometime in the next two weeks so that I can get into the new meat in Oregon," Newel said with an evil leer. Newel's father smiled at the thought of hunting in a new country with all the new smells and targets available. It made his mouth water.

* * * * *

As Detective Marsh sat at his desk trying to figure out the murders and analyze clues, something struck him. *What if the murderer he was searching for did as Jack the Ripper did way back when and just stopped the murder spree? Fuck, that would really be a kick in the teeth to have him just disappear!* Immediately, Detective Marsh ordered that the general description of the younger gentlemen be sent out to all airport security staff. He was officially a person of interest.

* * * * *

Newel's next two weeks were spent with family as much as possible. Newel and Liz planned to wed as soon as he returned. Newel had all the tools of his trade packed, and he said all his good-byes before leaving for the airport. He figured he'd stay the night before his flight near the airport in one of the local hotels and then get up early and head out to catch his flight.

Newel's Dream

In the past ... the dark shrouds, my very presence making me as a predator. My prey is not feeble or innocent but degrades humanity by their actions, reducing humans to products on an assembly line! I strike quickly, my knife as sharp as a razor, cleaving the flesh so fast that no alarming sounds alert anyone, leaving me to do my duty to my family.

Newel had been thinking and talking to himself in the dream. When he realized it was a strange voice talking to him, he woke violently. That had never happened before this past week.

Newel gathered himself. He awakened refreshed of his dream of his ancestors, which had recurred to him for more than a week. Getting up, he gathered his things, including his airline ticket to Portland, Oregon, via Seattle, Washington. It was time he left London for greener pastures and begin his missionary work. It would be a long flight, about nine and a half hours, until he arrived at his destination.

As Newel left the room, the door seemed to close all by itself, but Newel's mind was in control of it as evidenced by the door slamming so hard it shattered the doorjamb. As Newel rode to the airport, he remembered something his parents had taught all his brothers and sisters. They had said that as they went out into the world, they would all have a special skill and touch for the missionary work ahead.

Once Newel got to the airport and checked in, he traveled through security, which he tolerated until the very end when he passed a couple of police officers. Newel smiled politely and kept going, but one of the officers stopped and paused for a moment and looked back at Newel. The officer thought Newel's face looked a bit familiar.

Damn, he thought. *Where have I seen that face?*

Newel paid him no attention and went to a restaurant in the airport to have breakfast, a big feast before his feasting in America.

The officers from the airport finished their duties and arrived back at the police station late that afternoon. As they went to report in, they passed the bulletin board outside the task force room. On it was the general description and sketch of the younger man who was a person of interest in the last two murders.

Officer Bostwick stopped, and his mouth fell open. That was the face he had seen at the airport—or close to it. He had seen the sketch as he and his partner were headed to the airport early that morning, and because he was still new to the force, he hadn't picked up on it fast enough. Officer Bostwick went into the task force room and reported what he had seen to Detective Marsh. Marsh's face grew red with anger and frustration.

"Goddamn it. You just made this investigation that much more difficult by missing that chance. By now, he will have caught a flight and be gone!" Marsh shouted.

"I'm sorry, sir. I do remember where in the airport I saw him. Maybe if we show the sketch to the different terminals, we might get lucky and find out where he went, sir," Bostwick said slowly.

Marsh sent a group of men, including Bostwick, to the airport with instructions not to come back till they had gone and questioned all the airport staff. By the time they arrived back at the airport, Newel was enjoying his flight and had been in the air for two hours. Newel smiled and was feeling a bit devious. As he laid his head back in his seat, he reached out to Peter.

"Peter, I'm on my way to meet you. Beware!"

Peter had been taking a nap on the couch. He didn't have to drive his taxi till that night for a short shift. Suddenly, Peter woke with a start, as if he had just met death itself. Amy found him huddled over with his head in his hands.

"Peter, what's wrong?" she asked as she sat next to Peter.

"You know that person who communicates with me mentally, Amy?" Peter asked.

"Yes. Did he send you another message?"

"Yes, he wanted to let me know he was on his way, and he told me to beware," Peter said.

"Do you think he's dangerous, Peter?" Amy asked.

"I know he is, especially to me because I have the same abilities he does. He wants to prove who the stronger person is," Peter said.

Peter got on the phone to his police friend Bob. "Bob, that person who was communicating with me just sent me a new message. He's coming to Portland very soon, and he told me to beware," Peter said.

"That sounds like a very definite threat, Peter. Will you be able to sense when he gets here?" Bob asked.

"Yes, I'm sure of it, Bob," Peter said. After hanging up the phone, he turned his attention to Amy. "Amy, call our families and warn them that this creep is on his way and to watch for the things I told them about, anything occurring around them that is similar to my abilities."

Peter then decided to send a message of his own to Newel. "If you come to this city and create havoc, I will make sure you don't leave in the same condition that you arrived. *You will leave in worse condition!*"

When Newel received this message, he sat upright in his seat on the plane. His jaw set firmly as he stared out his window into the darkening sky, thinking. *We shall see about that, Peter!*

* * * * *

Back in London, Officer Bostwick and his squad had been showing the sketch to the airport staff all day long. As luck would have it, they found several people who had seen the person they were looking for. Bostwick went back to the station to report all the information to Detective Marsh.

"Detective Marsh, it seems that several people saw our suspect this morning, and we know where he is heading. He was on flight 666, stopping in Seattle, Washington. From there, he could have connected to anywhere," Bostwick said.

"Get the airline notified and get them a sketch to circulate at the Seattle airport to try to figure where he's gone!" Marsh yelled.

* * * * *

Newel couldn't believe how comfortable his traveling had been so far, except the security and the customs checks. He would be on his way to Portland, Oregon, in a matter of hours. As Newel walked past an open door in the Seattle airport, the shock of just how cold the area was this time of year hit him. It was fall, but there was still a cold bite in the wind as it blew along.

Newel remembered that he might have to buy some extra clothes for this type of weather. They would have to allow him freedom of movement and be all black of course. Since Newel had made his first kill all by himself, he felt an urge to kill prostitutes growing inside him. His father had warned him about this.

He realized that if he let these feelings take him over, he might become careless, which could lead to his capture or death by the authorities. Newel didn't intend on letting his bloodlust overtake his better judgment. He would be as famous as his great-great-grandfather who slew prostitutes right in the middle of London and then disappeared, never to be caught. Newel started to think of what else he would need for his work in Portland. A car and a place to stay were first, but he needed to make himself known to Peter. How would he do that? What Newel didn't know was that fate had already decided on how they would meet.

* * * * *

The airport security in Seattle recognized Newel's picture. He had stopped and gone through customs and boarded a flight to Portland. Several of the security staff recognized him. When Detective Marsh heard where he had gone, he smiled and made a call to the Portland Police Department. It was one of the strangest calls he had ever made. He talked to an officer in charge of a special squad, a man named Robert Meyer, who told him they were already aware of the killer coming to Portland, just not when.

"But how could you already be aware of the killer coming to your city?" Marsh asked.

"Well, Detective Marsh, we have someone on our special squad with unique abilities. Will you be coming to visit us, Detective Marsh?" Bob asked with a smile.

"Hell, yes. I'll be on the next flight into Portland, maybe fifteen or twenty hours from now," Marsh said.

"Good. We could use all the help we can get. I think this is going to be a nasty affair, Marsh," Bob said.

"I'll bring the case file and crime scene photos. You don't know just how right you are about this being a nasty one. Could I meet the person who gave you the advance warning about this, Bob?" Marsh asked.

"Sure, Detective Marsh. It would be my pleasure to introduce you," Bob said.

When Bob hung up the phone, he thought to himself, *I heard the doubt in your voice, Marsh, so I will be happy to introduce you to Peter and watch him blow your socks off as he clears your mind of any doubt you have about his abilities!*

Bob was a great believer in Peter's abilities. He had believed those abilities existed in all people to some degree; it was called the Power, or being touched. Some people had magnified degrees of these various abilities, and Bob had been a believer since he was a child. So when his friend Sam Bristol was telling him about his newborn son, Peter, Bob knew right away what was happening and had given as much information to his friend Sam as he could.

* * * * *

As Newel was flying over the state of Oregon from Seattle, he noticed one fact that had him smiling immediately. The moon was out, and it reflected off large rivers in the area, turning them into ribbons of silver. Newel would later find out that the largest river was the Columbia, and the biggest tributary to the Columbia that he saw was the Willamette River. It stretched right through Portland. How convenient this would be for getting rid of the clothes and anything else he needed to get rid of during his time here. As Newel's plane touched down in Portland, it was dark, and it had been raining off and on. Newel felt right at home.

Peter was on the night shift, driving only a half a shift for a friend of his who was sick. As Peter sat there at the section designated for cabs, he saw a man in a bowler hat and long trench coat coming down the line of cabs. He suddenly stopped by Peter's cab and got in.

"Where to, sir?" Peter asked.

"Downtown, where I can find a place to stay. I'm from out of town."

Peter caught the English accent, but he noticed something that bothered him. When Peter looked in his rearview mirror, the man blended into the darkness of the cab. And something about his voice seemed familiar.

As they got downtown among the hotels, the fare asked Peter to pull over. After stopping the car, he turned in his seat. "That will be forty dollars," Peter told him.

As the man passed the money to him, Peter momentarily touched the man's hand. Suddenly, Peter's vision was swimming and flowing red like a giant sea of blood. Peter heard the evil, guttural laughing that he had only heard once before. It was Newel in his cab! Peter's body was in shock, and he momentarily passed out for a second or two. When he regained his senses, the money was lying on the seat with a note that read: "I am here!"

Peter didn't touch the note and substituted forty dollars of his own money just in case Newel had gotten sloppy, but Peter thought the opposite of Newel. He felt Newel was crafty, smart, and an incredibly evil and dangerous killer. Peter phoned his boss at the cab company and then phoned Bob at the police station.

On the way to the station, Peter found himself getting angrier. Something had blocked his ability to sense Newel's presence. Could it be that because he had been working so much his exhaustion had caused him to be less focused, dulling his senses? Peter called into his taxi boss again and told him he couldn't work for a while, until he was finished with a special police project. He wasn't happy, but he promised Peter he could have his old job back whenever he wanted it. As Peter pulled into the evidence garage, the lab technicians and Bob were already there.

"Peter, did you get a look at the person's face who got in your cab?" Bob asked urgently.

"No, Bob. All I could tell was that he was young, in his twenties, about my build, but all dressed in black. And he was wearing a bowler hat," Peter said.

The technicians removed the note and the money. Like Peter thought, Newel wasn't sloppy. There were no fingerprints at all.

"Bob, I tried to see his face, but he seemed to blend right into the darkness in the back of my cab. Then when he paid the fare, our hands touched, and all I saw was red, like blood flowing in front of me. I blacked out for a couple of seconds," Peter said.

"Peter, you will never guess who called me today," Bob said. "A Detective Marsh from London. They've been investigating a case involving a group of murdered prostitutes with a special task force. And they think the killer is on his way here. The head of the investigation is on his way here with a case file and crime scene photos. Peter, this may be bigger than we first realized," Bob said.

"I wonder if the cases are related. That could mean a serial killer who has been active for some time," Peter said.

"You should have heard the surprise in Marsh's voice when I told him we were already aware of the killer's arrival. He instantly wanted to meet you, Peter."

"I'm sure he did. He has probably never run into anyone like me. It should be fun," Peter said with a smile.

When Newel checked in to a hotel, it was a nice one. He used a phony identification card. Newel had thought long and hard about a name for the card and came up with the first name Jack after his great-great-grandfather and the last name Listor, taken from the knife used for performing surgical amputations. And so, Jack Listor checked into a modestly priced hotel.

In the meantime, Bob had a talk with Peter. "Peter, if this gets as nasty as we all feel it will, we all need to get as much rest as we can, so we are at our peak performance. Go home and be with Amy and get rested up. Okay?" Bob urged.

"Okay, Bob," Peter said and begrudgingly went home to Amy.

Peter told Amy everything, and then they contacted their parents. Peter knew in his heart that now the real battle would start and that Newel's real mission here was to show Peter that he was the stronger person. He was sure Newel was determined to defeat Peter any way he could, including killing Peter, or anyone else who got in his way, if he had to.

The next morning Peter got a call from Bob. "Peter, how would you like to come to the police station to meet Detective Marsh from London?" Bob asked.

"Bob, why don't you swing by my place, and I'll ride out to the airport with you," Peter said.

"Okay, Peter. I'm picking him up at noon, so I'll pick you up at ten," Bob said.

"Sounds good, Bob."

Peter didn't realize Amy was awake and listening. Her arms came around Peter as she pressed her warm, naked body against him and started massaging him.

"Mm, Amy, that feels so good," Peter said as he leaned back. "But I have to meet Bob in a few hours. We're going to meet the detective from London at the airport."

"Well, you're not going anywhere until you give me more of what you gave me last night." Amy smiled as Peter turned to her.

"Woman, are you really that into me?" Peter asked.

Amy smiled. "Let me show you just how into you I am and how much I want you, Peter!" Amy said as she climbed on top of Peter and started making love to him passionately.

Peter barely made it out of his home as Bob pulled up in front to pick him up. Amy, wearing a long black robe, kissed Peter at the door and waved to Bob, who waved back.

Peter got in the car and apologized for oversleeping.

"Oversleeping? Is that what you call it?" Bob said, laughing out loud.

"Why are you laughing, Bob?" Peter asked.

"Peter, you came flying out of your home with everything looking just right except the zipper on your jeans. It's three-quarters undone," Bob said as he watched Peter turn red.

Peter laughed at himself.

The ride to the airport took about an hour. It gave Peter and Bob time to think about how Detective Marsh thought he might be able to help.

"Does Marsh really think that the murders in London are related to Newel's arrival here?" Peter asked.

"He seems to, Peter. Apparently, the newspapers are saying the London murders are a return of the son of Jack the Ripper, trying to sell more papers by sensationalizing the crimes probably." Bob guessed.

Peter and Bob walked through the Portland airport to where Marsh's plane was arriving. He was easy to pick out, as he looked very proper and authoritative.

"Hello, Detective Marsh. I'm Detective Meyer, and this is the member of our special squad I was telling you about, Peter Bristol," Bob said.

"So, Peter, you were aware of this person's arrival, and you didn't notify anybody?" Marsh questioned.

Before Peter could answer, Bob cautioned everyone. "I think we had better save the question-and-answer session till we are alone."

Once they had hiked to the car and were on their way, the questions started.

"Peter, how could you have known that this person was coming to your city in the first place?" Marsh asked.

"Peter has some very special abilities that most people don't have to his heightened level," Bob said.

"This sounds like a bunch of BS to me," Marsh said loudly.

"Detective Marsh, can I have your hand? Just like we are shaking hands?" Peter asked.

Peter took Marsh's hand and pushed and felt the rolling surge move toward the front of his brain.

"Marsh, your daughter is going to be just fine. She came through the operation fine, and there won't be any side effects," Peter said, smiling at Marsh.

Marsh's mouth just opened and closed without making any noise at all. "How did he do that? I haven't even told my closest friends at the police station back home," Marsh said once he got over his shock.

"Peter's mom was struck by lightning just as Peter was being born, and his abilities showed up as he entered puberty," Bob said, smiling. "Peter's already helped us on several cases, and he is documented with our police department. His abilities are kept away from the media so Peter can remain a useful tool for our department," Bob said.

"Peter, you could be very important in catching this person," Marsh admitted.

"Well, his name is Newel, and he and I have been communicating to each other for a few years, nothing long and drawn out, just little more than a sentence here or there. But I do know he is here to wreak the same type of havoc that he did back in London," Peter said.

"My God, if that's true, we will be hip deep in dead and mutilated prostitutes if we don't catch him," Marsh replied.

When they got to the police station, Bob made the introductions to his special squad. Next, Bob, Peter, and Marsh went to a private office to look at the file Marsh had brought with him, as well as the crime scene photos.

"I have to warn you that if this Newel character is the same person who was on the loose in London, everyone's going to have to develop a stronger stomach. He's a real butchering beast!" Marsh said, grinding his teeth.

"Can you show us some examples of his work, Marsh?" Bob asked.

Marsh took out the photos from the file he carried and the subsequent photos from past prostitute deaths involving mutilation, all separated chronologically. Bob and Peter both looked at the photos and felt their stomachs roll at the sheer horror of what they saw. The bodies were ravaged savagely in some cases and with the finesse of a surgeon from hell in other instances.

"Marsh, you have at least a decade of murders here. Do you think it's one person, or is there an accomplice?" Bob asked.

"Actually, I think there's an older person in his forties doing the exact same thing, and I think they know each other," Marsh said. "The more refined and skillful murders I believe were done by the older version of our murderer, while the more savage ones were done by this younger individual. Although skilled, he's impatient."

Peter picked up a couple of photos of murdered women. One was of Roxy, whom Newel's father had done, and one was of Coleen, Newel's first kill on his own. Peter pushed with his mind and saw their names rise to the surface of his mind.

"These two women were murdered by men from the same family," Peter said slowly.

Bob and Marsh were quiet as can be.

"How can you be sure, Peter?" Marsh asked.

"Detective Marsh, this one was known as Roxy and was killed by Newel's father. The other was called Coleen and was killed by Newel," Peter said, his voice cold as he stared at the photos.

"I think this case is going to be bigger than we thought," Bob told Peter and Marsh.

While having some coffee, the three of them were talking when Marsh's curiosity got the better of him.

"Peter, what else can you do ability-wise?" Marsh asked.

"Well, I can do levitation, receive and send impressions from people, receive impressions from objects, track anything used for criminal or evil purposes, and just about anything I can do with my hands and feet, I do with my mind. Plus, there are some abilities I haven't shown to anyone but my family. They are so dangerous that if I used them when I got angry, I could really hurt someone," Peter said with a slight smile.

Newel's First Night Out in Portland

Newel, posing as Jack Listor, walked out for the evening dressed all in black and carrying a small black bag. In London the waterfront was always good for finding prostitutes, so Newel headed for the waterfront of the Willamette River. He strolled along the riverfront for hours; either there were too many people around when he found who he wanted, or he couldn't find any hookers. The tension was growing in Newel to the point of frustration. Finally, he just waited by the wall near the river, and he was rewarded. A cute, slightly plump woman came by and smiled at him.

"Excuse me, sir, are you from out of town?" she asked Newel.

"Yes I am. Would you know of a place a man could get warmed up for a while?" Newel said.

"Hon, I know of a way to keep you nice and warm. Just follow me down the path under the bridge. By the way, I'm Sue."

As they walked under the bridge, Sue turned to Newel. "Okay, mister, it's going to cost you a hundred bucks if you want to fuck me. Is that okay with you?" Sue said with a smile.

Newel thought to himself, *You're overvaluing yourself, lady. Although you're nice looking, I won't be giving you any money for anything. All you get from me tonight is a razor-sharp blade!*

Newel nodded in agreement and leaned Sue onto a sidewalk bench.

"Oh yes, I know what you want, but if you want both holes, it's extra," Sue said with a smile. She pulled her skirt up over her hips, revealing she had no panties on.

As Newel got behind her, he couldn't help playing between her thighs a bit, just to keep her occupied. Then he used his mind to freeze her ability to scream as he drove the long, stainless steel knife through her back and heart. Newel sat Sue onto the bench, and using a surgical saw, he cut her feet off. As he was finishing marking his kill, he heard voices.

At that moment, a group of teenagers came down over the embankment and saw his silhouette and what was left of Sue. Newel took off at an unbelievable speed, soon outrunning his pursuers. Newel was sure they hadn't seen his face, but he would have to lay low till he was sure.

After Newel arrived back in his room, he had two problems to solve. One was easy—the growing sexual tension in him after the kill. The other was more difficult. He realized killing out in the open in this city was too dangerous. If he kept it up, he would be caught or killed by the local police easily and never become famous or meet Peter.

Newel decided to deal with one problem at a time. The first he spent the next three hours solving by reliving past murders and past sexual adventures with Liz. The second solution he found by eavesdropping on several conversations while enjoying a drink and some food in the hotel lounge. As Newel sat waiting for his order and sipping a drink called "a dirty whore," he overheard some guys behind him talking about where to meet women, really nasty whores. From what Newel gathered, there were websites you could access that offered nasty women—in other words, whores, in Newel's mind. After Newel finished his meal, he asked the desk clerk where he could hook up his laptop and surf the web.

"I'm sorry, Mr. Listor, our Wi-Fi access is limited in this hotel; however, there is a large coffee shop on the next block that has unlimited access. It's called The Brew," the clerk said to Newel.

Newel went to his room and started to form a plan in his head to solve his other problem. As he relaxed, he sent a mental message to Peter. "I have started my mission to rid this place of all prostitutes."

* * * * *

Peter was sitting at a desk speaking to Bob when all of a sudden he slumped forward like he had just fallen asleep. Bob tried to shake Peter to wake him up, but the only response that came from Peter was: "Noooo, not again!"

As Peter resumed a better frame of mind, Bob was at his side.

"Peter, what is it?" Bob asked.

"Bob, Newel has struck, and the victim is down by one of the bridges sitting on a park bench," Peter said.

Just then, Marsh walked back in, and Bob let him know what had happened.

"Peter, how do you know all this is true?" Marsh asked.

"Because Newel just showed me an image of the crime scene in my mind. And there's more. He says he's on some kind of mission to get rid of all prostitutes."

"I'm going to get the vice squad involved and have them spread the word to all the working girls that this nut is on the loose along with his general description," Bob said.

Bob checked to see if there had been any reports of disturbances near any of the bridges. He found only one, so the three of them got in one car and headed to the crime scene. When they arrived, the area was blanketed with police cars and yellow tape to mark the scene. The three men saw the witnesses being interviewed as they walked to the bench where Sue's body rested. Bob lifted the sheet covering the body. When they saw what Newel had done, they didn't feel like throwing up like some of the younger cops had done. Instead, they knew down in their hearts that this butcher had to be killed and erased from the gene pool for good.

"I can't believe he was so close to being caught tonight," Marsh said as they went back to the police station.

"We better go over the evidence as soon as possible," Bob said.

All three men were quiet on the ride back to the police station. All of them had made a promise to themselves to bring this murder to a deadly justice equal to the savageness of the murders he had already committed.

* * * * *

By the time the sun was coming up on a cold fall morning in Portland, Newel was dressed warmly and headed out toward The Brew for a light breakfast, something hot to drink, and information. As Newel arrived, he admitted to himself that the cold was just as bad here, if not more biting, than back in London.

"Excuse me, sir," Newel said to the manager, "Is it okay to eat while I use your internet services?"

"Sure, buddy," the man answered. "Go right ahead. It's free."

As Newel ordered his breakfast, he sat at one of the terminals toward the back for privacy and sat down. Newel thought about where he should look first and picked a general topic—hookups for adults. Newel had found a brand-new hunting ground for his mission work. As he scrolled through pages of listings, he smiled and realized he was licking his lips slowly, just like in movies about predators, such as tigers or other big cats. He was acting precisely as those animals did when they came upon a fruitful hunting ground. If Newel played it smart and didn't get caught, he could stay here for his whole missionary period, and to hell with Peter and his abilities. Newel felt that his were the stronger abilities, and if Peter needed to pay the full price to learn this, so be it.

Newel joined the website and filled out an online form for a free profile. As Newel left, the manager called out to him. "Did you find everything you were looking for, sir?" he asked.

Newel smiled as he turned back to the manager. "Thank you very much. I found everything I was looking for, and I will visit you again," Newel replied with a hint of malice.

As Newel walked back to his hotel, he started to wonder about how his plan would work. After all, he had looked through the profiles of many women on the site and came to one conclusion. These women were no better than the prostitutes he had been killing back in London. Actually, if you thought about it, they were less than the women he'd already murdered, because at least those women were being paid for their services. As Newel thought about it, he smiled a devilish grin, thinking that men always paid for women in one way or another. With that, he laid back on his bed, laughing hard.

* * * * *

The sun was up in the early morning over the Portland Police Station, and although it shone brightly with the promise of warmth, it was cold. An east wind chilled the air, making for a typical fall morning in Portland. The evidence room was quiet as the technicians methodically went about their tasks of collecting and organizing data, photos, and sketches to yield any possible clues for the special squad.

As Peter, Bob, and Marsh looked over the crime scene photos and the dead woman's effects, they were totally absorbed in the sheer horror that had been reaped on the woman's body.

"I believe this is the work of our visitor from London," Marsh stated.

"I think you're right, Marsh. Look how hurried and haphazardly the feet were removed and the lack of any further mutilation. Weren't there some murders with multiple mutilations other than the wounds that caused death?" Bob asked.

"Yes, there were, but remember this butcher was interrupted during his fun time by teenagers," Marsh said.

"I need to check something on the body," Peter said.

All three of the men headed toward the morgue.

"What on earth is he going to do, Detective Meyer?" Marsh asked.

"I don't know, but if Peter says he needs to do it, it's a necessity," Bob said with force.

As they entered the morgue, the coroner was pulling out the cabinet drawer holding Sue's body for Peter. Peter lifted the sheet just enough to grasp her hand. As Peter did this, he pushed with his mind, and the surge he felt was not like a slow, rolling wave but more like a locomotive crashing down on him. Peter held Sue's cold, stiff hand and fell back against the stainless-steel metal cabinet doors where the bodies were stored. Peter slowly dropped Sue's hand, but it remained like it was still holding onto Peter's hand.

"Peter, are you all right? Did you get something?" Bob asked.

"Yeah, Bob, I'm all right. I didn't expect a type of rebound effect when Newel's power and my power interacted."

"What do you mean interacted? He's not here," Marsh said.

"Yes, but he used his power on this woman, I suspect to freeze her throat so she couldn't scream as he killed her. Some of Newel's power was left over, and when it met mine, the effect was magnified a lot," Peter said.

"What did you see, Peter?" Marsh asked.

"I guessed that the woman Newel killed didn't die right off but bled to death. That made her a witness. Her mind recorded memories till she died. I just pushed with my mind as I held her hand in the hope that her last memories could still be accessed. I saw Newel when he heard the teenagers surprising him and almost catching him in the act. What he was thinking and feeling became embedded on his mind and relayed to Sue's mind by the Power.

"Newel was shocked and scared by the reality he now had to face. Killing someone here would be much more difficult than in London, which would make it easier for police to catch him. Realizing this means he will be more difficult to catch, because he is probably going to change the way he hunts these women, and he may go so far as to change how he kills them," Peter said in a grave voice.

"Holy Christ, that's all we need is for him to do either of those things when we are barely introduced to his methodology!" Marsh exclaimed.

They all decided to call it a day and catch some sleep before coming in later that afternoon somewhat refreshed. For Peter, he had the case so heavy on his mind that Amy saw it when she got home from City College. Peter had rested, but the dark circles under his eyes let her know he hadn't slept. Amy knew it had to be the case he was working with Bob and the London detective who had flown in.

"Peter, come here and curl up with me. Just let me hold you, so you can relax," Amy said soothingly.

Soon, Peter was sleeping against Amy's breast, and Amy quickly fell asleep next to Peter.

Newel's New Hunting Ground

While the special squad/task force was recharging their batteries with some sleep, Newel had already rested and was planning on hunting for his first victim that night. He had decided to try to organize several so-called dates for sex with women on the hookup site instead of doing one date at a time. That way, he could be prepared for future killings and hopefully confuse the police when they realized the women weren't prostitutes.

Like his father had taught him, strategy and planning ahead would keep him safe. As Newel dressed to go to The Brew, he sent a message to Peter. All Peter saw was the date and Newel leaving his room as the door shut behind him without anyone shutting it except Newel's mind. The message was clear. Newel was heading out and had already figured a new way of hunting women he considered prostitutes in Portland.

Peter woke quickly and phoned Bob. "Bob, Newel sent me a message while I was at home. He already figured out a way to hunt Portland's women, and he's going to start tonight!" Peter exclaimed.

"Shit, Peter, that was quick. What should we do?" Bob asked.

"Call Marsh. I think we need to spend the night at the station and monitor any assaults or murders," Peter said.

Amy stirred next to Peter; she saw that the dark circles under his eyes were gone, which made her happy. "Peter, is it the case again?" she asked.

"Yes, hon. He contacted me to let me know he was going hunting tonight," Peter said.

"Peter, you need to get this bastard so that other women won't be murdered," Amy said violently.

"Don't worry. I'm going to get him and end this insanity," Peter said.

Peter left home and headed to the police station to meet Bob and Marsh. After he arrived, Peter told Bob he was going to let Newel know he was out there. Peter went into an office and sat down. Concentrating, he just pushed with his mind. Peter felt Newel's mind acting like a receiver for his thoughts and pushed hard at Newel's mind. Newel felt the force of Peter's mind as a blinding headache. He laid his head on the table and passed out for a moment. Peter saw this in his mind's eye and smiled. He knew Newel had received the message.

"Peter, I left word that we are to be informed immediately of any female murders that occur," Bob said.

* * * * *

As Newel sat in the The Brew, the headache slowly subsided. *Goddamn you, Peter,* he thought to himself. *Because of that little trick, I'm going to make my first victim especially nasty just for you!*

Newel started going through the hookup site he was a member of now and picked out several women to contact for sex. They were of all different sizes and shapes, but the common element was that they wanted NSA sex, which meant no strings attached. At the end of his first two coffees, he had more than a dozen women contacted, and a third had already e-mailed him back wanting to meet or with a phone number to contact them. What a wonderful opportunity for a man with his skills, Newel thought with a smile.

Newel made his first contact by phone. Her name was Janice, and after talking to her and hearing the different ways she could make him feel good, Newel knew this was the right woman for his next kill. Janice invited Newel to her place so they could meet and decide what they would do from there. Newel caught a taxi and got out within a couple of blocks of the address Janice had given him. As Newel rang the doorbell, he saw someone peek out and smile.

"Hi. Are you Jack?" Janice said with a smile.

"Yes, Janice, I am, and you look wonderful," Newel said in his English accent as he smiled.

Janice definitely had sex on the agenda, as she was dressed only in a see-through nightie. "Well, Jack, do you like what you see?" Janice asked as she did a slow turn, dropping her nightie.

"Very nice, Janice," Newel said. He then walked up behind her and pulled her back against him, so she could feel how excited he was.

Janice hadn't noticed the bulkiness of Newel's trench coat, his tools hidden inside. Suddenly, Janice's throat was closing like invisible hands were strangling her. She struggled but couldn't free herself.

"Janice dear, don't worry. In a while you won't have any worries in the world. I must say you have a wonderful Christmas tree, but it doesn't have any presents yet. We'll just have to change that, won't we, Janice?" Newel said.

Newel had left his bag outside with a change of clothes. When he was done, he showered and changed, making sure no blood or hairs were present on him. Newel than called a taxi to pick him up a few blocks in the opposite direction. Everything had gone off without a hitch. Newel was so happy with himself that he ordered a large breakfast from room service and then fell fast asleep.

* * * * *

It was about ten in the morning when a call came in to the police station concerning a mysterious disappearance.

"I think we had better check this out," Peter said.

"Why, Peter? It's a disappearance not a murder, and this was a suburban lady not a working girl," Marsh exclaimed.

As they arrived at the address, the person who called it in was being interviewed.

"Mrs. Davis, why were you over here this morning?" Bob asked.

"Janice and I were going Christmas shopping so we could get finished early," Mrs. Davis replied.

Marsh questioned one of the officers as to what was inside the home when they entered and found out there was a Christmas tree with lots of wrapped presents under it.

"That's not possible. I know Janice hadn't done any shopping yet," Mrs. Davis said, surprised.

"Officers, clear everyone away from here within a two-block radius and get the crime lab down here. Tell them we have a bad one," Bob yelled.

Peter, Bob, and Marsh went inside the home. Wearing rubber gloves, they opened one of the presents under the tree. Inside they found a plastic bag containing Janice's hand.

"Oh Christ! She didn't leave! She's still here under the Christmas tree as the presents," Marsh replied.

Several officers and a few of the crime scene guys lost their lunch right there. As the crime scene technicians were looking around, one of them came up to Peter.

"Excuse me. Is your name Peter?" the technician asked.

"Yes. Why?"

"We found this envelope with your name on it," he replied.

Peter looked at it and found a Christmas card inside. It read: "Happy Holidays, Peter. Newel."

Peter gave the evidence to Bob and walked into the kitchen.

"Don't follow me!" he yelled as he walked away.

It was quiet for about five seconds, and then an explosion occurred in the kitchen. As they ran in to see what had happened, they saw Peter standing in front of one of the walls, and there was a hole in the wall big enough for a person to walk through standing up.

"Sorry, everyone. He kind of got to me, and I just had to vent some of my anger," Peter said calmly.

"I see why you warned us about following you," Marsh said.

"That's nothing," Bob said. "You see, that was Peter's idea of a controlled bout of anger. Imagine if he really let himself go."

"I hope if he ever does let himself go all the way that this Newel bastard is standing in the blast zone," Marsh said.

"I want everything we can find out about this woman—a full background check—ASAP," Bob said to one of the other officers. He then turned to Peter and Marsh. "We need to find out how this butcher is tracking his victims now."

"I believe he was trying to send us a message, daring us to catch him, as if to say, 'Look, I can be as violent and perverse a killer as I want, and you can't stop me,'" Marsh said.

"He wasn't sending us a message. He was sending it to me because of the little mental shove I gave him to let him know we were on to him," Peter said.

"Well, let's get back to the station and wait for the lab and coroner to finish their reports before we get in their way," Bob said.

As they left, all three of them were wondering just how deep Newel's sense of depravity went when it came to defiling a human body to accomplish his so-called missionary work.

When they got to the police station, the men started drinking coffee for the long haul ahead before the first reports came in. Five hours later they went down to the autopsy lab. As Marsh, Peter, and Bob approached the lab, they noticed some of the technicians standing in the hallway looking pale.

"What's going on here?" Bob asked.

"Well, Detective Meyer, everyone has been kind of hit hard by this murder, so we are working in pairs. We've never seen anything like this before," the technician said. As he caught his second wind, the color started returning to his face.

Peter and the two detectives entered the autopsy lab and were greeted with the equivalent of a chop shop of human remains, all belonging to Janice, Newel's most recent victim. The coroner greeted them and invited them to come closer if they felt they could stomach it.

"You see, gentlemen, the person who did this had training in both anatomy and surgical training. All the organs that were removed and packaged were removed with surgical precision, but the other body parts were haphazardly cut off either because of the murder's impatience or because daylight was coming and he wanted to be away from that location at a time when he could blend in with the other morning commuters headed into the city," the coroner said.

"Was there anything to tell us what this woman did for a living?" Bob asked.

"Yes, a guess would be some sort of office or receptionist work because of the calluses on her fingertips," the coroner said briefly.

As the three men left the autopsy lab, they stopped by the special squad investigating room and let them know to bring the background check on Janice to them and no one else when it was complete.

"How the *hell* did he figure out a new method to hunt for his victims so fast?" Marsh asked.

"Because he is smart," Peter said. "When he almost got caught, he realized that if he wanted to avoid getting caught, he would have to change to match his environment. Next he may change his killing method, although I doubt it."

"Why do you think he won't change his killing method? After all, you're not a cop like us, Peter," Marsh said.

"That's right, but I think the way Newel kills is how he creates the maximum excitement and justifies what he does," Peter explained.

As they were all waiting on the background check on Janice, a Detective Brown of the task force that Bob was in charge of came in suddenly. "Detective Meyer, I don't know if this means anything, but I've been putting in some overtime to see if there are any similar murders in the United states or through Interpol in Europe."

"Did you find anything from your search?" Bob asked urgently.

"As a matter of fact, I did. It seems there have been many unsolved cases involving prostitutes in the past five years, some in Europe, around Poland, and three in Texas," Detective Brown said.

"I want a time line on the murders all the way back to Poland. Work with Interpol and tell them we are in a hurry, and I want to know the exact times of the murders in Texas, as well as where they happened!" Bob said.

"How is this possible? Do we have several copycats out there?" Marsh said.

"I don't think so, Marsh," Peter said.

"Well, how would you explain this, Peter?" Bob asked.

"At the moment, my explanation would be too unreal and ultimately far more frightening to deal with," Peter said as he looked toward Bob and Marsh.

As Peter turned to walk away, he felt a tingling in his head, kind of like when an arm or leg falls asleep and you rub it to get the blood flowing again. As Peter tried to shake the feeling, he felt something unexpected. It was a brief touch on his mind by someone else; it wasn't violent, more probative. Peter realized that there was someone in the station who also had the Power. But why were they using it now, and who was it? The feeling disappeared as soon as it had begun and left Peter with no side effects, just questions.

Detective Brown caught up with Bob, Marsh, and Peter as they were going to the evidence lab.

"Detective Meyer, it seems that the murders in Texas occurred within two hours of the murders that occurred here by this creep," Brown said.

"So it was just a copycat, wasn't it?" Marsh stated.

"I don't think it's just a copycat, not when you look at the forensic data," Brown said.

"Let's compare the murders in London, Texas, and Portland for similarities," Bob said.

When they compared the murders, they found a startling and frightening thing. They were dealing with at least three murderers. The murders in London, for the most part, were well planned and thought out by a patient murderer, possibly older than Newel. The murders in Portland were chaotic and hurried and impatient, although just as savage in their use of surgical blades and techniques committed by Newel, who was the youngest of the three individuals. The third set of murders that were committed in Texas were done with an air of style. The bodies were positioned as if playing tea party, except around the bodies the organs were positioned relative to their location in the body. It all appeared very proper.

* * * * *

Across the Atlantic Ocean in London at the home of Newel's family, Newel's father walked in on his wife while she was reading a long letter.

"Is anything wrong, dear?" Newel's father asked.

"No. It's a letter from one of our children letting us know they are fine and doing well in all aspects of their life, including our family's mission."

"It looks like maybe we will have two of our children who will become legendary."

"That would be so wonderful, but you were right about raising them in different homes. After all, our relatives raise their children geared toward the success of our family mission. It did ensure that they would both have equal chances to become famous!"

"Be sure to write back and ask them to visit as soon as they are in our area," Newel's father said.

Texas

Police were baffled by the recent murders that had occurred in and around Austin. Recently, prostitutes had been murdered in the most bizarre ways, their corpses mutilated. The public was demanding the police do something, and the local media was on their asses! What the police didn't know was that the case was soon to take an unexpected twist that they weren't prepared for.

JoAnn was relaxing near a local hangout for prostitutes where they could shoot the bull and talk or warn each other about certain customers. As JoAnn rested, she heard footsteps and looked up and smiled.

"Where have you been?" she asked.

"Just around working. How about you?" the friend asked.

"The same, but I am so tired. I need some sort of pick-me-up," JoAnn said.

"Would you like to try one of my homemade candies? I put some caffeine in them to keep me awake when I'm trying to work and I'm exhausted," JoAnn's friend offered.

"Thanks. I hope they work," JoAnn said as she chewed the candies. After a few minutes, JoAnn's head was hung down, and she was groggy. "I thought these were supposed to wake you up. I'm more tired and sleepy than before!"

"Well, I guess I told you a little white lie, you skanky whore," her friend said quietly.

JoAnn mumbled something as she was maneuvered down an alley and behind a closed building. She felt her body being held by some force that she couldn't see, and the front of her clothes were ripped open by invisible hands before she was laid down on a wooden pallet. All of a sudden there was a glint of light as it shined on a stainless steel blade that flew through the night and pierced her throat. JoAnn could still breathe but couldn't scream. Her throat was paralyzed by something unseen.

JoAnn looked pleadingly at her friend and realized she was in the presence of someone who was deranged. As JoAnn slowly bled out, her friend proceeded to get ready to finish JoAnn for the police to find. If a passerby had looked onto the site, it would have looked like a magic show with knives going here and there and an adult dressing a life-sized doll and setting her on the pallet.

As JoAnn's friend left, she placed a slip of paper into JoAnn's pocket so it would be seen by police when they discovered the body. It was only a few days before JoAnn's body was found, and the police and the city of Austin went into a tailspin of fear!

* * * * *

The body was seated and dressed with all her organs arranged in a circle around her. Many of the cops lost their lunch as they investigated the scene. This made the third such murder in Austin that month. A serial killer was on the loose, and the serial killer had left a new clue and a name to be called by. There was a note found on the body, which was a first for this killer. It read:

Here lies a sad whore.

Now she is better as art.

Much more art to come!

The Poet

The word was out that a serial killer calling himself the Poet was killing prostitutes. The media had hold of it, the working girls were wise to it, and the public knew it caused a lot of pressure to be put on the local police. The request for information on the previous murders from Portland came in just as the clues and forensic data on the new murder of JoAnn were arriving at the Austin crime lab. A Detective Bolin read what came in from Portland and started shaking his head.

"It seems the police up in Portland, Oregon, are having a similar problem with a serial killer in their area and want to compare methodology of their killer and ours," Detective Bolin said. "Let's go ahead and send them what we have on all three murders and see what they come up with. It may help us on our case."

As the full case files came in, the three men in Portland noticed the date on the last case.

"Christ, this case just occurred a few hours ago. This is crazy. If they're not copycat killers, then what are we looking for?" Marsh asked.

"What if you had individuals who had the same purpose for their crimes?" Peter asked.

"Are you talking about organized crime, Peter?" Bob asked.

"No, I'm thinking more like a family of killers trained from birth to have perfect skills when it came to killing. Now imagine them with the abilities I have," Peter said.

"I don't know how we can fight something like that, Peter," Marsh said.

"Whenever I've had contact with Newel mentally, I've sensed that he is well organized, intelligent, and trained for the mission, as he calls it. It's a perception I get," Peter said gravely.

* * * * *

As the morning dawned, Victoria stretched and yawned. She had slept very well the night before and heard the morning paper being bounced at her apartment door. She smiled and went to get the paper after putting on her robe.

Let's see what the newspaper is about this morning, she thought to herself.

As she opened the paper, the headlines cried the news of a new serial killer called the Poet who was being pursued by local police. With that, Victoria—she never called herself Vicki or let anyone else do it because she felt it wasn't proper; her parents had given her the name, and she was proud of it—went into the kitchen and started breakfast after throwing the newspaper on the dining table. The paper was thrown a little too hard and slid slowly off the table.

"Damn it!" Victoria said.

As she finished making toast, she sat at the dining table with milk with ice in it and her hot, buttery toast with jam, her favorite. As she started to eat, she looked down at the newspaper on the floor where it had landed and smiled as the newspaper rose slowly off the floor and into her hands!

Portland's Hot Fall

Peter, Marsh, and Bob were pondering the incredible possibilities of what Peter had said and the more serious problem of how to capture the type of serial killer they were talking about. Just then, a member of the task force came in with the background check on Janice. She was indeed a receptionist at a business office and on the face of it seemed to be a very upstanding person.

The three men made arrangements to visit her office and interview some of her coworkers. The company manager and those employees who worked with Janice were very shocked still, and the company was still doing grief counseling. Bob, Peter, and Marsh asked to speak specifically with anyone who was close to Janice. That's when they met Cindy and Kerri, two friends of Janice's. They had started working together at the same time and grew to become good friends.

"Janice was really great until she broke up with a guy she had been dating for the past ten months or so," Kerri said.

"Yeah, she couldn't believe how lucky she had been to meet someone she thought was Mr. Right in a place like that, and then he dumps her because his interests changed," Cindy said.

"What do you mean in a place like that? Where was it?" Bob asked.

"She met him on an online hookup site, and she had decided if the guy who dumped her liked older women, then so be it. She would find a guy who liked her for who she was," Cindy said.

All three men looked at each other with disbelief. Newel had figured out how to hunt his prey using a computer website to lure women in.

"We'll need Janice's computer so we can check her accounts and activity on this hookup site," Bob said.

As they rode in the car back to the police station, they were talking out ideas.

"You realize what this means about Newel, don't you?" Marsh asked. "Newel has evolved as a serial killer. He started off only murdering prostitutes, but now he is murdering any woman who he sees as being no better than a prostitute. With Newel's state of mind, it could go all the way from some woman who dresses slutty to just being flirtatious, and he could bounce from one dating site to another."

"Just how many of those sites are around do you think?" Peter asked.

"More than we can hope to cover," Bob said.

Bob had radioed ahead for the crime lab to seize Janice's computer from her home and check her account activity and e-mails.

By the time they arrived at the police station and ate lunch, the report detailing the websites Janice had visited and the e-mails she had sent and received was in. The task force started pouring over them, separating sites visited most often and e-mails from the same person. What became apparent was that this was a lonely young lady searching for a special friend. Instead, she'd found a murderous maniac who was a born hunter. She had become his prey.

"Bob, I want to try something to see if I can zero in on Newel, but I'm going to need a quiet place to concentrate," Peter said.

"Use my office, Peter," Bob said.

Peter shut the door to Bob's office and started to send out pulses with his mind to see if he could get some mental acknowledgement and direction, like using sonar and waiting for it to ping, or bounce back, to its source. As Peter concentrated, nothing happened for about ten minutes, and then he received two mental registers. One was smaller than the other but definitely there, and the other was huge and filled Peter's mind.

Peter saw images from the larger mental ping and saw Newel's face and the crime scene down by the bridge. Suddenly, Peter started doing something his parents hadn't known about;

he started auto writing on a notepad on Bob's desk, just one word over and over again "Brew." When Peter came out, he was both excited and tired mentally.

"Bob, I did some auto writing, and this is what I wrote. Is there a coffee shop around with the word *brew* in the name?" Peter asked.

"I'll check, Peter," Bob said.

As Bob looked on his computer, Marsh questioned him about auto writing. "Peter, how do you do auto writing?"

"Well, I just concentrate my thoughts outward, and if I feel a contact, my hand just picks up something to write with," Peter said. "It's kind of like when you see waves rolling onto a beach. Only this is just steady pulses of my mind until I get a response of some sort. It was funny, because for a moment, I thought I felt two kinds of contacts, almost like an echo of mental touches," Peter said.

By this time, it was getting late in the day, and all three of the men were exhausted. They all agreed to go home and get some rest before hitting it hard in the morning.

When Peter got home to Amy, she urged him to talk and get it out of his system so he could rest.

"It's a gruesome case, dear. He's a real butcher when it comes to killing," Peter said.

"I want to know it all, Peter, so I can help you deal with it," Amy said.

So Peter told Amy everything, even describing some of the police crime scene photos. Amy was horrified that anyone could be that brutal to another person. The other thing that scared Amy was the fact that the murderer Peter was seeking had the same powers as Peter.

The next morning Peter arrived before Marsh and Bob. He was curious as to who might be the other person he had detected with his mind a few days earlier. Just then, Marsh came in.

"Peter, do I have it correct in my mind that when you detected two mental registrations yesterday it means you detected two people with your mental abilities?" Marsh asked.

While Marsh and Peter were talking, Bob entered the room and settled into a chair.

"Yes, it does, though I have no idea who. Bob, have you had any luck with your computer search?" Peter asked.

"Yes, Peter, I did, and you won't believe it. There's a coffee shop six blocks from here actually called The Brew," Bob said.

"Let's go and visit this place and see if our friend Newel has been having his coffee there," Marsh said.

As they headed to the coffee shop, Peter spoke quietly. "Let me go in first; if he's here, we may get involved in a situation where everyday weapons are useless!"

Peter slowly opened the door to the coffee shop, slowly pushing his mind and looking around for anything giving off the gray glow he was familiar with after things came into contact with evil or evil deeds. As Peter looked around, everything seemed normal until he noticed sunlight hitting a patch of gray, glowing material surrounding a computer terminal in the corner of the shop. Peter led the other two men to the terminal.

"That son of a bitch was just here," Peter said angrily but quietly to his two companions.

"How do you know?" Marsh said.

"Because I can feel him!" Peter said, turning swiftly. "Get down behind something!" he yelled.

Suddenly, the door to the restroom flew open, and Newel came out using his mind to paralyze the people in the shop and keep them pinned to the floor. The only people who weren't paralyzed were Peter, Bob, and Marsh. Suddenly, Peter tried to grab Newel with his mind, forcing the tentacles of mental energy at Newel. But as they started closing around him, Newel pushed with his own mind, causing a blinding flash of light and a loud explosion like thunder right in the shop as their minds met.

Both men leaned into each other, fighting with their minds. All of a sudden a stool from the counter flew at Newel, catching him along the shoulder and surprising him. He cursed in pain. Both Marsh and Peter looked in amazement as Newel broke his concentration and fell to the side. Newel took off through the coffee shop door like he was on fire.

"What the hell just happened here?" Marsh said. "Quick, let's go after him!"

"Never mind, Marsh. Newel's already gone. I don't feel him anymore, but I do feel another mental energy present," Peter said

"Who, Peter? Who do you feel?" Marsh asked.

Peter turned to face his longtime friend. "It's you, isn't it, Bob? You have the Power!" Peter said.

Bob smiled a sly smile, and Peter smiled.

"I don't believe it. How can this be? You've known each other since Peter was a youngster," Marsh said.

Peter held up a metal spoon from one of the tables. Bob knew what Peter wanted him to do. Bob concentrated on the spoon, and it started bending in half in a slow, calculated way until the two halves were crushed together. Bob then went to a phone and called in the disturbance at the coffee shop. Once the police had arrived and taken their statements; minus the telekinesis details, the three men headed back to the station.

Once they were alone, the three of them talked.

"Bob, why didn't you tell my parents that you had the same thing that I have? It would have explained how you knew so much about these abilities and were able to help my dad to understand them," Peter said.

"Peter, I'm sorry, but I like to keep that side of me private unless I can help someone; it's like my secret weapon," Bob said.

"You mean, like being able to help my dad understand about me and throwing the stool in the coffee shop?" Peter asked.

"Yes. Your dad needed to know that everything would be okay to ease his stress. In the coffee shop I thought if Newel was distracted, his ability would decrease. Besides, it felt good to put him on the receiving end of some pain for a change after all the pain he's caused," Bob said. "After all, Newel's victims are people too, and they don't deserve to be brutalized like this."

* * * * *

Newel headed for his hotel, making sure he wasn't followed by any of the men who had come looking for him. He started to think about his future plans for this bountiful hunting ground. Would he have to change the way he hunted so soon after finding this unique method for selecting his prey? How much risk was there of being caught by Peter and his police friends if he kept hunting?

Newel felt he would have to think on this more. In the meantime, he would take a brief break to let the police think he had been scared off for the moment. This was not the case. In fact, Newel was more determined than ever to stay in Portland near Peter and prove that his abilities were far more formidable than Peter's.

Newel lay there in bed thinking of Liz. His hand went between his legs as he fantasized that she was there with him and what wonderful things they would be doing to each other. Eventually, Newel fell asleep. As he dreamed, he couldn't get out of his head one troubling aspect of his most recent meeting with Peter. While he and Peter had been mentally fighting each other, a counter stool had come flying through the air and crashed into his shoulder. His shoulder was bruised and still hurt, but the thing that troubled him was that he didn't see anyone pick up the stool and throw it, at least no one who was strong enough to throw it across the shop with that kind of force. Peter couldn't have done it because he was engaged in fighting. The only answer was that someone else in the shop also had the Power, but who was it? Newel swore to himself if he ever found out who had thrown the stool, he would make them sorry for butting into his business.

Later, when Newel woke up, he was watching some TV. He found he really enjoyed the variety of shows Americans had to choose from for their entertainment. The channel he was watching interrupted the current program for a news bulletin. A suspected serial killer had recently been questioned in London, and although the police couldn't hold him, he still remained a person of interest. Newel thought instantly of his father and got on the webcam at one of the terminals in the private-use area near the lobby.

"Hello, Mother. Was father the one who the cops detained?" Newel asked quietly.

Newel could tell she had been crying but recently had stopped. "Yes, Newel, he was, but the stupid cops were so eager to make an arrest they just grabbed the first person they saw; he was just in the wrong place at the wrong time. Since they had no direct evidence, they had to let him go," Newel's mother said.

"Is he home yet, Mother?" Newel asked.

In answer to his question, he saw his father walk up next to his mother and sit down. His face was a little swollen where the police had roughed him up a bit before taking him in.

"Father, how are you doing?" Newel asked.

His father smiled gingerly because of a split lip. "I'm doing okay, Newel. I guess I made too many evening appointments in my favorite area, and they surprised me right after finishing with a client."

Newel knew that this meant his father had just murdered a prostitute and was leaving when the police stopped and arrested him.

"Father, you got very lucky. It might be a good idea to not take any evening appointments for a while to keep you and the family safe," Newel said.

"That's probably a good idea. How are you doing, Newel?" Newel's father asked.

"Very good. This area is a hunter's paradise, Father," Newel said with a smile.

"Just remember what I said about being overly confident, Newel," his father warned.

"I remember. If I get overly confident, that's when I'm most likely to make a mistake. Father, I remember!" Newel said, a bit exasperated.

Newel didn't really believe he could ever be caught, and to prove it, he was going out today to buy a wedding ring for Liz for when they saw each other again. Peter and his police friends were only an annoyance and could be dealt with easily.

* * * * *

After the encounter with Newel, the order of business, and maybe the most obvious, was to get the names of the sites Janice had visited, an IP address if possible, and the online name that Newel was using so they could track his activity. As they expected, when they received the report back on Janice's computer, the IP address led back to the coffee shop. But Janice's computer showed she had visited three separate such sites, making their job a good deal harder to narrow their suspect down and monitor.

"What is Newel's handle on the website?" Marsh asked.

"JackL is what he used on his e-mails to Janice," Bob said.

"He is definitely that, but now that he knows we are on to him, he could change his handle and jump to any dating site that he wants and keep killing all the women he wants," Peter said.

"We have to get a plan into place and figure out a type of trap to lure Newel out into the open," Marsh said.

"Bob, would it be possible to monitor the site that Janice was on and have them contact us if they see any suspicious handles or verbiage open up?" Peter asked.

"Sure, Peter. We could even have one of our lady police detectives go undercover for the meet if Newel comes out of his hole," Bob said.

"Do you have someone in mind who is tough enough for this assignment, Bob?" Marsh asked.

Bob smiled and made a phone call, asking the officer who answered to come and meet them. A short time later, an attractive lady detective joined them.

"Gentlemen, let me introduce you to Det. Miranda Scott. Detective, this is Detective Marsh from London, and this is Peter, who you may already know is on the special squad," Bob said.

"I think that because of the nature of these crimes, Detective Scott should have an opportunity to look at the case file and decide if she wants to work this case," Marsh said.

Both Peter and Bob agreed and waited as Detective Scott went through the materials, including the photos.

"Well, Detective Scott, what do you think?" Bob asked.

"Do you want my honest opinion, Bob?" Miranda asked.

"Yes, of course, Detective Scott," Bob said.

"I think we should go and erase this shithead from the face of the earth before any more women are killed," Miranda replied. "What do you guys have in mind?"

"We are looking at doing an undercover operation to try to lure Newel back out to his hunting grounds, using you as a decoy and the guys in the computer section," Bob said.

"I imagine that the sex dating site that the last murder victim was on will need a profile," Miranda said.

"Don't worry about that. The computer guys can come up with something," Bob said.

Miranda laughed out loud. "Bob, I thought the idea was to lure this creep out so we could nail him, not scare him away. Thanks anyway. I can do my own profile and get him interested," Miranda said, smiling.

Miranda headed to the computer lab in the police station to create her profile. In the meantime, the conversation in the squad room changed to coming up with a plan to catch Newel if he fell for the trap.

"How do we reduce Newel's ability so that we can handle him if this works?" Marsh asked.

"Well, how about a sedative combined with an antiseizure drug of some sort?" Bob suggested.

"That might give us a chance to get him restrained and back to the station. We had better find a doctor, fill him in on what we are dealing with, and see what he suggests," Peter said.

After consulting with a doctor, it was recommended they use a type of drug cocktail administered through a hypodermic needle from an air rifle. The same process is used on large cats, such as lions or tigers, when zoos have to examine them.

"All we have to do now is wait and see if Newel comes out of hiding to take the bait," Bob said.

"Yes, but we have to be ready to move quickly if he appears so that Detective Scott isn't harmed," Marsh said.

They all agreed. This was going to be a tricky sort of sting, if it worked at all. The day ended quietly enough until all of them went home for the night. After Peter walked into his home, he sat down and was talking with Amy when the phone rang. As Peter went to answer it, the receiver floated out of the cradle and moved toward him. A voice came over the phone as clear as day and somehow amplified.

"Hello, Peter. Did you have a good day at work?" Newel said over the receiver.

"Not an especially good day, because you are still out there, Newel," Peter said in a calm voice.

Just then, Amy came into the room in time to see the receiver floating in midair as Peter talked to Newel. Her mouth fell open, and she sat down to listen.

"Peter, I know you and your friends are probably planning some sort of trap for me, but it will do no good. After I've hunted here for a while, I will go home and marry my true love. Then I'll come back, maybe for our honeymoon, and have some more fun in Portland," Newel said.

Then the receiver dropped and bounced off the arm of the couch. Amy ran over to Peter, and they hugged tightly. Peter could feel Amy trembling.

"Peter, you need to catch that murdering bastard," Amy whispered.

"I will, Amy, but why are you so upset? You've seen things like that floating phone receiver when you and I played as kids, and you helped me practice my abilities," Peter said.

"Peter, I think I'm pregnant. I'll have to go to the doctor to be sure. I didn't want to tell you this way with this case on your mind, but I don't want our child coming into the world with him on the loose," Amy said, leaning on Peter's shoulder as he smiled.

"I'm going to be a dad," Peter said out loud in awe.

* * * * *

Newel had waited for three long, boring days to let things quiet down a bit before he considered going out again, but now he realized that thanks to the interference by Peter and his cop friends at the coffee shop, he would have to find a new place to use a computer terminal. Newel talked with the hotel staff and was told about another spot called Morning Lion, which was about four blocks in the opposite direction of the first coffee shop he had frequented. Morning Lion had a very English atmosphere to it with its ornately carved dark woods of older rustic pubs laced with modern technologies such as flat-screen TVs and computer terminals. Newel loved it as soon as he walked in.

Newel ordered tea and a scone and went to an out-of-the-way terminal to start the day's hunting. Before long, he had answered all his e-mails on the sex dating site and set up several dates. Newel was feeling very pleased with himself for finding a new place to work from in such short time, but as he left his new coffee shop, Newel spotted something that made him avert his face. It was one of the police detectives who had been with Peter at The Brew; he was the one who had the accent. Newel knew he had seen his face, and if he didn't avert his face now, all this effort of finding a new place to use computers would be for nothing. Although Newel hated doing it, he slowly turned and walked in the opposite direction of Detective Marsh. Newel never walked away from a challenge, and now he was forced to do just that to avoid a commotion and be able to use his new coffee shop. Newel was so mad that he had to do this he was seething.

I'll give that English cop something to remember me by, Newel thought as he glanced back to see Marsh open the door to his new coffee shop.

Newel used his mind and forced the coffee shop door to close faster and with much more force than anyone had ever seen. It caught Marsh's hand, and although it didn't break it, it gave Detective Marsh a pair of nasty cuts deep enough to leave permanent scars on the back of his hand in the shape of a check mark.

Newel smiled, *That will give you something to remember me by, you snoopy bastard!*

As Marsh received medical attention at the hospital, he called Peter and Bob at the police station and told them what had happened. They were a bit shocked, but Marsh assured them he was fine and would come in after he was done at the hospital.

When Marsh arrived with his hand all bandaged, the questions flew from Peter and Bob at light speed.

"Did you see any evidence that Newel was in the area of this new coffee shop?" Bob asked.

"No, not at all. I just went to a new coffee shop this morning for some coffee. It was probably just bad luck," Marsh offered.

"Marsh, would you let me try something on you so we can be sure that it was just bad luck?" Peter asked.

"What are you going to do, Peter?" Marsh asked.

"I'm going to try to see it happen as if I were standing near you watching," Peter said.

"Do I need to do anything?" Marsh asked.

"Just see the door in your mind as you start to open it," Peter said.

Peter took Marsh gently by his injured hand. As Marsh concentrated, Peter pushed with his mind. Peter saw Marsh opening the door slowly and walking into the coffee shop as he let go of the door, which was designed not to slam on people's hands or fingers. Then, all at once, the door started closing so fast that Marsh never had a chance to move his hand, even if he would have seen it closing. Peter noticed something very important about the door. Around the edges Peter could see a glowing gray film, which could only mean one thing—Newel was near.

"Marsh, Newel was there. The gray film that glows was all around the edges of the door. You pissed him off somehow, and he was just letting you know it as a sort of warning," Peter said.

"Marsh, did you notice him the previous time when we saw him at the other coffee shop a few days ago?" Bob asked.

"No, the only thing that I really questioned was a man who was heading in the opposite direction, away from me. I could have sworn he was going to turn and walk toward me, but he slowly turned and headed away from me," Marsh said.

"That may have been Newel. Marsh, somehow he recognized you from our previous encounter and didn't want to make a scene in public in the daylight," Peter said. "We all need to be very aware of our surroundings and the people around us. Newel is not only hunting for his next victim, but he is also looking for any chance to eliminate us, because we are the primary people pursuing him and know the most about him."

* * * * *

As Newel rested before going out for the night, he drifted off to sleep. As he slept, he started to feel like someone was trying to make contact with him on a mental level through his dream. It started with two babies separated at birth and raised by separate families, and then he heard a woman's voice. All it would say was, "I'm here, Newel. I can feel you."

The voice was not his mother's, and Newel was very confused by this dream, because this was the second time it had occurred. Newel tried to shrug the dream off as being homesick for his family and Liz, his future bride, but it wasn't working. Although the presence of the dream bothered Newel, it felt comfortable and safe.

Newel got up and shook himself hard until his head had cleared of the sleep he had just had. He had a date and didn't want to keep the young lady waiting. After all, she had practically begged him to sleep with her after chatting only a couple of times. Newel headed for Morning Lion dressed all in black. When he arrived, he ordered a warm drink called a Warm Willamette, which when made was so thick it was like a coffee milkshake, only warm.

As Newel logged on to his hookup website, he saw that his date had sent him an e-mail saying that she was sick and couldn't make it. Newel was seething with anger. How dare she cancel on him. Newel felt that she should have gotten off her ass and still met him, sick or not. Now he had no one to use that night, and he was all set mentally and physically. He stormed out of the coffee shop and walked toward the Willamette River. The cold air was helping to ease his temper a little bit but not enough.

A man in his twenties started to walk past, and Newel just stared because he had a dyed white Mohawk, white sleeveless shirt, white pants, and a furry loin cloth. As Newel watched him, he smirked at his costume, and the young man saw his smirk.

"What the *hell* are you smirking at, you bastard?!" the man with the Mohawk yelled.

Newel didn't answer him, which provoked the young man more.

"I bet someone like you is down here looking for a guy to fuck," the young man said.

"That's not what I usually do here when I go out for the evening," Newel replied slowly.

"So what do you do when you go out at night?" the Mohawk man said.

At this time, Newel and the Mohawk man found themselves alone on the sidewalk. "Would you really like to know why I'm out here, young man?" Newel said.

"Sure. If it's what I think, let's go over here under the freeway overpass," Mohawk man said.

As they got into the dark, the Mohawk man addressed Newel "Well, if you want me to go down on you, mister, go ahead and take it out, but it's going to cost you twenty bucks."

Newel smiled at the young man. "I'm here to take care of people like you," Newel whispered.

And within seconds, the young man couldn't speak and was pinned against the concrete pillar of the overpass by invisible hands from Newel's mind. Newel's rage boiled over, and suddenly, he forced the young man's head to turn a complete revolution, snapping his neck.

"You are not worthy of any further attention from me. You shouldn't have insulted me with your conversation when I was in the mood I was in," Newel said over the body under his breath as he walked quietly away.

Newel felt a little better, not great but better.

The next day the task force that Bob was in charge of met in the squad room. One of the tasks that had become an everyday item was to check all assaults and murders for any possible links to Newel. Bob noticed one of the officers who had been given the task that day was barely glancing at the cases that had come in from the previous evening.

"Officer, are you in some kind of hurry to finish your work here on the task force?" Bob asked with a grumble in his voice.

"No, sir. It's just since this creep is only going after women that he considers no better than prostitutes, I just rule everyone else out. I thought it would speed up the sorting process," the officer replied.

"Well, give me the files you eliminated already, and let's see if you missed anything," Bob said, taking the files.

The officer felt confident that he hadn't missed anything of importance, but when Bob pulled the third file out of the stack, the younger officer started to sweat profusely.

"Officer, why did you eliminate this file as not possibly having anything to do with our killer?" Bob asked.

"Because it was a guy who had been murdered, Detective," the officer replied.

"Did you read the crime scene notes and the autopsy report?" Bob asked the young officer.

"No, Detective, I didn't," the officer replied, quietly knowing he had made a mistake somewhere.

"According to the crime scene notes, there were traces of blood on the concrete pillar under the overpass starting about ten feet high, which means the victim had to be pinned at that height while being killed. Next the autopsy shows that his neck was broken by twisting his head in a complete circle. Wouldn't you say, Officer, that this is an unusual way to snap a person's neck?" Bob asked.

"I'll try to be more careful going through these files, Detective," the officer said.

"Was the guy in the police system, Bob?" Peter asked.

"Yes. He had been picked up a few times as a male prostitute but always made bail," Bob said.

* * * * *

Austin, Texas, was pleasant on this fine morning. Victoria had gotten up early to get some chores done. The biggest was making candy for the kids' food drive where they sold it to earn money for field trips and such for their classes. Victoria always gave of herself and always made a large quantity of candy, because truth be told, she enjoyed some candy once in a while—more than she should. As she finished, she sat down and opened a locket she wore around her neck and looked at the two pictures inside. Both pictures looked like Victoria as a baby.

Don't worry, Brother. One day we will meet, she thought to herself.

Victoria finished and left her home to complete her errands, one of which included a stop at the pharmacy. Some of the working girls in the area recognized her and waved a hello to her, and she waved back to be courteous and not to raise any bad blood between them and her. After all, it would be best to stay on their good side if she was going to stick around for a while. With all the work to be done around here, she would have to stick around for a long while.

* * * * *

The detectives in Portland were shocked when they learned that Newel had probably killed the male prostitute they had found under the freeway overpass.

"I wonder if the guy Newel killed had somehow insulted him, causing Newel to blow up with anger," Marsh said.

"If that's the case, we could all be in harm's way if he gets really pissed off," Bob said.

"Well, look what he did to Marsh's hand just because he thought Marsh had discovered his new place to work," Peter said.

Just as the three of them were talking over the case, the phone rang. Marsh grabbed it. "Hello, Portland Police Task Force. Marsh speaking ... Okay, that is unusual. And how many murders has this occurred in? ... Okay, thank you for the heads up. We'll be looking at the details as you send them to us, Detective." Marsh then ended the call.

"Something unusual has occurred in the murders in Austin, Texas," Marsh told Peter and Bob. "It seems the women who were murdered were first given candy of various sorts that was drugged to make them easier to handle, and then they were taken to a more private place to be killed and placed in their peculiar positions after being killed.

"It seems they have a serial killer of prostitutes down there too, all of who ate candy that was drugged and all who were positioned in some weird tea party fashion after being killed. And get this, at the last murder, the murderer left a poem and signed it 'the Poet.' The local media is going nuts and causing a public scare."

"How's your hand doing, Marsh?" Peter asked.

"It's doing fine. It will take a while to heal, and I guess I'm going to have a nice scar in the shape of a check mark to remember Newel by," Marsh said with a grin. Suddenly, Marsh yelped in pain and collapsed, holding his injured hand.

"What's wrong, Marsh?" Peter asked as he helped Marsh up. Peter held Marsh's injured hand and felt Newel's mind, so Peter pushed back with his mind, hard.

Newel flew off the bed he was lying on in his room and slammed into the wall and slid down the wall, trying to get his wits about him.

"You're going to pay for that, Peter. The whole *fucking* lot of you are going to die!" Newel communicated to Peter.

"Not if I have any say about it, you stinking bastard," Peter shot back at Newel mentally.

"Peter, what just happened?" Bob asked.

"Newel just threatened to kill us all. I emphasized my point by pushing hard with my mind, and he got upset," Peter said. "Marsh, Newel didn't just injure your hand. He marked you so that he could track you with his mind and give you pain anytime he wanted. What did it feel like?"

"The area of the cuts started to burn like they were on fire," Marsh said.

"Has your hand ever done that before, Marsh?" Bob asked.

"No, that was the very first time," Marsh said.

"If you start having that sensation again, tell me by using a code word that only we know the meaning of, like volcano. That will tell me that Newel is near and trying to get to you, and I can give him a taste of his own medicine," Peter said.

"Okay, Peter, will do. That sure hurt like hell when it happened," Marsh said.

* * * * *

A couple of days had passed since the task force had enlisted Det. Miranda Scott's help as an undercover to try to lure Newel out of his sanctuary so the squad could have a shot at capturing him. She had made up a very convincing profile on the sex dating site, which was drawing a lot of attention from men and a few women.

"Wow, Miranda. I'm glad we had you write the profile rather than some of our tech people. You're drawing a lot of attention," Bob said, smiling and congratulating her.

Miranda laughed. "Well, a woman knows how to get a man's juices stirred up."

"As well as some ladies," Marsh said as they all laughed a bit.

They got a printout of all the handles of people who had responded to Miranda's profile and started looking them over. One of the e-mails was particularly creepy. The person started talking about how it would be wonderful to die while having sex with each other. His handle was the Hyena. Miranda set up a date with him in a location that was a police safe house.

When he arrived, the guy introduced himself as Robert, and Miranda invited him in. Miranda wasn't wearing much, playing the part of a woman who was just there to get laid. She had hidden her weapon in a wraparound thigh holster so it wouldn't be seen. However, if he got very touchy-feely, she would have to discourage him from finding out her secret.

Robert grabbed at Miranda, kissing her hard. Then he did the craziest thing. He started cackling and laughing as he imitated a real hyena and began roughly throwing Miranda from side to side. Miranda gave Robert a judo throw, and he ended up in a corner of the room, not knowing what had happened. Miranda gave the signal to the others to come in and get Robert. He was not who they were looking for by any means.

"Damn it! We wasted a whole night waiting for this nut case," Miranda said, exasperated.

Once they all got back to the station and did their reports of the evening's activities, they agreed to hit it fresh tomorrow morning.

After a good night's sleep and lots of morning coffee, they all met in the squad room to go over more handles of people interested in Miranda's profile. They felt pretty confident in eliminating some of the hits, like the females and transgender individuals. They were looking for a killing machine who had started out killing only prostitutes for some demented mission and had evolved into a killer who would murder any woman he deemed easy or slutty, whether it was the way she acted or dressed.

Capturing Newel would stop him for a short time, but with his abilities, he wouldn't remain in prison. He could trick guards into not seeing him or escape by knocking out all the prison staff just like Peter could with his mind. The abilities that Newel and Peter had were kept from the local media to avoid any type of higher panic being created. The only real way to put Newel out of commission was to have him die or become a mental vegetable so he couldn't use his abilities.

As they started looking through the list of handles, one of them stuck out to Peter for no reason but a gut feeling: JackL. Peter touched the name on the paper printout and saw Newel's face, a deadly smile upon it.

"That's Newel right there!" Peter exclaimed.

"But why that handle?" Bob asked.

"Remember your Jack the Ripper history? Jack being the first name of the Ripper's nickname, and I think the *L* is for the type of surgical knife he used to dismember his victims with. I believe it's called a Listor knife used for amputations," Marsh said.

With that, the team started looking over all JackL's e-mails to Miranda. There were five in all, talking about how he would do things to her that she had never had done and how he would love to hear the sounds she would make when she was with him. They informed Miranda that they had got the attention of Newel and were going to set up a new sting, one where they hoped to try out their medical cocktail to subdue Newel until they could get him confined.

Miranda e-mailed Newel that she would love to experience his body from head to toe, and if he wanted, he could come by her home the following evening about five in the afternoon. She would fix them something to eat, and for dessert, they could have each other. Miranda got an e-mail from Newel within five minutes.

It read: "Give me your address, and I'll be there at five."

Miranda sent a reply, and the team prepared to spring the trap the following day.

The idea was to get Newel alone with Miranda. Then, when he began to commit his crime, they would shoot him with the special tranquilizing dart containing the drug cocktail. They hoped this would render Newel easier to handle and transport. As the hour approached for the meeting, all the squad members were in their assigned places. Miranda was wired for sound with a two-way receiver/transmitter so the team could hear everything and move in on a moment's notice.

As everyone watched, an older gentleman in a dark trench coat passed by the safe house slowly and paused. He looked right at the house and then continued on to the next block and disappeared. At a little after five, a man approached all dressed in black and carrying a black bag. It was Newel, and he walked right up to the safe-house door and knocked.

"Hello. Are you Miranda?" Newel asked with a smile.

"Yes I am. Are you Jack?" Miranda asked then smiled.

"Yes. You don't strike me as someone who would have any trouble finding men to have sex with, Miranda. Maybe if you quit your second job, you would have more time for fucking," Newel said.

"What do you mean, Jack?" Miranda replied.

Suddenly, Miranda couldn't speak, and she knew she was in trouble as Newel forced his way in the door.

"I mean your job as a police detective must really mess with your social life, you lying whore," Newel whispered in her ear.

Miranda knew this was her chance, maybe her only one, to get out of this alive. It was going bad fast. While Newel was close to her ear, Miranda brought her knee up hard into Newel's groin twice, making him gasp in pain but breaking his concentration. For a moment, Miranda had her voice back and cried out into her receiver for help.

Peter and Bob crashed through the front door just in time to see two knives headed toward Miranda's throat and chest. Peter used his mind to stop the knives just inches from Miranda and turned them toward Newel. Because of the tremendous energy of Newel's and Peter's minds colliding, thunder and lightning crashed above the safe house. Bob shot the drug dart at Newel, which he stopped in midair and shot back at Bob. He was not ready for Newel's action and took the dart in his thigh before collapsing to the ground.

Peter saw this and saw how his friends were being hurt, which made him very angry. He pushed full strength with his mind at Newel, making him fly backward through the door into the front yard and slamming him onto the ground. Peter kept pushing, making a protective force in front of Newel so the only thing Newel could do was retreat. Newel moved away from the safe house, but it didn't look as if his feet were touching the ground. Slowly, it seemed that Newel just disappeared from sight.

But as Newel seemed to disappear, Peter's raging anger reached a fever pitch. Suddenly, a burst of blue-white electricity shot from Peter's hands right at the point where Newel had disappeared. It exploded with the force of a lightning bolt and just as loud. Everyone was staring at Peter and noticed the strong smell of ozone in the air like after a thunderstorm.

"How in the world did you do that, Peter?" Marsh asked.

"I'm not sure. When I let my anger go unrestrained, just about anything can happen. Is Bob okay?" Peter asked.

"I think Bob's just fine, but I think you should keep that specific ability you just showed us at hand and maybe practice it in case we need it again," Marsh said.

About an hour after they got back to the police station, Bob started to wake up.

"Hi there. Did you think you could get a bit of a rest by taking the tranquilizing dart instead of moving out of the way?" Marsh said.

"Hell no. Did you see how fast that bastard shot the dart back at me? *Christ!*" Bob said groggily.

Marsh smiled, and Bob knew he was just being teased a bit. Peter was smirking the whole time this was going on.

"So what happened? Is Miranda all right?" Bob asked.

"She's fine, Bob," Peter said.

They proceeded to tell Bob everything that happened, including how Newel seemed to vanish and Peter's newest ability.

"I think because I received the Power when my mom was struck by a lightning bolt as I was being born, I'm a sort of conductor for electricity more than most people," Peter said.

"That makes sense, Peter, and I agree with Marsh that you should practice that ability and learn to control it," Bob said.

"I know a place you could practice—at the old police firing range. It's deserted, and it's in an out-of-the-way place, very off the beaten path," Bob said.

"Peter, do you feel up to going out there now?" Marsh asked.

"I think I need to rest a bit, guys. Let's start in the morning. Okay?" Peter said.

"I'm going to check on Miranda before I leave," Bob said.

"Bob, wait. I'll go with you. Besides, I'm not sure you should drive yet; that was a pretty strong tranquilizer dart you got hit with," Peter said.

As they went by Miranda's office, Peter was unintentionally lagging a step or two behind. As he rounded the corner, he saw Bob and Miranda kissing passionately and hugging. When they noticed Peter, they parted, and after Peter made sure Miranda was okay, he and Bob went to the unmarked car they'd driven there.

"Bob, how long have you and Miranda been seeing each other, if you don't mind me asking?" Peter asked.

Bob was quiet for a moment and just looked at Peter. "About a month. We kind of would like to keep it to ourselves until we know where it's going, if anywhere. Okay?" Bob said.

"That's not a problem," Peter said, smiling at Bob.

When Peter got home, he walked in and found Amy on the sofa bundled in blankets and shivering!

"Amy, what's wrong, hon?" Peter asked.

"Earlier today I was outside in the backyard and looking at the rosebush when all at once the red blossoms turned black." Peter ran to the back door and looked.

Sure enough, when Peter went to the bush, all the rosebuds were black. Peter smelled something like the remnants of a smoking fire but with a hint of an odor mixed in that was familiar but he couldn't quite place. This set Peter's alarm off! Somehow Newel had found out where he lived and was telling him that by turning the rosebush blossoms black. But the smell that Peter detected didn't make sense. Why would the smell like the remnants of a smoking fire be present, and what was the added odor that seemed familiar?

Peter quickly got on the phone to his and Amy's parents to warn them. Then he made a call to Marsh, Bob, and Miranda, telling them what had happened with all the details.

That Burning Feeling

The previous night when Newel was almost trapped by the special squad, something had happened when he escaped and ended up near his hotel. Newel didn't notice it right away, but there was a slight burning sensation on the heel of one foot; he didn't think too much about it. At the time, he thought it might just be a blister coming up and figured he would deal with it later, but now, a day later, his heel was on fire.

When Newel examined his heel, he noticed that the cuff of his pants on that leg had been charred like from a fire. His heel was not a simple blister from shoes but an angry red blister like you might get if burned by fire. It looked like it might even be a second-degree burn. Newel called down to the desk for a first-aid kit for burns, which they brought right away without questioning their mysterious guest.

"Goddamn it, Peter!" Newel said out loud in his room.

Newel knew that Peter had tried to do something. He'd even expected it, which is why Newel left the way he did as he escaped the safe-house trap. But Newel didn't think he had been harmed. As Newel doctored his heel, he realized maybe for the first time since he had left England that he was vulnerable.

Newel wondered what Peter had done or projected at him as he escaped that would cause so much damage from a brief touch. Newel laid back on his bed and decided to sleep for a while. As he slept, the dream he found so comforting returned.

A female voice called to him. "Newel, I am not just your friend, but I am also your sister."

Newel was tossing and turning because of the dream, and it was causing pain in his heel. He didn't believe that this voice in his dream could be his sister, so he decided to test it.

"If you are my sister, are you hunting to fulfill our family mission?" he asked the person in the dream.

"Yes, I am, Newel. There are many whores out there to hunt," the voice said.

"Yes, there are, Sister, but to prove to me that you are my sister and not a figment of my mind, I want you to kill a whore for me and send me what I tell you to. Do you know where I am?" Newel asked the voice.

In the dream, it seemed like a long pause followed his question, and then, without warning or reason, the voice spoke. "Yesssss."

Newel woke up with a start and in a cold sweat. The dream had shocked the hell out of him. After a while, Newel was wondering if he had just had the crazy type of dream you deal with from too much stress or pain.

Well, I guess I'll wait and see if the person in his dream does what I requested, he thought.

Just then, there was a knock at the door of Newel's room. Newel walked over to the door and was greeted by a member of the hotel staff.

"Sorry to disturb you, Mr. Listor. I came to retrieve the burn kit if you are done with it," the staff member said.

"Sure. Just let me change the bandage once more," Newel told the staff member.

As Newel unwrapped the bandage on his heel, the staff member saw the wound.

"That's a nasty electrical burn you have on your heel. My uncle was an electrician and was always getting burns like that from electricity," the staff member said.

Newel was shocked. *Peter has control of and the ability to use electricity. He may even generate it from his body under the right situations,* Newel thought.

Peter must have projected a spike of electricity at Newel as he tried to escape the safe house, and just before he disappeared, it struck his heel and wounded him. This caused Newel to stop and think of how he could deal with this new aspect of Peter's abilities. Then Newel smiled a very sinister grin, showing lots of teeth covered in warm saliva. The grin was definitely one of a predator who had just figured a possible way to get to his prey.

The Gift

It was a clear night in Austin, Texas, with very few people roaming about. Bethany was taking a break and wondering how she was going to pay this month's rent if she didn't get a couple of more guys to service. She'd even take a woman. That always cost extra, but Bethany really got into it because she was bisexual. Whoever she was servicing, if it was obvious the person was having a good time, it turned Bethany on even more, which made the whole experience better for both of them.

But these slow nights were rough on working girls. If things didn't pick up, Bethany may have to consider getting a regular nine-to-five job to pay her bills. Just then, Bethany noticed a person walking toward her in the shadows. As she got closer, Bethany realized it was a smartly dressed woman in classy clothes, except the skirt, which was slit up the side to her hip. As the woman got closer, Bethany said hi in her sexiest voice.

"Well, hello, and what is your name, miss?" the woman inquired.

"My name is Bethany. Are you just out for a walk?" Bethany asked.

"Not exactly. I was feeling a bit horny, so I thought a walk would help take my mind off things," the woman said with a sly smile.

Just then, Bethany caught the familiar perfume of a woman who was excited. Bethany breathed the musky scent in deeply as the woman watched her smiling.

"Bethany, are you smelling something you like?" the woman asked, moving closer to Bethany.

There was no one near them, so the woman parted the slit in her skirt so Bethany could enjoy a bit of easier access. Bethany took the hint and started letting her fingers roam under the skirt, finding no panties on the woman.

The woman realized she was taking a risk, but it felt so good she thought she would indulge herself with this wanton little whore.

"Bethany, let's find a place that's a bit more private so we can play together," the woman offered.

"Come with me. A friend has an apartment near here that I can use. By the way, what is your name?" Bethany asked.

"You can call me Pleasure, Bethany," the woman said with a smile.

In ten minutes, they were at Bethany's place, and fifteen minutes after that, Bethany and Pleasure were engaging in as many ways to give each other pleasure as possible. Pleasure was really amazed at this young whore's skills with her body and a variety of special toys. It was a shame that she was going to have to be killed for the family mission and to get her brother his gift. As they were lying next to each other for one last embrace, Pleasure looked into Bethany's eyes. Bethany saw contempt, sorrow, rage, and lastly evil as Pleasure's eyes grew almost black from their beautiful blue. Suddenly, Bethany's throat collapsed, almost killing her.

"Oh, sweet Bethany, this next part I must do for my brother and my family mission, which is why I chose the hands-on approach." Pleasure proceeded with what she was doing and stored her brother's gift in an ice cooler that looked like a canvas lunch sack. As Pleasure left, her eyes changed back to their brilliant blue.

Pleasure had taken special precautions so as not to get any blood on herself. She wore latex gloves with sleeves that extended up to her shoulders for the close work. When Pleasure arrived back home, she took the items from the cooler and packed them in boxes with dry ice. One she labeled for Portland, Oregon, for Jack Listor, and the other she labeled to the Austin Police Department. She included a note that read:

> There was a young tart with despair that needed to service me fair. We serviced each other with great flair

and then when she stopped breathing air, I took this
pair.

The Poet

With that chore finished, Pleasure showered and went off to sleep. She wanted to get up early to drop off the packages at the post office.

* * * * *

The morning was a tough one, not just because mornings always came too early for the detectives in Austin Police Homicide Division, but because they brought new cases on top of the cases they were already trying to solve with very little sleep usually under their belts. This morning was going to prove to be special. As the mail came in, the newest member of the group, Dennis Kim, picked up a small, cold package.

"Well, since there's no name on it, whatever's in here, I claim it," Detective Kim announced.

Kim opened the package and saw what was inside. The color drained from his face, and he started sweating as he stayed silent.

"Kim, what's the matter? What's in the box?" the other detectives asked.

Suddenly, Kim dropped the box and grabbed a wastebasket as he threw up. Luckily, the box landed flat on its bottom, keeping the contents from spilling out. As the other detectives checked the contents, they found out why Kim was so distraught. One bloody ear was in the box, along with a neatly folded piece of paper with a poem. The Poet had struck again, and they didn't even have the body yet. The Poet was playing a dangerous game by toying with the police the way a cat plays with a mouse.

The Plan

Newel woke in his room to the unexpected pleasure of no pain in his injured heel. Suddenly, the phone rang.

"Hello, Mr. Listor. This is the front desk. We have a package for you," the staff member said.

"Thank you. I will be right down." Newel couldn't keep the excitement out of his voice. Could this be the package he was hoping for?

Newel reached the front desk in record time. He signed for his package and returned to his room. As Newel sat, he savored the coolness of the package and opened it slowly. Inside, he found an ear with a small note that read: TO MY BROTHER, FROM YOUR SISTER.

Newel could not have smiled any broader without breaking his face. He had a sister he never knew about, and she had powers like his. Newel sat looking at the ear and mentally sent an image to his sister, thanking her.

"My name is Newel, but I'm going by the name Jack Listor in honor of our great-great-grandfather. What is your name?" Newel asked his sister.

"The name I go by here is Pleasure, but my given name is Victoria," she said to Newel mentally.

Automatically, Newel knew not to call her Vicki because she liked being called by her formal name. Newel responded mentally in that way, which made Victoria smile broadly.

What a wonderful day this has been, she thought.

The Team at the Range

The next day, Peter, Bob, and Marsh were going to head to the deserted firing range after they met at police headquarters. As they walked through the building, they passed some maintenance people working on an electrical panel. As they passed by, a section of the panel shorted out and arched with a small electrical charge. It was followed by the smell of burning caused by the arch of electricity.

Peter stopped suddenly and recognized the smell he had missed at the roses. It was the same burning smell caused by electricity when he shot the electric charge at Newel. Peter realized he must have hit Newel with the charge and burned him somewhat.

"Everyone, I finally figured out the underlying odor at my home where the rosebush had turned black. It's from an electrical burn. I think I injured Newel just before he disappeared!" Peter exclaimed.

"Well, let's put out a bulletin to all hospitals and clinics to be on the lookout for such wounds and report them to us," Bob said.

Peter made a quick call to Amy and told her all he had found out and to warn his parents also. As the trio left for the shooting range, they were all very quiet. Newel had been injured, and that meant he was vulnerable and could be stopped.

As they arrived at the shooting range, Peter was thinking that the word *deserted* was an understatement. It was an open area of several acres with stacks of hay bales and dilapidated wooden buildings, and the nearest occupied building was at least fifteen miles away. The cool air hit all of them as their breathing made clouds of fog in the cold air.

"Peter, why don't you give us another demonstration of your electrical ability," Bob suggested.

"Okay, Bob," he agreed.

Peter made the same motion that he had when he first used the electric bolt, but all that happened was a small burned black area appeared three feet in front of him. Peter looked amazed with his mouth hanging open.

"I don't understand; it was so easy before. It seemed automatic," Peter said.

"Peter, maybe you need strong emotions as an incentive to help you trigger the ability," Marsh said.

"Think of some violent act that would raise your anger to its highest level if it happened, and then try the electricity as a fluid motion," Bob suggested.

Peter thought, and his brow became furrowed as darkness came over his face. Suddenly, Peter turned in one single motion and pointed with his hands across the open area at a stack of hay bales. The stack exploded as the electricity jumped from Peter's hands at incredible speed, making all of them jump from surprise.

"Holy shit, Peter! What were you thinking about?" Bob asked.

"I was thinking what if Newel came after my family and how I would treat him," Peter told Bob.

"Peter, how much control do you have over where the electric bolt strikes?" Marsh asked.

"I don't know, but let's find out," Peter said

Peter concentrated and threw the next bolt, but as he threw it, he pointed a finger as he concentrated. The electricity jumped from his finger and hit a corner of one of the old buildings fifty feet away, blowing a hole through just the corner of the building and charring the edges.

"How did you direct the electric bolt with less intensity, Peter?" Bob asked.

Peter smiled broadly. "I'm learning how to control this new ability by using one finger and concentrating on a specific spot. The bolt strength and where it strikes can be controlled," Peter told them.

"It's no wonder when you used both hands with your anger raging it was like being in the middle of a lightning storm," Bob said, smiling.

"Bob, to what extent do you have the Power?" Peter asked.

"My abilities were passed down through my parents. You already know I can bend objects with my mind, as we saw in my office, but I have a few other abilities such as ESP, and one that I have a bit of a problem controlling no matter how much I practice. I can control water and make it do anything I want, from something pleasant to something very deadly," Bob said quietly.

"Well, that makes me the odd man out. I have no special abilities except an in-depth knowledge of Jack the Ripper and this damn scar he gave me," Marsh said.

"But that's important. Not only does it allow Newel to locate you, but through you, we can locate him. It's a two-way street," Peter said, smiling.

They suddenly realized that to defeat Newel they would need to work as a team, because they all had something to offer to capture this murderer. Just then, they noticed Bob standing off to the side and concentrating. A small column of water appeared across the open area. It was a column of water from a small creek nearby that had been muddied by recent rains. Bob dropped the water over the smoldering hay that Peter had exploded earlier.

"Well, you didn't expect me to leave things burning out here, did you?" Bob said with a smile.

They all laughed and decided they had done enough practicing for the day and headed back to the station.

Newel's Plan

In Newel's mind, he felt that if he attacked members of the special squad's family, it would distract the special squad members. As a result, they would slip up and make errors. That would be when Newel would strike at the three special members he hated so much: Peter, Bob, and Marsh. Then a fierce grin grew on Newel's face.

Let's not forget about that slut bitch who lured me into that trap at the safe house where I was injured, he thought to himself. *She will have to pay as well!* "I think her name was Miranda," Newel said out loud to no one.

Newel had decided on his first target. It seemed ironic and made him laugh out loud. He would give his heel one more day to heal, and then he would start his revenge. Instead of borrowing a medical kit if he got injured, Newel decided to get his own to be prepared. He realized all too well that he could be hurt.

"Where could I purchase a first-aid kit like the one I borrowed the other day?" Newel asked at the front desk.

"At the corner store called Baker's," the staff member said.

Newel thanked him with a tip and left. When he arrived at the store, he asked for a first-aid kit to treat a wide range of problems, including electrical burns. The clerk helped Newel find one that met his needs, and he left with an eagerness to put his plan into effect, feeling he was prepared for the worst.

The next day he set out to arrive on the block where Sam and Paula lived. Newel walked around the block for about five minutes until he saw the car that Peter's dad drove. Newel was going to make this up close and personal. As Sam got out of his car, his years of experience and Peter's warning kicked in as he saw the figure all dressed in black in front of his home.

"Can I help you find an address?" Sam asked Newel.

As Newel turned and passed the flowers along the front fence, they turned black, and Sam caught the odor that Peter had described from electrical burning. Sam's cop instincts took over, and he dove toward Newel instead of away so as to surprise him and gain an upper hand for what he planned to do.

Newel was surprised as Sam rolled to the ground and came up with a Taser gun. Sam was hoping he could cause this killer enough pain to mess his aim up no matter what his powers were. Sam fired the Taser at Newel and hit him in the arm and shoulder, but the effect was instant as Newel yelled out loud and disappeared. Paula came running out of the house to see what was going on just in time to see Sam getting up off the ground.

"Paula, Newel was here, outside our home, waiting for me. He just walked right up to me, and if it wasn't for Peter's warning, I wouldn't have realized it was Newel. See our flowers?" Sam said.

However, as she turned to say something to Sam, her mouth fell open and all she could do was point to Sam's shoulder. Two knifelike darts were sticking out of it courtesy of Newel. Sam was in shock, and the adrenaline in his system didn't let him realize he was even wounded. Paula got a towel to apply pressure to the wound and drove Sam to the hospital at a speed even Sam had never seen.

When they arrived back home, Peter was pacing in the driveway, mad and worried all at the same time. But when he saw his dad and heard the story of what had happened, his anger exploded and overflowed like molten lava. Peter knew he had to direct it somewhere, and because Newel wasn't there, Peter went to the backyard. He focused his anger on a large rock about the size of a man and let go. The rock disintegrated, and Peter cleaned up by levitating the pieces and placing them along the fence at the back of the yard. When Peter was done, Paula was smiling.

"Thanks, Peter, I always wanted a rock garden there," Paula said.

Peter just looked at her with a kind of exasperated look, and then he smiled too. "How are you feeling, Dad?" Peter asked.

"Not bad. They gave me some pain killers, and they're helping," Sam said through drowsy eyes.

Peter spent the next hour calling all his friends and warning them about what had just happened to his dad. Peter needed to think about how to catch or kill this son of a bitch and do it for good. Peter went home to meet with Amy, and she and Peter talked seriously about their respective families moving out of town for a while.

"Peter, I knew the work that you do with the police can be dangerous, and I am not going to run and hide. I'm staying with you through this," Amy said as she kissed him deeply.

Peter sensed Amy's resolve and her passion for him, which only served to intensify the moment. Amy went to bed late that night, and Peter was still furious that Newel had attacked his family. Peter sent something special to Newel, an electric charge focused right at Newel's mind. Peter didn't know if it would have the desired effect, but the idea that it might was too inviting not to try. As Peter concentrated, he found Newel's thoughts and pushed with his mind toward Newel. All of a sudden, the connection with Newel was broken. What Peter couldn't see was Newel collapsing on his bed and having a seizure with only the following words repeating in his head: Stay away from our families!

Newel awoke from the seizure feeling drained and still remembering the words that had repeated in his head and were now imprinted there because of the seizure he had experienced. Newel's attention was quickly drawn from his thoughts to the pain in his arm and shoulder. It was a familiar pain like the pain he had in his heel. When he checked it out, he found spots on his arm and shoulder where the Taser electrodes had struck him. Newel used his first-aid kit and bandaged his wounds and then used the hotel computer terminal downstairs to check out what type of weapon he had been wounded by. Newel soon found out that many police departments had their officers carry what was called a Taser gun that imparted an electrical charge through two electrodes fired from the gun. Newel got up from the terminal and went back to his room, cursing under his breath and vowing to get revenge on the special group of people who were after him. They would all be so sorry they messed with him.

* * * * *

The next day at police headquarters, there was an early-morning phone call for Bob long distance. As Bob took the call, his face grew grim and lost all color.

"Bob, what's the matter?" Peter asked urgently.

"That was the Austin, Texas, homicide squad detective in charge of some similar murders they have had there. They just found another body and a poem from the Poet. Apparently, this time the murderer took a trophy from the prostitute who was murdered. The murderer took both ears from the victim and shipped one to the Austin Police Station. They don't know what was done with the other ear," Bob said slowly.

"We had all better be extra careful. Apparently, Newel can track us down by locking in on our thoughts with his mental abilities, acting like a GPS, and then find us directly," Peter said.

Just then, Miranda came in to see how the case was going. "Hey, everyone, I just had the strangest thing happen. A package was left for me that arrived this morning, and all it said on the outside was, 'from an admirer.'"

Bob took the package from Miranda. It was cold, and that sent up a red flag. He put on a pair of latex gloves and took the package from Miranda. He immediately went to the forensic lab to have it checked for prints. Once it was dusted for prints, the package was slowly opened. Inside was the ear that Newel's sister had sent him packed in dry ice with a short note that read: "My sister sent me this, so I thought I would share it with you!"

"You know what this means, don't you?" Bob asked.

"That Newel can target all of us and will try to kill us," Peter said grimly.

"It also means that I'm going to be staying with you for a while, Miranda," Bob said sternly.

Miranda started to protest until she saw the look in Bob's eyes that told her it was no use.

"So is this your plan to get into my house and stay with me, mister?" Miranda asked Bob.

"Who, me?" Bob asked, trying not to smile. "Miranda, I'm just worried about you."

"It might not be a bad idea, Miranda, since you are the only one of us without any special abilities," Peter said.

"What is Peter talking about, Bob?" Miranda asked.

"I'll tell you everything on the way home tonight. Promise," Bob said.

By the time Bob and Miranda headed home for the evening, she knew all about everyone's abilities, including his, but Bob also got a surprise when Miranda informed him that she lived on a deluxe houseboat on the river. The area was beautiful, and Miranda was curious about Bob's ability to control water.

"Bob, can you show me how you control water? Just a little example?" Miranda asked.

Bob smiled, and after making sure no one else was watching, Bob made the river water rise up and form a fence in front of Miranda's houseboat about three feet high and a foot thick and then held it there. Miranda stood there with her mouth hanging open as she watched Bob, who she realized was even more special than she had realized. Then Bob let the water gently go back to the way it had been. Suddenly, Miranda kissed Bob passionately and warmly. Later that night, Bob woke to find the bed next to him empty.

"Miranda, are you okay?" Bob asked.

"Yes, Bob. I just came out to get something to drink and a snack," Miranda said, giggling a little and thinking to herself that Bob was going to need some extra energy for the late-night activities she had planned.

As Bob laid there waiting for Miranda, he couldn't help thinking how lucky he was to have met her. Suddenly, Miranda screamed, and there was a crashing coming from the living room of the houseboat. Bob sprang from the bed and darted into the living room, but the sight that met his eyes stopped him dead in his tracks.

Miranda was being slammed into the ceiling with terrific force as she screamed Bob's name. Then Bob saw him, a dark shadow in the doorway moving his head up and down, causing Miranda's poor unconscious, bleeding body to keep slamming into the ceiling. It was Newel. If this kept up, Newel would kill Miranda.

Bob moved like lightning. Not toward Newel but to the sink in the kitchen where he turned on the hot water full force. Newel thought this amusing, but then his expression changed from an evil smirk to a knowing frown as Newel heard in his head Bob's thought: "*Die, you bastard!*"

At that instant, the stream of hot water from the sink shot at Newel with the force of a red-hot bullet. Newel screamed as the water hit him and knocked him off the houseboat, landing him thirty feet out in the river. Bob didn't have time to check to see if Newel lived or died. He went straight to Miranda as he called for an ambulance. Luckily, Miranda was still alive and started to regain consciousness as they loaded her in the ambulance. Bob rode with Miranda to the hospital and talked to her all the way.

Bob had called Peter and Marsh, and by the time they arrived at the hospital, Miranda was out of surgery and asleep in her room.

"Bob, how bad was Miranda hurt?" Peter asked.

"Broken bones and a punctured lung. He was trying to kill her, Peter," Bob said.

"What did you do to him to stop him?" Marsh asked.

"I used hot water on full force to knock him out into the river. I don't know what shape he's in. I was only concerned with Miranda," Bob said.

They all kept Bob company at the hospital until Miranda woke in the morning.

* * * * *

The morning after attacking Miranda, Newel sat in his room in pain from his wounds. He was sweating and frustrated. He knew he needed something to put things back on track with his goal and mission, which was twofold now—to get rid of the sleazy whores who roamed the world and to make this so-called special group of individuals who kept getting in his way pay dearly, with their lives if possible.

Newel smiled through his pain when he realized just what he needed to get things back on track, and it involved the use of one of the local whores in Portland. Newel started laughing uncontrollably as he saw the plan unfold in his mind's eye. As it did, Newel's laughter became more throaty and wet. Tomorrow would be the day he started to strike and show the people who were wanting to capture him just how dark and like his great-great-grandfather, Jack the Ripper, he really was.

* * * * *

Susan was an outspoken, independent woman who was Asian and very beautiful. On this particular night, she felt like traveling on the MAX line to downtown Portland and to do some barhopping. Maybe if she met the right kind of guy, she would invite him to come back to her place, unless his place was closer. Susan was the type of woman who knew what she liked when it came to sex, and she wasn't afraid to tell the guy she was with. She also relished her sexual activities deeply.

While in a downtown nightspot that was modeled after an English pub, she noticed a man dressed all in black staring at her. Granted, she had dressed to catch men's eyes tonight, black leather vest unbuttoned, black jeans tight, and a bright red fishnet top with a wide weave that allowed anyone watching to glimpse her breasts and nipples when her vest opened. Susan had a smile that was inviting, and she flashed one in the direction of the guy who had been staring in her direction. The guy waved her over, and Susan went willingly and sat down like a moth to a flame.

"Hi. I'm Susan. Do you like what you've been staring at?" she asked.

"My name is Jack, and yes, I like what I've been staring at very much. I wish I could see more though."

"Well, do you live close by or near the MAX line?" Susan asked.

"Not exactly. What I had in mind, Susan, was going somewhere dark but public, getting you naked, and doing you right out in the open, if you don't think that's too kinky," Jack said with a smile.

"Mm, Jack, that sounds wonderfully kinky, and I like that. Let's finish our drinks and go. Okay?" Susan said, smiling.

The two of them caught the MAX train to the special location Jack had been thinking about. On the ride out, Susan and Jack were French kissing, and Jack was even groping Susan, making her moan and squirm. Because they were alone in the MAX car, they could have done anything they wanted. When they got off the MAX train, Newel took Susan and started walking her down the block.

"How far is this place, Jack?" Susan asked.

"Just over here, Susan," Newel said, pointing to a nearby bench.

Newel had her sit next to him, and as he kissed her neck, he whispered to her. "I told you a bit of a lie, Susan. My real name isn't Jack. It's Newel."

"I don't care, Newel. You have me so horny, just fuck me right here," Susan said in a deep voice as she breathed hard with excitement.

"I'm sorry, Susan. I lied about that too. Although it would be nice to enjoy your body that way, my soon-to-be wife waits for me back in England, and she is the only one I will be making love to *ever*! But I do intend to use you tonight to send a special message to some friends of mine," Newel said, smiling.

"Fuck you, Newel, or whatever you want to call yourself. You're not using me for anything," Susan said with venom in her voice.

As Susan went to get up and leave, she stopped as she stood straight and gasped low in her throat. She sat back down hard. She lived just long enough to see blood running down her chest in a river from her neck. Newel had used his mental abilities to command the surgical knife that severed her neck ear to ear.

"Now, my dear Susan, your real usefulness comes into play," Newel said to himself as he started to work on her body.

When Newel was done, he cleaned up and discarded his bloody clothes in a trash can at the MAX station on his way back to town. Before Newel left the area, he looked across the street at the house across from the bench where Susan's body now sat. Newel could feel the thoughts of Peter, Marsh, and Bob, who, for whatever reason, had decided to go to Peter's home that night. Newel would have really enjoyed seeing the look on their faces when they discovered the surprise he had left the special squad.

* * * * *

Peter had called Amy to let her know that he and some of his friends from the special squad were coming to his place to do some brainstorming about the case, and they would probably stay the night. Amy made a sarcastic remark about feeding the whole police force, but it wasn't biting. It was with humor in her voice.

"Okay, Peter, but you owe me big time, mister," Amy said with a laugh to Peter.

"I'll be ready for you and your friends," Amy said.

When they arrived at Peter's home, the smell of tomato soup and grilled cheese sandwiches greeted them as they walked in.

"Amy, thanks for allowing us to invade your home," Bob said.

"It's okay, Bob. Why don't all of you come into the dining room and eat before you start talking business," Amy said with a smile after she kissed Peter.

While they ate, Peter asked Bob, "How is Miranda doing?"

"Miranda is getting better and feeling stronger every day. Thanks for asking." Bob had been constantly thinking about Miranda, even more so since she had been injured.

Soon, the conversation switched back to more pleasant thoughts as they finished their meal and moved into the living room to work on the case.

"I think the reason this Newel character is evolving is because he believes he is the second coming of the original Jack the Ripper, his so-called ancestor. Newel might be thinking of himself as a sort of reincarnation of him," Marsh proposed.

"How in the world would we know if that's what he is thinking?" Bob asked.

"Well, when he murders again, that should help us decide. Of course, Peter could probe Newel's mind and see if he gets any clues," Marsh said.

"You have got to be kidding, Marsh. Any time I go into that junk pile Newel calls a mind, it drains me like a nightmare does," Peter said.

"Peter, it was just a thought, if you were up for it," Marsh said.

After everyone was situated for the night, almost everyone was tossing and turning with thoughts of Newel except for Marsh. He slept flat on his back and didn't move. The mark on his hand glowed red, and even though he had experienced a great deal of pain when it did this before, Marsh felt nothing. When they woke, Peter was the first one up and saw Marsh sitting on the sofa rubbing his hand.

"Anything wrong with your hand?" Peter asked.

"Not really. It's just a bit sore this morning," Marsh said.

As Peter walked into the kitchen, he met Amy, and they kissed as they both got coffee. Peter happened to glance out the window at the cold, foggy morning when he noticed a person sitting on the new bench across from their house. Peter may not have noticed except the person wasn't dressed for a cold Oregon morning like this. Peter's mental abilities started working like loud sirens going off in his head.

"Wake everyone else up and have them meet me out here, but you stay in the house until I'm sure it's safe," Peter said.

Amy had learned from past experience to heed Peter's warnings, so she went and woke up the others. As Peter approached the person on the bench, he found out several things. The person was a woman, she was dead—given the amount of blood under the bench—and there was a note next to her. It read: "Just thought I would drop in on your little meeting and give you a personal message. I took part of this lady home with me, much like my great-great-grandfather would have to sample. Can you tell which part? Newel."

Peter's mouth fell wide open. Newel had been right outside as they tried to figure out how to catch him.

As Bob and Marsh arrived, they saw the note, and the crime lab was called.

"No breakfast at home today, just stale doughnuts at work," Bob said.

"Oh, no you don't, you three. Here you go." Amy handed a sack to each person, and they were warm. "Now go and kill this son of a bitch and take him out of the gene pool," Amy said sternly.

"Amy, we usually try to capture them first," Bob said, smiling.

"Oh yeah, guess it was a slip of the tongue," Amy said with a smile.

When the men opened the sacks, they found warm bacon-and-egg sandwiches inside, which they wolfed down with gusto. When they finished eating in the car, they talked about what had happened that morning.

"I told the lab boys to do nothing to the victim unless it was in front of us and the exam room was to only have the coroner and his assistant and us in there. We don't want to get rumors or the media circus started in on this," Peter said.

"That was a good idea, Peter. The press has been nosing around the station trying to get a lead on this story, along with some of the officers who leak information to the press for a few extra bucks," Bob said.

As they arrived at the station, the three of them made a beeline for the autopsy room. They arrived at the same moment as Susan's body, and the room was cleared as requested by the special squad. As the coroner undressed the body, he was shocked at what he found.

On Susan's body, cuts had been made deeply to write all three of the names of the lead workers on the special squad. On her arms were Bob's and Marsh's names, and right over her heart was Peter's name. If that wasn't shocking enough, Susan's abdomen had been opened up. At the sight of this, Bob told the coroner what the note had said.

"Doctor, is she missing any body parts?" Bob asked.

After checking, the doctor got a strange look on his face, and he lost all color. "She is missing a kidney," the doctor said and then excused himself for a breath of fresh air as he walked unsteadily outside.

"I think we have confirmation as to Newel's intentions and how closely he feels related to Jack the Ripper," Marsh said.

"I think that Newel is telling us that we will end up like this woman he butchered if we stay on the case," Peter said.

"Peter, would you consider doing something that might be preemptive where Newel's activities are concerned. It might save some people," Marsh asked.

"Well, sure. If I could be convinced it would save people, I would do it," Peter said.

"Peter, we need to take a few things to be true. First, that Newel's great-great-grandfather was indeed Jack the Ripper and that Newel's family trains future generations of serial killers in that fashion. What would happen if you could convince Newel to talk about his family by using the Power? Specifically, his brothers and sisters and their names. If we knew their names, we could be forewarned of potential serial killers," Marsh suggested.

"I see your point, but I would need to try it when I'm alone in a quiet place so that I could concentrate," Peter said.

"Maybe when you're home and trying to sleep. That way Amy could be there if you need to be woken up," Bob said.

"And you could keep a notepad near your bed with a pen to write down whatever you remember. Then we could go over it with you," Marsh said.

Peter just nodded his head. He didn't much like involving Amy. Even though the danger was slight, it still bothered him. He would want to talk to Amy later that night and be completely honest with her before he tried it.

* * * * *

Newel was completely rested after his night with Susan, and his frustration and anxiety were gone. Newel was hoping that his message got through to all three men. If they pursued him, they would pay with their lives. Peter had guessed right about this message, but the other part of the message Newel was sure was loud and clear—he was the descendant of Jack the Ripper. Newel smiled to himself while gazing at Susan's kidney in the refrigerator.

* * * * *

When Peter got home that night, he sat brooding in the living room, trying to broach the subject with Amy about him trying to psychically connect with Newel to find out some of his siblings' names. Peter decided the straightforward approach would be best.

"Amy, we think we may have come up with an idea that could prove to be beneficial in saving some lives where Newel is concerned, but I wanted to talk to you about it first."

"Peter, if it's going to save lives, it would be a great move, and you should put it into effect," she said.

"Amy, this idea would involve me getting into contact with Newel mentally and trying to find out the names of some of his family, mostly his brothers and/or sisters. If we had names, we could use them as an early warning system to other police groups about these highly trained serial killers. This plan would involve you too," Peter said quietly.

"How would I be involved? I don't have any special talents like the rest of you," Amy noted.

"Amy, you would have one of the most important jobs—keeping me safe. When I communicate with Newel, it's possible for me to get too wrapped up in the nightmare that is Newel's subconscious. If that happens, I am going to need you to wake me out of the nightmare sleep violently so that Newel doesn't draw me down mentally into his mind where I can't return to my own body or retain my sanity," Peter said gravely.

Amy sat quietly, considering everything Peter had just told her. "Peter, if it might save lives, then let's do it together. But how will I know if you're back and the connection has been broken?" Amy asked.

"When my eyes clear and I speak to you in my own voice, you can be sure the connection is broken."

Peter called Bob and Marsh and told them that Amy agreed to help and that they were going to try that night for the first time. As Peter set everything up, including the notepad and pen, Amy watched and hugged him.

"Peter, I am so proud of you that you would take a risk like this to protect people you don't even know." Amy then kissed Peter.

"I have a selfish reason for doing this also," he said. "I'm protecting my family."

"Peter, I understand wanting to keep your parents safe," Amy said a bit shyly.

Peter lifted Amy's chin gently. "Amy, I wasn't just talking about my parents. I was talking of my future family. After all this is over, I would like to marry you, if you will have me with all this weirdness," Peter said with a big smile as he pulled a small box from his pocket. He showed Amy the ring inside.

Amy smiled as tears ran down her cheeks.

"I take it that is a yes?" Peter asked.

"Oh, yes! Right after we get rid of the butcher called Newel," Amy said.

As they went to bed, Peter began to try to connect with Newel. But as he did, he seemed to be getting a connection from another source, one that kept trying to divert his efforts away from connecting with Newel, almost like a mental wall. Peter was sweating buckets and tossing all over so much that he woke Amy. It was obvious to Amy that Peter needed to be awakened quickly, so she smacked him violently across the face. Peter's eyes snapped open, and he spoke to Amy in his normal voice.

"Peter, are you okay? You were sweating and tossing and turning. What do you remember? Tell me everything, and I will write it down," Amy said as she held Peter.

"For some reason, I couldn't connect with Newel's mind. Every time I tried, something diverted my efforts and pushed my thoughts away from Newel."

"Did you get anything useful at all, Peter?" Amy asked.

"Possibly. Just before you smacked me, I was trying so hard to break through the barrier that I tried using my mental energy like a lightning bolt and directed a concentrated shot at the barrier. For an instant, it seemed like the barrier faded away, and I saw a name. Victoria. I also thought I heard a woman scream in surprise and pain," Peter said.

Amy wrote everything down. Peter had told her it may take several tries before he connected with Newel, because it seemed someone was trying to prevent the connection from being made.

* * * * *

In Austin, Texas, Victoria was waking to the morning with an unpleasant sensation on the back of her neck. Then she remembered where she got it from. She had been trying to communicate with her brother in Portland, just to see how he was doing, when she sensed another mind also pushing to reach him. It was a powerful force, and Victoria knew by instinct that she needed to block this other mind from connecting with her brother. She was able to fend off the mental powers of the individual for a short while until she saw a bright flash of light and felt a severe pain on the back of her neck. At that point, her connection with her brother and the other mind was broken.

Victoria went into the bathroom for a hand mirror to check out the source of the neck pain. What she found shocked her. At the source of the pain on her neck was a burn about one inch in diameter and bright red. Whomever she had made contact with also had the same Power as her brother and her but with some unusual differences, which might even make this other mind stronger than them. Victoria bandaged her wound and consoled herself that it was hidden by her hair so there wouldn't be any unnecessary questions being asked of her.

When Peter got to the squad room, Bob and Marsh were already waiting for him. As he walked in, he got himself coffee and placed the notepad with all the notes that Amy had jotted down in front of him.

"Well, Peter, how did it go last night? Were you able to contact Newel and learn anything?" Bob asked.

"Well, it was good and bad. As I started to contact Newel's mind in the way I had done before, a strange thing happened. A kind of wall was forcing me away from connecting with Newel, like a mental force field. I got so frustrated that I focused the Power like I did the lightning bolt at the block, and it cleared for a moment. I heard a woman scream and then saw the name Victoria. I think this is one of Newel's siblings, and she has the same abilities as Newel and me to some extent," Peter said.

"Forgive me for saying this, Peter, but that doesn't seem like much in the way of good news," Marsh said.

"That's because it's not the really good news, which is that I asked Amy to marry me as soon as all this is over. I gave her the ring, and she said yes!" Peter said, smiling from ear to ear.

Everyone in the room started cheering and telling Peter it was about time.

"Well, Peter, we had better take care of Newel as quickly as possible," Bob said, smiling.

"I think that if I don't run into any more interference, I may be able to make contact with Newel tonight," Peter told the squad.

"Just make sure you're up to it. If there is another mind out there with similar abilities as you and Newel, you don't want to get blindsided when you least expect it," Marsh said.

* * * * *

Newel was napping when his sister contacted him. "Newel, someone was trying to contact you last night. I tried to prevent it, but at one point, they were able to push me away and I saw a bright flash of light. I got a burn on the back of my neck like an electrical burn. Does anyone who's trying to find you have abilities like that?"

"Yes, Sister. His name is Peter. He was the one I was communicating with while I was still in England. I'm sorry you got hurt."

"We must make this person pay for what he has done, for the pain and for the embarrassment to us and our family," Victoria told Newel.

Newel's eyes slowly opened, and he was looking through bloodshot eyes even though he'd had plenty of sleep. Newel was angry, not just a little mad but ready to rip apart the person who had hurt his sister. And like any brother to a sister, he would do it slowly so he could relish every moment of agony his victim experienced, making him sorry he had touched his sister. No matter what Newel had to do, he made a promise to himself that Peter would pay with his life for hurting his sister.

Newel was curious as to why Peter was trying to contact him. *What could he be after?* Newel thought.

As the day finished, Peter, Bob, and Marsh gathered at Peter's home to congratulate Amy and Peter officially and as a precaution. Peter was going to try to contact Newel again, but because of how Peter had reacted the first time he tried to contact Newel, it was agreed that having the members of the special squad there was good idea. They could protect both Peter and Amy. If Newel got an idea of what they were trying to do, there was no telling how savagely he could be and at whom his anger would be directed.

After dinner, Peter went in to sleep, while the others kept watch from their sleeping arrangements in the home. Of course, Amy was with Peter as he slept, ready to call the others if she needed help waking him. This time, Peter's thoughts found Newel waiting for him.

"Why the hell have you been trying to contact me, Peter?" Newel said mentally.

"I was curious. I have never met anyone like you who had a famous relative. Do you come from a big family, Newel?" Peter asked mentally.

"Oh, so you do believe my great-great-grandfather was Jack the Ripper," Newel said with pride.

"How can I not believe that? The way you have removed some of the wanton women in Portland in such a short time." Peter complimented Newel.

"It would be a much faster process if my brothers and sisters were here to help," Newel boasted.

"How big is your family?" Peter asked calmly.

"I have four brothers and three sisters, and they will visit the cities of the world when they are of age and their training is complete to keep getting rid of the women who prostitute themselves for money," Newel bragged.

"Newel, is one of your sisters named Victoria?" Peter asked.

Newel was deadly quiet, almost brooding. "How did you know that?" he asked with caution.

Peter sensed the danger in Newel's thought and in his question. "I tried to contact you the other night. I couldn't get through, so I pushed with my mind focused at the force that was blocking me. When I did that, the block cleared, and I saw a name. Victoria was the name."

"Do you know what your little mental push did to my sister, you bastard? It gave her a burn on the back of her neck, which you will have to pay for starting right *now*!" Newel shouted mentally at Peter.

But before Peter could break the connection with Newel, he gave a mental push right at Peter, making him somersault out of bed and land hard on the bedroom floor. Amy woke to the commotion and saw Peter lying on the floor, eyes still glazed, not speaking.

"Bob, Marsh, come quickly! Peter's in trouble!" Amy screamed.

As the men came running in, they saw Peter convulsing on the floor.

"We have to shock Peter awake until he speaks with his own voice!" Amy yelled.

Marsh went to Peter and smacked him hard across the face, openhanded. Peter's eyes opened, and Amy tried to talk to Peter.

"Peter, can you hear me?" Amy screamed.

"Yes, everyone, I'm back, but who the hell smacked me so hard?" Peter asked.

"I'm afraid you have me to thank for that, Peter. I smacked you harder than maybe I should have. You may have a black eye by morning," Marsh said.

"That's all right. At least I'm back, and I did find out some things," Peter said. "Newel has seven brothers and sisters all together, four brothers and three sisters, and one of his sisters is named Victoria. Also, he mentioned that there is a certain age at which the children in his family are unleashed on the world." Amy wrote everything down as he spoke.

"I'm going to make an educated guess that it's when they reach their early twenties, gauging by Newel's age, maybe the legal age of twenty-one," Bob said.

"That's not a bad guess. Now all we have to do is figure out who the other five serial killers are to warn other authorities about them," Marsh said.

Peter was trying to recuperate when Bob spoke up. "Do you remember when we got the ear from Newel?"

"Sure. That was a gruesome piece of mail," Marsh said.

"Well, I believe we should compare the DNA of that ear to the DNA of the ear in Austin, Texas, and we might just locate one of Newel's sisters and help solve a murder in another city," Bob said with a smile.

With that, they all cleaned up and ate breakfast. As they talked about Bob's idea, they were all amazed that the idea hadn't occurred to them earlier. On the ride to the station, it was very quiet as the men were lost in thought.

"We need to work together as a team with everyone watching one another's backs. And if we have ideas, we need to share them quickly, no matter how crazy they seem," Marsh said.

They were all quiet, considering what Marsh had just said. It was sinking in that if they all were to survive this case, they had to not only outsmart Newel but also to use their abilities in new and creative ways that Newel wasn't expecting.

While the group was waiting for the DNA comparison with the DNA from the ear in Austin to come in from the lab, the squad members started kicking around some ideas on how to find Newel.

"Marsh, you told me that scar you got from Newel sometimes hurts," Peter noted. "When were the times that it hurt? What was going on?"

"Well, when I first got the scar and when we had the meeting at Peter's home when we found the body of that woman on the bench across the street," Marsh said.

"Is it a dull ache or an obvious pain that you feel?" Bob asked.

"It's an obvious pain. It hurts like hell, like someone just burned the back of my hand. I noticed when we were at Peter's home, the scar got very warm to the touch," Marsh said.

"If you're willing, Marsh, we could devise a plan to try to locate Newel by using your scar to find out where he is staying," Peter said.

"Peter, didn't you say you were sure you had hit Newel with that first bolt of electricity that night at the safe house when he disappeared?" Bob asked.

"Yes I did, Bob. Why do you ask?" Peter said.

"Because electrical burns require special first-aid treatment from an emergency room or a first-aid kit for treating those types of injuries. We could put a search out not just to emergency rooms but to those places that have those types of first-aid kits for sale or hotels that have those kits," Bob said.

Bob got on the phone and amended his first alert to only hospitals and clinics to include the places that include the sale of burn kits like they were looking for. The squad would start the tedious work of calling hotels in the area one by one and finding out which places had those first-aid kits. It was good, old-fashioned police work. They spent the rest of the day making calls to hotels locally.

It wasn't until the end of the day that they got some news. It was the DNA results from the two ears. Both ears belonged to the murder victim in Austin, Texas. Bob made the Austin authorities aware of this. They also informed them that their murderer was a female who called herself Victoria and that she was the sister of Newel, the murderer who was currently on the loose in Portland, Oregon.

When the Austin police heard that these killers were keying in on prostitutes, they started going back through past cases that involved any type of mutilation or arranging the body after death. To their shock, they found three right off the bat and were still searching.

"But you haven't heard the wildest part yet. The individuals doing these murders have some extraordinary abilities due to the fact that they are able to use all their minds' capabilities," Bob told the chief of detectives in Austin.

"What the hell do you mean by that?" the detective asked in disbelief.

"I have seen it with my own eyes, things like teleportation, levitation, and psychic abilities. Anything that can be done with our hands, they can do with their minds," Bob told him.

"You aren't kidding around, are you, Bob?" the detective asked.

"No, it's some very scary shit, and it makes these people the ultimate killers," Bob said.

All at once, the door to the squad room burst open. One of the detectives who had been making phone calls to motels rushed in.

"I think we just got a small break in locating where this murderer is!" Officer Davis said to the room.

Bob rushed to Officer Davis, along with Peter and Marsh. "Davis, what do you mean?" Bob asked.

"Do you remember the location of the first murder, when we found the woman sitting on the bench with her feet amputated near the bridge by the Willamette River in Waterfront Park?"

"Yes, that's what let us know that Newel was here in Portland," Bob said.

"Well, we located three hotels in the area that carry first-aid kits of the type you told us to look for. The hotel managers confirmed it," Davis said. "And when we checked on places that sell those first-aid kits, one turned up just a couple of blocks away from the hotels we contacted."

"Good work, Davis. Tell your team they did great," Bob said. "Marsh, how would you feel about going on a hunting trip to get this butcher?"

"I would really enjoy nailing this bastard to the wall, regardless of the pain it will inflict through this goddamn scar," Marsh said with venom in his voice.

"Very good, everyone. Let's go on a walk around the area that Davis told us about and see if by using the scar on Marsh's hand, we can pin down Newel's location," Bob said as they left the squad room.

* * * * *

Newel sat in front of his room's large window, enjoying the rare bit of warm sun that this Oregon day was providing. Suddenly, he got an impression of Peter and the rest of the special squad searching for him. Newel was not only aware they were searching for him, but he knew they were coming to the general area where his hotel was located.

"They must have figured out how to use the scar I gave Marsh to act as a locater beacon. *Damn it!*"

In his own mind, Newel started to go over various actions he could take. The truth of the matter was that he had underestimated the ingenuity of these foes, and it had put him into a precarious position.

Without warning, a voice spoke to Newel out of nowhere in his head. "Newel, calm yourself. There is a way to deal with this situation easily. Just listen to me, and I will tell you what to do," said Victoria's voice telepathically to Newel.

As Newel listened, he smiled and relished the simple evil of the plan. Because it came from his sister, Newel once again realized that his sister was watching over him at all times in every way. Because they had similar abilities they were linked physically, emotionally, and mentally forever.

* * * * *

The first place the men stopped was the location that sold the type of first-aid kits they were looking for. When they questioned the manager, he told them he had sold only three in the past couple of weeks.

"Did any of your customers who bought those types of kits have an accent?" Peter asked.

"As a matter of fact, one of them had an English accent, pleasant but a bit guttural," the manager told Peter. The manager hadn't noticed which way the customer had left by, just that he had a bit of a limp.

"We had better stick together as we look for Newel and start asking questions at each of the hotels that Davis located," Peter suggested.

As the trio walked to the next hotel, they started talking about getting some lunch. Marsh started rubbing his hand with the scar.

"Marsh, is your hand hurting?" Peter asked.

"Yeah, but it's not just hurting. It's like I'm being burned," Marsh said.

Peter grabbed Marsh's hand and felt the intense heat coming from the scar. It was obvious that Newel was close by! "Everyone, Newel is close. Be ready for anything!" Peter said.

As the three men passed an alley, Peter felt Newel's presence like itching powder on his brain and also felt Newel's intent. Peter whirled around, pushing Marsh and Bob to either side and ended up looking down the semidark, shadowed alley at the dark figure that was Newel. Peter could see his eyes glisten with evil, and as Newel smiled, Peter saw his saliva-covered teeth in a predator's smile just before it strikes its prey. Peter sensed Newel was attacking, but with what? The block Peter had encountered before was back.

Enough of this bullshit! Peter thought to himself.

Peter focused his energy into a concentrated point at the block, and it cleared with a scream just in time for Peter to see the knife-sharp darts that Newel had thrown with his mind toward one member of the group. Marsh! Peter pushed with his mind to protect Marsh and at the same time snapped an exterior water faucet off, which shot water across the alleyway. Bob took the hint and bent the direction of the water toward Newel, knocking him into the back of the alley thirty feet away.

All anyone heard was Newel exclaim, "*Fuck!*" as he slipped away from the alley.

Both Bob and Peter smiled and turned to Marsh, who was collapsed on the sidewalk. They rushed to Marsh's side to see how badly he was hurt. As they turned him over, they saw one of Newel's darts sticking out of his chest just above his right lung.

While they were waiting for the ambulance, Marsh spoke to them both. "Peter and Bob, you be sure to get that bastard for me. Amy was right, Peter; he needs to be killed, not captured. Him and his whole sick family," Marsh said.

"We'll get him, Marsh. I'm just sorry that I missed that dart that got you," Peter said.

"It's okay, Peter. You got the others," Marsh said as he looked higher on the alley's brick wall.

Both Bob and Peter looked where Marsh was looking and higher on the brick wall of the alley were Newel's three other darts. They were each six inches long, razor sharp, an inch apart, and all buried half their length into the brick wall. Peter realized that Newel had thrown those darts not just with killing purpose but with an evil hatred.

* * * * *

Newel made his way back to his hotel room, changed his clothes, packed, and made reservations at another hotel a few blocks away. Before he left, he mentally linked with his sister.

"Victoria, are you okay?" Newel asked.

"Yes, Brother. I will survive, but that person you call Peter has harmed me again with a burn across the back of my hand," Victoria said with pain in her voice.

Newel heard her pain, which made him blind with rage. Suddenly, the bathroom door exploded into splinters as Newel needed something to direct his anger at right then.

"That's it, Brother, but the next time you meet this Peter, direct all your anger and vengeance toward him. I can't stand being hurt by him anymore."

And to emphasize her point to Newel, she mentally raised the king-sized bed three feet off the floor and slammed it back down hard enough to break all four of the legs.

"Don't worry, Sister. I will not let anyone hurt you again. I promise!" Newel told his sister mentally.

All Newel sensed was reassurance from his sister as he left his old hotel room. Newel was at his new location within thirty minutes and very comfortable.

* * * * *

Peter and Bob followed the ambulance to the hospital and waited for any word from the doctors about his condition. As Peter and Bob waited, they both ended up thinking the same thing: how could they get to this butcher and kill him? Yes, they were all right. Newel had to be taken out of the gene pool permanently. Amy, Marsh, Miranda, and now Bob and Peter were all of the same opinion. But how was the big question.

Waiting for Marsh to get out of surgery was a long tedious, period. Coupled with the frustration of working out how to get Newel, both Peter and Bob had fallen asleep and were awakened by the doctor still wearing hospital scrubs.

"Gentlemen, your friend is going to be all right, but I'm afraid he will need some downtime to let his wounds heal. He was very lucky. If he had been hit a few inches to the right, he wouldn't have made it to the hospital. He would have bled out," the surgeon said.

"When can we see him, Doctor?" Peter asked.

"Not till tomorrow. He's in recovery right now," the doctor told Peter.

"Okay, Doctor, and thank you," Peter and Bob both said.

* * * * *

Newel was resting in his new room. He had just communicated where he was with his sister and found out she was feeling better after being burned the second time by Peter's mind-block-breaking abilities. Without warning, Newel suddenly smiled from ear to ear. His sister had just suggested to him an idea that was both unexpected and delicious, and it would help to defeat this so-called special squad once and for all so that he could resume with his family's work.

* * * * *

The next morning the whole group met at the hospital—Bob, Amy, and Peter. Even Miranda came down in a wheelchair to visit Marsh, because they were both in the same hospital. As they came in the room, Marsh waved from the bed and smiled.

"Hey, Amy, did you happen to bring any of those bacon-and-egg sandwiches with you? I don't know what food is like in this hospital, but I've heard rumors that some of the patients are here because of the food," Marsh joked.

Everybody laughed, and it felt good to see their friend feeling good enough to laugh as well. When they all left, the talk turned to how to trap Newel. Even Amy and Miranda were trying hard to think of ways to lure him to where he could be dealt with in the most severe manner. Nothing was thought of that they could be sure would defeat Newel permanently, but this team was just getting started. And with the injury to a second member of their group, the squad was more determined than ever before. Newel would be put down like a rabid dog.

* * * * *

The flight attendant noticed a well-dressed lady sitting in first class holding a small decorative box with a red ribbon.

"That looks very nice. Is it for someone special?" the attendant asked the woman.

"Why, yes it is," the woman responded.

"Well, I'm sure it will make whomever it's for very happy," the attendant said with a smile.

"It will make me happier to give this gift to her. You see, I like to make people happy," the woman said with a pleasing smile.

When the plane landed, the lady from first class got into a cab and gave the driver an address. As they traveled through Portland, the lady smiled, thinking very private thoughts. When she arrived at her hotel, she was escorted to her room. She immediately put out the do-not-disturb sign. Then she placed the box that she had been carrying in the refrigerator and unpacked before lying back on the bed to relax. But as she rested, her body went rigid. Her lips were moving, but no sound came out of her mouth.

* * * * *

Newel was resting in his new room at the hotel he had moved to when he felt a presence like a warm embrace on his mind, and he heard three words mentally.

"Portland is beautiful."

Newel smiled so broad it would have broken his face if he smiled any larger. *It is going to be a great day,* Newel thought to himself as he sat down to relish this moment. Newel was mentally communicating with his sister later that day about what to do about the members of the so-called special squad who were interfering with their family mission to such a great degree.

His sister was curious who the other members were. Newel told her about Miranda and Marsh being injured and in a hospital. He explained that Bob and Peter were the only two members who were uninjured but that they were the most dangerous because of their special abilities, which he told his sister about. Newel heard his sister laughing, and she told him that Portland and its special squad were going to be changed soon. As Newel listened to what his sister was telling him, he got that special smile on his face of impending chaos and satisfaction.

* * * * *

Miranda had returned to her room, and the nurse informed her that the doctor had ordered a test for her, so off in her wheel chair she went with the nurse. A short time later, a woman walked up to the nurse's station on Miranda's floor and inquired of the nurse.

"I just got into town, and I was told that a friend of mine was injured and was in this hospital. I was hoping to visit her for just a few moments to see how she was doing," the woman said politely.

"What is the name of your friend?" the nurse asked.

"She is a Portland detective. Her name is Miranda." The woman smiled as she talked.

"She just went for some quick tests, but she should be back in about fifteen minutes if you would like to wait," the nurse told her as she showed her to Miranda's room.

Miranda returned from her tests to find a small box with a ribbon sitting on her nightstand next to her hospital bed. The card just said it was from a friend. Miranda thought Bob had left her a little something to cheer her up, and as she opened the box, she found two caramel-filled chocolates inside. She ate one and decided to save the other for later. Soon, Miranda became quite drowsy and couldn't seem to stay awake. As Miranda fought to stay awake, she sensed a presence next to her bed. When she opened her eyes, all she could see was a blurry image of a nurse's white uniform.

"It's all right, dear. You just rest. It's time for your medication. Doctor's orders," the woman in white said.

As Miranda laid back, the nurse gave her the medication through her IV. "There, dear. Now everything is in its proper place as the Poet says."

Miranda snapped her eyes open at the sound of the word *poet*. She recognized it but couldn't think straight, and then she realized something else. It was getting harder for her to breathe. Suddenly, the alarm went off at the nurse's station for Miranda's monitors, and the nurses called a code for decreased breathing. The doctor on call rushed in as the nurses worked on Miranda as her breathing grew shallower.

She was slowly dying. The doctor ordered a ventilator to help her breathe, but she was getting worse. The doctor got the strangest look on his face and told the nurses to draw blood and get him a shot of cholinesterase inhibitor. *Stat!* The doctor injected the shot directly into the IV and waited. Within minutes, Miranda was breathing on her own, and her breaths were becoming regular and full.

"Doctor, what do you think was the cause of the detective's distress?" asked one of the nurses.

"I believe this young lady had an attempt made on her life using a rare poison. Would you please see if the other police officers are still here, and don't touch anything in this room," the doctor said.

Bob, Peter, and Amy were still visiting Marsh when they got the news. Bob was nearly running at full speed to get to Miranda's room because of how much he cared about her. When they reached the room, Miranda was able to talk clearly, although she was still a bit groggy. Miranda told Bob that when she came back from her tests, she found the box with two candies. She ate one and left the other on the nightstand to save for later. Then she got really sleepy and realized someone was standing by her bed dressed in white.

"I thought it was one of the nurses, but I couldn't make her face out. My eyes just wouldn't focus," Miranda said.

"It sounds like you were drugged, Miranda, and then poisoned," Bob said.

"But with what? Why drug her and then poison her?" Peter asked.

"I think I can answer that," the doctor said, speaking up.

"I've seen only one reaction similar to this when I was in South America. It's curare poisoning. Curare does nothing if eaten, but if injected, it causes paralysis of the respiratory system and eventually death if not treated quickly. You have to keep the person breathing and administer a shot of a cholinesterase inhibitor to bring the victim completely back to health.

"So the candy was probably used to drug Miranda so that the person trying to poison her wouldn't have to fight her to give her the shot of curare," Peter said. "Bob, we need to document all this and have the lab check out that other candy to see what's in it."

"Bob, I just remembered something odd," Miranda said. "The woman who gave me the shot said for me to rest and that everything was in its proper place as the Poet says."

When Bob and Peter heard the name the Poet, their mouths dropped. Like Miranda, they both recognized it. That was the name of the serial killer in Austin, Texas.

"That can't be, Peter!" Bob exclaimed.

"I think we had better be prepared for the worst, because if what we think has happened, happened, our troubles have just doubled," Peter said.

After the CSI team left with all the evidence and fingerprints to analyze, Bob and Peter did two things. Bob kissed Miranda good-bye and told her he would be back in the morning, and then Bob stationed two police officers in front of Miranda's room. Next, Bob and Peter headed back to police headquarters. If what they thought had happened were true, the body count of not just prostitutes but of any woman who looked in the least bit easy or provocative was going to increase because of some perverse mission of Newel's family. As they drove through the streets of Portland, they could feel the fall air chilling the glass windows on their car. Bob was gripping the steering wheel so tight that his knuckles were white.

"Bob, Miranda is all right. The doctors were able to help her in time," Peter said with feeling.

"Peter, that bastard's bitch sister came after Miranda. We have to consider that all our family members are in danger!" Bob said.

Peter took the hint and called Amy, telling her to be prepared for anything that could possibly happen in the realm of weird.

"What did Amy say, Peter?" Bob asked slowly.

"She said she knew what to look for as far as clues for weird shit happening because she's been around me for so long. Then she laughed, which made me feel better."

"Peter, you're a lucky man, and you and Amy will make a great married couple," Bob said as he smiled.

"What about you and Miranda? Are you two considering anything more serious than dating?" Peter asked with a smile.

"Well, just between you and me, I've been considering asking Miranda to move in with me to see if she can tolerate a slob like me, but don't say anything till I ask her," Bob said.

"Sure, Bob, I won't say a thing," Peter said, grinning from ear to ear.

As Bob and Peter arrived at the police station, they hurried to the lab to see how things were progressing. The lab techs saw them coming and gave them the sign to slow down.

"You guys will have to give us a little while to sift through all this evidence. Go grab a cup of coffee and see us in about an hour. All right?" the head lab tech said.

Both Peter and Bob were fidgeting like crazy waiting for the hour to pass so they could get something to go on from the lab technicians. As Bob and Peter hurried back to the lab, the head tech was working on some paperwork related to the case and eating a tuna fish sandwich.

"Well, did you finish with the evidence, or did you just need a break, Max?" Bob asked sarcastically.

"Oh, I'm done with the evidence, gentlemen. I was just catching up on the related paperwork for this case," Max said, smiling. "It's interesting what I found. Apparently, after ruling out hospital staff, the only prints that were found were without fingerprints. I believe that whoever poisoned the detective used latex gloves that were right in the hospital room, which is how most hospitals operate. They store latex gloves in the rooms so they will be handy for various procedures," Max said.

"So did you find anything of interest?" Peter asked.

"Yes, I did. I got the lab work from Miranda's blood work, and it confirmed the use of curare. Also, we analyzed the one candy that remained and found that a powerful opiate-based sedative in liquid form had been injected into the candy. A person of a couple of hundred pounds would have been knocked out," Max told them.

"Talk about overkill. Newel's sister wanted to make sure that whoever ate the candy wouldn't wake up until she was done," Bob said quietly.

* * * * *

Portland, Oregon, was cold that dark fall evening as a woman strolled downtown and stepped into a local nightspot. She took a seat at a booth by herself and ordered a drink, a black widow. As she sipped it slowly, another drink of the same type was brought to her by the waitress.

"I didn't order that, miss," she told the waitress as she sipped at her raspberry-flavored drink. It had a reddish tint, almost like blood.

"Miss, this is the compliments of the lady at the end of the bar," the waitress replied with a smile.

The lady at the end of the bar lifted her drink to the woman in the booth and smiled, and the woman with now two drinks smiled back and motioned her over.

"Hi. My name is Sherry. Would it be all right if I join you?" Sherry asked the woman she had bought the drink for.

"Sure, Sherry. Please join me, and thank you for the drink," the woman said.

"You know my name. Would you mind if I ask yours?" Sherry asked.

"My name is Pleasure, Sherry. Glad to meet you," the woman in the booth said.

"Watching you sip that drink reminds me of a female vampire in the movies," Sherry said, smiling.

"Oh, Sherry. I'm no vampire, but I am a creature of the night," Pleasure said, whispering close to Sherry's ear.

As Sherry and Pleasure talked, they sat very close and were soon fondling each other under the table away from prying eyes. The only obvious thing was that every so often they would slowly and passionately kiss, which didn't seem to bother anybody.

"Pleasure, I think I would like to go someplace more private. Would that be all right with you?" Sherry asked.

"I want to so badly, Sherry, but are you doing this because you really want to be with me, or are you a working girl?" Pleasure asked, cautiously making like she was a bit shy for suggesting that Sherry was a prostitute. "I'm sorry if I offended you by asking."

"I'm not offended, Pleasure. I am a working girl, as they say, but I enjoy both men and women, and I only charge the men," Sherry said as they both smiled and laughed to each other quietly.

As the two women left, the bartender wished them both a good night, and they were lucky to catch a cab right outside. Sherry gave an address to the driver, and he took them to one of the nicer hotels downtown. When they got to Sherry's room, Pleasure stripped down as she held Sherry, and Sherry rubbed and kissed her all over.

Pleasure was enjoying this indulgence a great deal. It hadn't been since Austin, Texas, that she had felt such wild yearnings. As the two women moved to the bedroom, they indulged each other's passions completely. Afterward, Pleasure got a candy from her handbag and gave it to Sherry. After Sherry ate the candy, she got a little drowsy.

Pleasure spoke to her calmly. "I really have enjoyed being with you, Sherry, but there's something I have to do, which you aren't going to like I'm afraid. You see, sweetheart, like the drink I was drinking when we met, I am also a black widow." Pleasure smiled, with teeth showing. "Sherry, it's really for the best for all concerned—for me, my brother, and, of course, to get rid of another prostitute from the world."

Sherry's eyes bulged wide even though she was groggy. She was scared to death, because she saw how Pleasure's eyes gleamed and how her teeth glistened wet with saliva as she smiled. She was sure she was going to die tonight. Suddenly, a metal knitting needle came out of Pleasure's handbag, and with the speed of a bullet, it pierced Sherry through her ear and brain and straight out the ear on the opposite side effortlessly.

As Sherry died, Pleasure talked to her soothingly. "I tried to take your life quickly, Sherry dear, with as little pain as possible because you have been such a wonderful lover. But what I'm about to do now to you will not be painful, because I will have already sacrificed you for the cause. It will send a message to that damn special squad!"

And then Victoria proceeded to use her abilities, along with hand motions, to disembowel Sherry and redress her, all without getting a spot of blood anywhere on herself. As Victoria left, she put an envelope on the dresser. It was addressed to "Peter, Bob, and anyone else who pokes their nose into our family business."

Sherry's body was found the next day by housekeeping, and Bob and Peter were called to the scene. When the note to them was opened, the following words greeted them: "There was a lady from Portland whose love was sweet as strawberries, but she had to go to make it known that now I am here too! The Poet."

When Bob and Peter heard this their worst suspicions were confirmed. The serial killer from Austin, Texas, Newel's sister Victoria, was in Portland, and all hell was going to break loose if these two serial killers joined forces with their abilities.

* * * * *

Newel rested and felt his sister's mind trying to contact him. "Newel, is there anything you can tell me about Peter, the person you said uses electricity?" Victoria asked her brother.

Newel rolled his mind over like sorting through a card catalog at the library of facts about Peter, Bob, and the special squad and relayed the information to his sister.

"My, my, this is an interesting bit of information, Brother dear." Victoria smiled with an almost demonic evil that most people wouldn't have imagined possible from a well-to-do woman.

Newel was receiving and reading his sister's thoughts, and he started to smile the same type of smile.

"But, Sister, be careful. I have experienced what Peter is like when he loses control of his anger. He becomes violent and vengeful, releasing a dark side against those who cross him. I don't want you to be hurt again, or maybe worse!"

"Don't worry about me, Brother. I can take care of myself!" Victoria said, laughing.

* * * * *

Bob and Peter had checked in on both Miranda and Marsh and found that they were doing well but recovering slowly. Then a call came in from the lab. Max wanted to see them both right away.

"Peter, Bob, you look a bit frayed, guys," Max said, smiling.

"Max, you would too if you were dealing with a murderer who was not only attacking people in your city but also people who are close to you," Bob said with a bit of a growl.

"Max, do you have anything for us?" Peter asked.

"I think the lady from the hospital has struck again. I found a piece of candy in the stomach contents of the victim from the hotel, and it was laced with the same type of opiate that knocked out Miranda," Max told them.

"So, Bob, it's started. The attacks by these two super serial killers have begun, and it won't stop till they leave our city on their own or in a box," Peter said, gritting his teeth.

"Peter, I was wondering. Do you remember how Newel used the scar on Marsh's hand to keep us located?" Bob asked.

"Yes, I do. Why?" Peter asked.

"Well, couldn't you try using your abilities to block Newel's and his sister's ability to know when we were getting close to them or setting a trap for them?" Bob asked.

"Kind of like how I concentrated my mental powers to break the block that Newel's sister was putting up when I tried to contact Newel or when we found him in the alleyway," Peter said.

"That's right, Peter, but I think it would have to be like a bubble of your energy rather than a spike of your mental energy concentrated at one point. That way, it would occupy both Newel and his sister at the same time," Bob said.

Peter started reflecting on how he could use his Power in that way. He would have to figure this out, and they would have to try it at the firing range to see how successful he was before they confronted this pair of predators who had taken up residence in their city.

The day was a chilly fall morning with a light frost on the flowers in the flower boxes that Amy had started. Maybe the overcast would burn off and it would be sunny that afternoon, which was a common occurrence in Portland this time of year. As Amy cleaned the dishes in the sink, there was a knock at the front door.

When Amy answered the door, a well-dressed woman holding a clipboard of papers was standing there smiling. "Hello. Are you the lady of the house?" the woman asked.

Amy smiled at that, thinking how she would have to get used to being called that after she and Peter got married. "Yes, I am. Can I help you?" Amy asked.

"We are doing surveys to see how people feel about the proposed light rail extensions into this area. Would it be all right if I came in and asked you a few questions?"

Just then, the bell on the washing machine went off, signaling that the cycle was done. Amy excused herself, telling the woman she would be right back and shutting the door slowly. Amy felt that something was not right. The woman referred to the MAX line as the light rail, but all the locals called it the MAX line. Then after turning off the washing machine, Amy looked out the window at the flower box she had planted. All the flowers had withered and turned black. Then it occurred to her that

Peter's dad saw the same thing just before being attacked by Newel.

Amy felt her vest pocket, and the bulge was still there. She walked out, and suddenly, three knives shot past her face, almost impaling her. They buried themselves into the wall next to her. Amy heard the familiar voice of the woman at the door now inside her home.

"I came in to see if you were all right, miss. You were taking so long," the woman said.

"I'm fine, you murdering *bitch*!" Amy yelled.

"Such a mouth you have. Does Peter know how foul your mouth and thoughts are, Amy?" Victoria said.

"My Peter is going to see that you and your brother are sent straight to hell, express!" Amy said as she pulled a knife from the wall and threw it in Victoria's direction.

Victoria used her mind to divert the knife and laughed out loud. "You might as well come out. I know you don't have any special powers, Amy, and I'm here to do only one thing—to hurt you badly enough to get through to Peter to leave us alone," Victoria said.

Amy didn't move, but all of a sudden a force picked her up and threw her across the room, slamming her against the wall. Amy felt like a rag doll as she was repeatedly lifted and battered. Finally, she lay at Victoria's feet, bloody and semiconscious.

"I think I will pose you outside for your future husband to see and the public also," Victoria said as she lifted Amy by the arms and dragged her outside.

Victoria was right. Amy had no special powers, but what she did have was something that made Peter fall in love with her from the start, a fighting spirit to never give up. As Victoria posed Amy for Peter to find, Amy reached into the vest pocket that she had checked earlier and found what she wanted. She pulled from her vest pocket a stun gun that she had received from Peter's dad for protection. While Victoria was close to her, she jammed the stun gun hard to Victoria's right breast and pressed the trigger. Victoria screamed like a wounded banshee, and Amy could smell burning flesh.

Victoria dropped Amy on the front lawn. "Oh, you little bitch. You'll pay for that!"

Amy passed out, and when she came to, she saw Peter and the paramedics loading her into an ambulance.

"Excuse me, sir, we have to get this lady to the hospital for medical help quickly," the paramedic told Peter.

"Not without me you don't. I'm riding with her. She's my fiancée," Peter said.

Bob followed in the police car and looked ashen over the idea that Newel and his sister had struck their group so many times and so seriously. Peter held Amy's hand the whole way as the paramedics gave her pain medication. She even managed a small smile for Peter as encouragement. When the ambulance arrived at the hospital, they were met by a trauma team, and Amy was rushed into emergency. Bob took Peter to the waiting room forcibly, so the doctors could do their work without Peter getting in the way.

"Don't worry, Peter. The doctors got to Amy right away, just like with Miranda. She's in good hands. Just remember all the things you told me when I was worried sick about Miranda," Bob said as Peter's friend.

Bob watched as Peter turned toward him. His eyes were watery, very bloodshot, and narrowed down to slits, giving Peter the look of hell itself. The look of Peter even shocked Bob, sending a cold chill down his spine and making him believe that the persons he would least like to be right now were Newel and Victoria.

"I'm going to kill both those assholes or make sure that they no longer function as humans!" Peter said, growling in a whisper.

"Well, Peter, let's do this together and get the garbage out of Portland permanently," Bob said.

"First, Bob, I have to let those two know they that they messed around with the *wrong* people!" Peter said as he went into a vacant room and closed and locked the door.

Peter began concentrating. Using his mind and abilities to locate Newel's and Victoria's minds, he pushed hard, forcing an electrical charge at the two of them accompanied by three words: "I warned you!"

Suddenly, both Newel and Victoria were convulsing, their bodies contorted by the energy of Peter's warning and his anger. Unfortunately, both Newel and his sister were in their rooms when this occurred; otherwise, someone would have called for medical attention, and the special squad may have learned of their location. Afterward, when Peter came out, Bob was waiting for him. Bob got a glimpse of the interior of the room Peter had been in. The walls were scorched, but there was no smell of burning, and some cracks could be seen running up the walls.

"Peter, have you had any thoughts as to how you could prevent those two from catching on to the fact that we are coming for them or laying a trap for them?"

Peter looked at Bob as he spoke. "Bob, my mind has only been concerned with how Amy is. *Please!*" Peter said woefully.

After that, both men sat quietly for the next two hours as they waited for news from the doctors. Finally, the doctor came out and walked up to Peter. "Your fiancée is going to be fine, but she is going to need some time to mend. She has some broken bones and a concussion, but she will heal fine with rest," the doctor told Peter.

"Can I see her, Doctor?" Peter asked.

"I'm afraid not. She's in recovery and sleeping. She probably won't wake up till tomorrow morning."

"Bob, you should go ahead and go home. I'm going to be staying the night at least," Peter said, the tiredness and worry showing in his voice.

"To hell with that, Peter. You're my friend and my partner, and now three people we care about are in this hospital because of those sons of bitches. I'm going upstairs to see Miranda if she's awake, and I'll let her know about Amy in case she wants to visit," Bob said as he clapped Peter on the back as a sign of support.

As Bob left, Peter's guilt and worries came flooding in on him like a waterfall. If only he had never gotten Amy involved in this shit, she wouldn't be in a hospital right now. Peter sat looking out across the waiting room, which was right across from the gift shop. The clerk was in the gift shop and preparing for the next day's customers by inflating balloons and tying them to a rack. Suddenly, Peter took great interest in the clerk's technique. First, he would stretch out the balloon lengthwise and then use the helium from a tank to inflate the balloon, making it fat and round. Although any bystander would have thought that Peter had never seen balloons inflated before, this was not the case. Peter had the seed of an idea, and even though he still stared at the clerk in the gift shop, he no longer saw him because his mind was working on an inspired idea. His mental wheels were turning, and his mind was in full gear.

Peter borrowed a pen and made a few notes to himself as Bob came back from seeing Miranda.

"How is Miranda doing, Bob?" Peter asked.

"She is great, well enough to cover my face in kisses after I asked her to move in with me," Bob said, smiling broadly.

"That's great," Peter said. But Peter couldn't keep the regret out of his voice, and Bob picked up on it right away.

"What's wrong, Peter?" Bob asked, pointing out that Amy was going to be all right.

"Bob, that's not it. If it weren't for me, Amy wouldn't have been hurt," he said, confessing his worries.

"Now you listen to me, Peter. Stop feeling sorry for yourself and Amy! Amy has been aware of your abilities and your quirks since you were in grade school, and she has stuck by you the whole time, even when you decided to help the police. And with all that, she agreed to marry you and share your life no matter what. You need to get off your ass mentally, stop feeling sorry for the past, and concentrate on the future. When we get these two sickos put away, you and Amy can start your life as husband and wife," Bob said, getting right in Peter's face.

Peter listened to Bob and what he had said, and it got through to Peter like no other wake-up call had ever gotten through to him. Peter took a deep breath, stood up, and smiled at Bob.

"Thanks, Bob. That was the best get-back-in-the-game speech I have ever heard," Peter said, smiling at Bob.

"What do you say we go up and visit Marsh for a while?" Peter said.

"And before you ask, Peter, there are already police stationed outside Amy's room," Bob said, smiling.

"Thanks again, Bob," Peter said, looking a little less stressed.

As Bob and Peter entered Marsh's room, he was telling off a nurse for apparently waking him up to take his vital signs and to give him his medication, which included a sleeping pill.

"Marsh, I see you are well enough to tell off the nursing staff. I guess when you are well enough to tell off the doctors, you'll be ready to get out of this place," Peter said, smiling.

"You're damn right, Peter," Marsh said. "Hi, Bob. What are you two doing here this time of night?"

"Newel's sister, Victoria, paid a visit to Amy today and beat her very badly," Peter said.

"Is Amy all right, Peter?" Marsh asked, deeply concerned.

"The doctors say she will be fine. She suffered from a few broken bones and a concussion, but the reason she's still alive, I think, is because of the medical staff and the little gift my dad gave her to protect herself," Peter said, smiling.

"What do you mean, Peter?" Marsh said.

"When all this started with Newel and after Peter's dad was attacked, Peter's dad bought a police-issue stun gun from the department, which the public can't usually get their hands on. Peter's dad gave it to Amy so that if she were attacked, she could use it for protection," Bob said, smiling.

"We won't know exactly what happened until tomorrow, because Amy is under sedation and probably won't wake till tomorrow morning," Peter said.

Peter asked if he could stay in the room with Amy, which the nurse said was fine. Bob asked if he could stay with Miranda.

The nurse smiled. "These two ladies you mentioned must be very special to you."

Both Peter and Bob answered yes together, making the nurse laugh out loud.

"Men are so funny when they are in love," she said as she left, shaking her head and giggling to herself.

As Peter and Bob settled down in their rooms with the people they cared about, sleep came quickly, enveloping them like a dark, black cloud full of mystery.

* * * * *

In the center of Portland, Newel laid back to rest. The urge to kill more wanton women, prostitutes, or slutty-looking women didn't matter. It was like an itch inside his body that he could not reach but needed to scratch. Just as Newel was about to fall asleep, he heard a scream of intense pain followed by cursing and hard sobbing. At first, he thought it was coming from an adjacent room, but then he realized it was inside his head.

"Victoria, what's wrong?" He called out mentally.

"Oh, Newel, that bitch Amy has disfigured me!" Victoria sobbed to her brother mentally.

"How do you mean, Victoria? How have you been disfigured?" Newel said urgently to Victoria's mind.

Victoria looked down at her injured right breast and relayed the image to Newel's mind. Newel's mouth opened in shock at the image he saw. His sister's once-beautiful breast was burned across the nipple, and on either side of the burn, two dime-sized red, angry chunks of flesh had been opened and were weeping where the electrodes had made contact with her breast. It was hard for Newel to see this image and at the same time hear his sister's painful crying.

"That looks like the same type of injury that I had when I confronted Peter's father on the way home. It's called a stun gun, and it imparts an electrical charge when it contacts a person," Newel told his sister. "Victoria, call the front desk and ask if they have a first-aid kit for electrical burns. If they do, follow the directions for treating and bandaging the wound, but I warn you, Sister, you will be very tender for several days, maybe a week."

"Thank you, but the only thing I want right now is to have that bitch dead!" Victoria screamed in Newel's head.

"How did she surprise you like that, Sister?" Newel asked.

"I really don't know, Brother. At first, everything was going well, and then a washing machine bell went off, and she excused herself for a moment. When she came back, she was fully alerted to who I was and what I was going to do to her. When I was posing her outside for her precious Peter to find, I leaned over her, and that was when she shocked me with the stun gun. And as badly as she was hurt, she didn't just touch me with it. She jammed it hard to my flesh and held it there with the trigger depressed until I passed out. It's very lucky I came to before people came around. That's the only reason I got away."

Newel's anger at this new development made him feel hot with anger, and beads of perspiration appeared on his brow. It outraged him, and he went down to the park in front of his hotel and unleashed his anger on the public. Suddenly, cars were driving into one another and into buildings, and many people were hurt, but Newel didn't care. If anyone were to blame for this chaos, it was the people on the special squad and their family members who had injured his sister and him.

Police headquarters was in a pandemonium with dozens of calls coming into the station and 911 for police and medical help down at the waterfront. By the time morning rolled around, the final cleanup was complete, and the police presence in the area of the waterfront had been cleared so that a seminormal day could resume.

Bob brought Miranda down to Amy's room in a wheelchair after she got over the shock of Bob telling her about Amy's encounter with Victoria. As Amy opened her eyes, she felt sore and groggy and lucky to be alive.

"Hi, beautiful. Good morning," Peter said, smiling as he kissed her softly.

Amy tried to move but found she was restricted by two casts, one on her leg and one on her arm, and her head pounded and ached terribly. "Peter, how bad am I hurt?" Amy asked.

"Amy, you have a few broken bones and a concussion. It's going to take some time for you to heal properly," Peter said. "Do you remember what happened to you?"

"Yes, I remember every detail of that nightmare!" Amy said, gritting her teeth.

"Do you feel like some company, Amy?" Peter asked.

"Yes, for a short visit," Amy said.

Peter brought Bob and Miranda in to visit. Both of them got tears in their eyes when they saw how beaten and battered Amy was, but she managed a smile, using her fighting spirit to put on a brave face. As Miranda visited with Amy, Peter talked with Bob.

"Peter, does she remember anything?" Bob asked.

"She remembers everything, and if we get a sketch artist down here, we will know what Newel's sister looks like," Peter said.

Bob called police headquarters right away, and as he requested the sketch artist, he told the chief of detectives what had happened to Amy. When he was done, Bob found out about the chaos on the waterfront. Bob's face drained of all its color.

"Bob, what's wrong?" Peter asked Bob quickly.

"Peter, after Victoria's encounter with Amy, Newel flew off the handle and created mass chaos on the waterfront. A dozen people were injured, and there's property damage," Bob said quietly to everyone.

"Why the *hell* would that monster do that?" Peter exclaimed.

"I think Amy must have hurt Victoria *very* badly and she relayed her pain to Newel mentally, maybe even showed Newel how bad her wounds were. After all, what makes a brother madder than someone who hurts his sister?" Miranda said.

"Amy, do you remember where you connected with the stun gun when you shocked Victoria?" Peter asked.

Amy got a big smile on her face. "Damn right I do. She was leaning over me and dragging me outside when I grabbed the stun gun and shoved it hard into her breast. I held the trigger down hard and pinned the gun to her flesh," Amy said proudly.

All the people in Amy's room looked at one another, and then Miranda gave Amy a high five. Bob and Peter both laughed a bit.

"That should teach that bitch who not to mess with; my lady can be tough as can be!" Peter said. "Amy, I'm proud of you, but what tipped you off that the woman was Newel's sister?"

"When I went back to shut off the washing machine buzzer, I noticed the flower box I had just planted the day before out one of the windows. All the flowers had withered and turned black, just like when Newel attacked your dad. Otherwise, I would have walked into three knives that bitch had waiting for me," Amy said.

"Bob, I may have an idea on how to block Newel and his sister from detecting us as we set a trap for them, but we need to get some supplies to try it out," Peter said.

As Peter and Bob left, they passed the sketch artist, whom they both knew, and headed back to the police station. When Peter and Bob got back to the station, Peter put together an unusual shopping list that was made from Peter's and Bob's experiences in this case so far, their knowledge of electricity, and their own special abilities. After that, they headed out to the deserted firing range and began to set up a unique test. If successful, it could give them an edge over Newel and Victoria. Once out at the range, Peter and Bob started setting things up and putting rebar into the ground a foot deep. Then they hooked a car battery to wires and to the rebar.

"Peter, can you pick up the electrical charge from the two pieces of rebar with your mind?" Bob asked.

Peter concentrated like when he tried to communicate with Newel. His hair stood up off the back of his head like he was standing in a windstorm. "Yes, Bob, I can definitely pick out two energy sources!" Peter exclaimed.

"What now?" Bob asked.

"Bob, what I want you to do is use your ability to control water, and when I say so, throw a stream of water over the rebar connected to the battery."

"But, Peter, what will that prove?" Bob asked.

"If I can isolate the two pieces of rebar from the stream of water by using my mind, then I should be able to isolate Newel and his sister from detecting our efforts to find them and trap them," Peter said.

"And if this doesn't work?" Bob asked with concern.

"Well, the first thing that will happen is that the fully charged car battery is going to explode violently, which is why we need to be a safe distance away. Second, we will have no edge the next time we confront these two killers," Peter said guardedly.

As Peter and Bob moved back to a safe distance, both men were thinking the same thing.

"Bob, I really hope this works for all our sakes," Peter said.

"Me too, Peter. It would sure help all of us involved directly in the case," Bob noted.

All of a sudden, both Bob and Peter stopped dead in their tracks. They looked at each other and realized they had communicated without talking. For a moment, they were in shock and just stared at each other, and then a smile broke on both their faces.

"Have you ever done that before, Bob?" Peter asked out loud.

"Never. I was just relaxing, getting ready for the test, and not thinking about anything, and I felt your thoughts," Bob said.

"Well, maybe you can do more with your mind than you think, more than just control water and bend metal."

As Peter and Bob were at the firing range, Victoria was nursing her wounds, which she was able to do with the help of the front desk first-aid kit. Her brother was right. She was sensitive around the burn, but it felt a little better after applying first aid. She had to be very careful not to bump her breast or right side. She found this out the hard way when she accidently bumped gently into the edge of a door, and it sent waves of hot pain through her body.

Peter and Bob were still at the firing range and about to test their idea.

"Bob, when I tell you to go ahead and try, let the water start falling as much as you can, and don't stop till I tell you," Peter said.

"Okay, Peter, let's give it a try," Bob said.

Bob watched as the hair stood up from the back of Peter's head like before, and his eyes narrowed with intensity.

"Okay, Bob, bring the water!" Peter yelled.

From the small creek, water flew through the air above the electrically charged pieces of rebar and suddenly stopped flowing over and around the rebar without touching it or the battery. It formed a big, glistening, wet bubble. As Bob watched, the bubble seemed to increase in size, the wet sides shining in the sun. All at once, the bubble collapsed, allowing a sheet of water to make contact with the rebar and the battery, which exploded.

Bob ran to Peter. "Are you all right?" he asked.

"Yeah, Bob, just not used to that kind of power surge coming back at me," Peter said, smiling. "So how long did I have the rebar protected?"

"About twenty to thirty minutes, not bad for a first try," Bob commented.

* * * * *

Victoria had recovered from Peter's warning jolt and had been resting when the front desk at her hotel called her room.

"Excuse me, miss, but you have a telegram from Dover, England," the desk clerk said.

"I'm not feeling very well. Could you please deliver it to my room as quickly as possible?" Victoria said.

Within five minutes, the telegram was delivered, and Victoria was reading it. It was from their mother in Dover, and she was concerned about the both of them.

> Victoria, I hope you are making our family proud as you both see to our family's mission. But I am concerned about your brother; sometimes he can get single-minded when he has a goal in mind, and combined with his anger, it might endanger his life with the authorities. Victoria, I have one request of you; if the worst happens and Newel dies or is severely injured, please bring him back to our family in Dover.

As Victoria read this, she was tearful but sent an immediate telegram to their mother, saying she would do as she wished. Victoria made a promise to herself that no matter what happened, she would make sure that she and her brother returned back to England together.

As Peter and Bob rode back from the firing range, they were both quiet, lost deep in thought.

"Peter, have you given any thought as to how we might trap Newel and his sister once we've located them?" Bob asked.

"No, but I am sure of one thing. If we are to defeat these two, it will take both of us with all our abilities and smarts to make it work," Peter said.

"Peter, what do you say we stop by the hospital and let our friends know how things went at the range and maybe pick everybody's brain as to how to trap these two killers?" Bob suggested.

"That's a good idea, and besides, I want to visit Amy and see how she is doing," Peter said.

As they entered the hospital, they saw the sketch artist was still there and just coming out of Amy's room.

"You're still here, Jim?" Bob said.

"Yes, the lady inside was going in and out with the pain meds they are giving her, so I just took it slow and concentrated on one aspect of the suspect's face each time she was awake. Peter, it is amazing the details Amy recalls from her encounter with Victoria. It allowed me to make a good enough sketch for an all-points bulletin, which I already sent by fax," the sketch artist said to Bob and Peter.

"Jim, can we get a copy of that sketch you made?" Bob asked.

"I had a feeling the two of you would want to see it. Here you go." Jim handed a copy of the sketch to both Peter and to Bob.

Looking back at them was the first glimpse of Newel's sister Victoria. She was beautiful, with long hair and a devilish gleam in her eyes. It was uncanny how the sketch transformed the face of this lady who in any other situation would have been asked by any man for a date, but who was in actuality a deadly murderer like her brother.

As Peter and Bob went into Amy's room, Miranda was sitting with her and holding her hand. Amy was awake, and Peter sat by her side.

"Amy, I need to ask you a question. Is this sketch that the police artist made an accurate picture of Victoria?" Peter asked gently.

Amy looked long at the sketch and smiled. "Peter, that's the bitch who beat the hell out of me. I remembered which side I jammed the stun gun into; it's her right breast, so she's going to be very sensitive on her right side for some time."

"Thanks. That could help when we confront these two killers, a definite weak spot for Victoria," Bob said.

"When you two find her, would you do me a favor?" Amy asked.

"Sure, anything, Amy. What is it?" Peter said.

"Give that bitch a good hard jolt to her right side and let her know it's from me for all the pain she put me through," Amy said, gritting her teeth.

"We will both make sure. Plus, Peter and I have a surprise or two up our sleeves," Bob said, smiling.

"What are you talking about? You two come on and give. Tell us what happened at the range," Miranda said.

So Peter and Bob described the experiment and what had happened with their efforts for isolating Newel and his sister.

"All we have to do now is come up with a plan to entrap Newel and his sister in one location to spring the trap," Peter said.

Amy was intently listening to the group, and slowly she spoke up. "Peter, do you think you can extend the length of time that you can block Newel and his sister to give you and Bob more time to carry out your plan?"

"Maybe in a large area, if I pushed harder making the electronic field bellow out, I could get Bob and I more time," Peter said.

"Well, all this worries me, and enough people have been hurt already by these two people," Amy said.

"Bob, we need to get a copy of that sketch to the Austin Police Department to see if they can clear up a few more of their murders," Peter said.

"Did anything else important happen while you two were out at the range that we should know about?" Miranda asked sarcastically.

Bob smiled and took Miranda's hand, and she got the funniest look on her face.

"Miranda, I know what you're thinking right now," Bob said with a smile.

"Yeah, sure you do, Bob," Miranda said disbelievingly.

Then Bob leaned down to Miranda's ear and whispered for a long time. Suddenly, Miranda's face went beet red.

"How did you know that?" Miranda asked, smiling and a bit surprised.

"We found out by accident that I can read minds to some degree," he answered.

"What were you thinking, Miranda?" Amy asked.

"Just a passionate, warm thought about Bob and I, which, if he's good to me, he will enjoy once I'm well," Miranda said.

All at once, everyone in the room burst out laughing at the implied thought.

* * * * *

Newel was so enraged by how badly his sister had been hurt by Amy that his rage was fueling him on still, even after creating the chaos on the waterfront. Newel still had that itch that needed scratching to kill prostitutes in large numbers, or anyone he thought looked like a prostitute, for that matter. Newel went outside and walked until he happened upon several hookers at a corner.

"Hey, tall, dark, and mysterious, do you need some company?" one woman named Ally questioned.

Newel smirked. "Do you think you have what I need, miss?"

"Oh, sweetheart, call me Ally, and as for what you need, I have it all for the right price." She laughed, quietly showing lots of thigh and cleavage.

Newel took the opportunity to grab Ally in a close, entirely sexual embrace in front of her friends as he let his hands slip under her skirt and probe wherever he wanted. Ally sighed her approval, encouraging Newel's attention.

"Hon, did you want to do this right here or go back to your room?" Ally asked, breathing heavily.

"I don't think I could wait that long to get back to my room. As a matter of fact, I want all three of you at once. We can go to the back of this alley," Newel said lecherously.

"Hey, if you want us all, you are going to have to show us the money before we party," one of Ally's friends said.

Newel smiled, fished a thick wallet from his pocket, and opened it. It was full of one hundred-dollar bills, which caused the women's eyes to glisten with greed.

"Well, Ally, let's take your friend way back here, and we can have some major fun," the women commented.

As all of them walked into the alleyway, the women started taking their clothes off and flirting with Newel. Little did they realize that this was antagonizing Newel more than it was arousing him. When they looked into Newel's eyes, they saw the evil and the anger that was dwelling there. It was like a caldron on a hot fire, boiling and about to overflow right in front of them.

Suddenly, Newel brought his arms in front of him in a hard pushing motion, causing all the women to be thrown off their feet into a brick wall at the back of the alley. The women were not only shocked as to what had happened but dazed from the collision with the brick wall.

As Ally stood, she turned to Newel. "Hey, you asshole, what's going on? I think for this kind of treatment we should relieve you of all your cash and spank your ass for mistreating ladies like this!"

"Oh, Ally, I already know how to treat skanky whores like the three of you!" Newel growled as he grinned.

Ally started to say something but was interrupted by four daggers, which Newel had thrown with his mind. They hit her in the chest, mouth, and abdomen. The shock that went through the other ladies was paralyzing.

Newel proceeded to cause one of the women to run into a brick wall so many times and with such force she was dead before she fell to the ground. The final victim was in so much shock that she couldn't move, so Newel gave this lady his personal touch as he dissected her while she was still alive.

Newel felt fully vindicated, and that irritating itch he had was now satisfied for a while. Newel took a roundabout way back to his hotel, getting rid of his blood-stained clothes in obscure locations.

The bodies of the women in the alley were found the next evening by a homeless man who was searching for odds and ends he might be able to use. When the murders were reported, Bob was notified right away with all the specifics.

"Peter, there has been another murder. Three hookers were brutally murdered last night, and it was very Jack the Ripperish, according to the report I got," Bob said quietly.

"Bob, we may have to face a grim fact, that Newel has gone completely insane with this so-called family mission of his," Peter said.

"That's a scary idea, Peter, because that means that between Newel and Victoria, Victoria is the sane one," Bob said.

"Can Marsh travel by wheelchair, Bob, or is he bedbound still?" Peter asked.

Bob smirked. "I don't think the doctors or anyone else could keep him away for any reason. He would want to be part of this planning session."

Bob went to go and retrieve Marsh from his room so that the whole special squad could be in on the planning of the trap for Newel and his sister, not only to pick all their brains but to give them all closure since this hell-bound case began. As Marsh was wheeled into the room, everyone called out to him and asked how he was. Bob and Peter brought Marsh up to speed.

"I can't believe all this you're telling me—advanced special abilities, and Peter having come up with a way to shield Newel and his sister from being aware of an impending trap," Marsh exclaimed. "What the hell do you need me here for?"

"Marsh, you are every bit a part of this team, and you do have a special ability," Peter said.

"And what would that special ability be?" Marsh said.

"You know everything about Jack the Ripper, who is supposed to be the relative of Newel. You are our navigator through Newel's and Victoria's behavior as the Ripper's descendants, and with that knowledge, you may be able to tell us how these two will react in a given situation," Peter said.

"All right, let's see what we can cook up for these two," Marsh said.

After a few hours, they were all very worn out from coming up with ideas and then tossing them out for one reason or another.

Finally, Marsh asked the million-dollar question. "Holy crap! I can't believe I didn't approach the problem like this sooner, must be the pain meds that are effecting me," Marsh exclaimed.

"What is it, Marsh?" Bob asked.

"The first thing any good profiler does when he is looking at someone new is ask himself, what does the subject want?" Marsh said to the group.

The room was silent for a few minutes as they pondered Marsh's question. Then Miranda smiled.

"Newel and Victoria want the same thing—to kill prostitutes. Or, in Newel's case, anyone who looks like a prostitute."

"That's right, Miranda, so if we create a situation that will be unavoidable for Newel and his sister not to attend, we could localize them, and Peter and Bob could put their plan into action to nail these two," Marsh said with a smile. "Bob, how is your relationship with the chief of police these days?"

Suddenly, Marsh started outlining a possible plan, and as the room full of people heard the idea, they started nodding their heads and pointing out contingencies they needed to be prepared for.

"Peter, have you had any time to practice with your shielding ability to better protect you and Bob?" Marsh asked.

"No, I haven't. We just worked the possibility out this morning at the firing range," Peter said.

"Peter, I was just reading an article as I was in my hospital bed that may help. It was about something called astral projection. Have you heard of it?" Marsh asked.

"Yes, I have, but I don't see how that will help us," Peter said.

"Peter, think about the balloons you watched being inflated, first being stretched out and then expanded to the size you wish.

What if you didn't think of the balloon as being inflated but as being projected in a three-dimensional plane," Marsh proposed.

All at once, Peter's face lit up, and they could not only see the wheels turning in his head but a big grin creasing his face. "That might make it possible for me to cover a huge area just by projecting the will of my mind over Newel and his sister's approximate location."

"But we don't know their location yet," Bob said.

"Maybe we can get an idea of where they are from where they last struck and then lure them in to a planned trap in that area," Marsh said.

"Bob, we need the list of hotels that had the special first-aid kits for electrical burns, the location of the stores that sell them, and the location of the last murders as quickly as possible," Marsh said.

Bob had to return to the police headquarters to catch up on paperwork for this case, and Peter went along to help. They both promised to return as soon as possible. Peter helped out as much as he could, but sleep took over, and he crashed in the police lounge. Bob was used to going long hours without sleep and had just finished all the paperwork, so he decided to try out his new abilities to see just what he might be able to do.

All of a sudden, Bob's face went into shock, and then he was smiling broadly and jumping at his desk. Bob had just made a discovery that could prove very helpful to the special squad and catching Newel and his sister if given the chance to use it. It was then that Bob remembered Amy's request to Peter and Bob about giving Victoria a hard jolt to her right side, and he turned his head hard and pushed. There was a crash, and Bob sat down as Peter came running in. He, along with the rest of the station, had heard the crash. As Peter entered, he looked at Bob who was looking very guilty. Then he spotted the hole in the wall of Bob's office.

"Bob, are you all right?" Peter asked with concern.

Others came running, but Peter relayed that everything was fine. Peter closed the door. "Bob, what the hell happened?" Peter said.

"Peter, see the hole in the wall? Why don't you reach in to it and pull out what's inside," Bob said.

Peter did as Bob asked and pulled out one of the pieces of rebar that they had used in the experiment that morning, except now it was twisted into the shape of a pretzel.

"Bob, did you do this?"

Bob's face broke into a big smile as he nodded yes.

"But how? Show me," Peter said, smiling.

Peter pulled the blinds on Bob's office, and then Bob took the bent rebar. As he held it, he concentrated. The rebar acted as if it had a mind of its own, unbending to an almost straight piece of iron again.

"All right, Bob, you've been playing to see just what you could do, but what was the explosive impact the station heard?" Peter asked.

"Well, you remember when Amy asked us to give Victoria a good, hard jolt just for her?" Bob asked.

"Yes, I do," Peter said.

"Well, just as I bent the rebar, I thought of what Amy said, and it made me angry. I turned my head, concentrating on a spot on the wall, and pushed with my anger," Bob said.

"The next thing I knew, there was a hole in my wall where I was concentrating on, and the rebar was buried in the wall," Bob said.

"Bob, I think between your abilities, my abilities, and the brainpower of the rest of the squad, we just might have a chance of pulling this off," Peter said.

"Peter, have you tried to locate Newel and his sister's minds like you located the electrically charged rebar this morning?" Bob asked.

"Why, Bob?" Peter said.

"Well, wouldn't it drive Newel a bit crazy if he couldn't find your mind emanations since you two have been in such close mental contact that at any instant you could communicate with each other?" Bob said with a smirk.

Peter smiled broadly. "I think you're right, Bob. It might just drive Newel batshit trying to figure out what was going on," Peter said.

"Do you want me to leave so you can concentrate?" Bob asked.

"No, I want you here to tell me what happens when I do this, and in case there's an emergency," Peter said.

As Peter searched using his mind, first projecting his energies outward until he felt Newel's and Victoria's minds, Peter said one phrase mentally. "We are coming for you!"

Then Peter expanded his mental energies, which cloaked Newel's and Victoria's thought process from contacting them.

Newel and his sister shot thoughts back and forth between each other rapidly.

"Newel, can you still feel Peter's mind and connect with it?" Victoria asked her brother.

Newel didn't answer his sister right away.

"Newel!" Victoria shouted at her brother mentally.

"No! I can't find his mind, Sister, and I don't know why. I have the superior mind between Peter and myself. *Why is this happening?*" Newel shouted mentally.

As Newel shouted to his sister, Victoria heard something in his voice as he communicated with her that worried her. It was the sound of a trapped animal that would do anything to escape the danger that was coming.

Secretly, Victoria was glad that her mother had sent her the telegram asking that Victoria bring Newel home no matter what happened. At that thought, a tear ran down Victoria's cheek, slowly betraying what she thought was going to happen to herself and her brother.

As Bob and Peter went to talk to the chief of police, they passed a television that had several officers gathered around. It was a breaking story about the three murdered prostitutes who had been found a day ago and whose bodies were lying in the morgue downstairs at that very moment. The news was saying that sources close to police had indicated they were looking for a serial killer in connection with several other murders of prostitutes.

"How the hell did that information get out? The chief gave a direct order that all this information was to be kept quiet until a handle could be gotten on it," Bob said.

"You don't think Max would have leaked the information, do you, Bob?" Peter asked.

"No, but there is someone I'm familiar with who would sell shit to his relatives if he thought he could get away with it," Bob said as they both headed down to the morgue. As they arrived at the morgue, they noticed the summer intern who worked with Max sitting at his desk, a brand-new leather jacket hanging on the back of his chair.

"Carl, how much did you get for leaking that information about the three hookers who were brought in last night?" Bob asked.

"What the hell do you care, you asshole? You make more than I do. I'm a struggling student!" Carl said with a smirk on his face and arrogance in his voice.

Bob grabbed Carl by the lapels and lifted him right out of his chair, pinning him against the wall. "Do you realize that you could have compromised our investigation for the little piece of change you collected? And delayed us catching these killers? If any more people die because of this stunt you pulled, it's on your fucking head!"

Bob then informed Max what his intern had done, which, needless to say, cost Carl his job right then and there.

Peter had not seen Bob that mad in a while, and he was sure that he had gotten through to the intern. As Bob and Peter walked into the chief of police's office, he looked like a man with not enough hands and arms as he tried to answer several phone lines, watch the news broadcast, and check his e-mails. It was all about the serial killer in Portland, which the whole city was learning about.

"Bob, what the hell happened? I wanted this information restricted until we got a handle on it so as to not cause panic," the chief said.

"You can blame the greedy little intern down in the morgue for leaking the information to make a few bucks, sir," Bob said.

"I hope you and your special squad have a plan in mind to capture this killer, Bob," the chief said.

"Well, first off, sir, we do. Second, it's two serial killers who are in Portland. They're brother and sister and have been trained by their family since they were kids on their heritage and best methods to kill," Bob said.

"What do you mean their heritage?" the chief asked.

"They believe they are descendants of Jack the Ripper and are on a family mission to rid the earth of all prostitutes," Bob explained.

The chief's mouth hung open in disbelief for a few seconds as he tried to absorb what he was hearing.

"And the children in this family, once trained, go out into the world to carry out their mission of killing," Bob said.

"Do you have any idea how big their family is?" the chief asked as sweat glistened on his brow.

"Well, in Newel's family, counting his sister and himself, there are seven kids who, when they reach the age of twenty-one, will go on their missions out into the world," Peter pointed out.

"And you say you have a plan to take these two killers out of commission?" the chief asked.

"Yes, sir, we believe we do. Using all the assets of the special squad, we have put together a plan that will require some cooperation from the media, the mayor, and you, Chief," Bob said with conviction.

The chief looked skeptical and wary at the same time, because he didn't plan on being the chief of police forever. His ambitions were aimed higher, at a political office in the future. So Bob and Peter started to outline their plan to capture, kill, or incapacitate this savage pair of killers.

* * * * *

In his hotel room, Newel was like an impending storm developing to its full fury the longer it sat and churned. Things kept flying through Newel's room, thrown by his mind in frustration and shattering against a wall every so often. Victoria sensed Newel's turmoil and said she would come over to comfort him. Newel relented. Victoria found her brother easy enough just by tuning in to his mental signals, but when she knocked on his door, she had to wait a very long time before her brother opened the door.

Newel's eyes were dark and sunken sockets of evil intent, which shocked Victoria and also aroused her sexually. She entered Newel's room and hugged her brother, stroking his back lightly.

"Don't worry, Newel. We will end up surviving the special squad no matter what they try to do to us," Victoria whispered in his ear.

For an instant, Newel felt something he didn't expect as he held his twin sister, a purely sexual arousal for her. As they held each other, their minds connected, imagining a lustful sexual encounter. Before they both knew it, an hour had gone by, and they had been locked in a physical and mental embrace that left them both surprised and relaxed.

"Sister, I have never expected that of you. I hope you aren't ashamed of me," Newel said apologetically.

"Not at all, Newel. I was enjoying those feelings about you as much as you were about me, and besides, it got our minds off our worries for a little bit and allowed us to relax so we can be better prepared for whatever the special squad throws at us," Victoria said with an evil grin.

* * * * *

The chief of police listened to Bob and Peter, and he was intrigued. "Do you really think that plan will work, you two?" the chief asked.

"Yes, and we can have everything arranged by day after tomorrow," Bob said.

"Good. I'm leaving a bit early to meet a friend. You go and put your plan into action," the chief said as he left.

By the time the chief arrived at his friend's hotel, he was relaxed and ready to meet a unique lady. They had met previously in the lounge, and he had been attracted by her long hair and beautiful face. As they talked, she seemed to know a lot about him. Although they had just met, she suggested they get a room so they could be alone. They arranged to meet the next day.

The chief went straight to the room they had agreed to meet in. He found her waiting for him, nude and ready to please. She stripped the chief, and as he sat, she smiled.

"Let me serve you." She knelt between his legs and put her head into his lap. The chief gasped with excitement as the woman looked up and smiled into his eyes as she pleasured him. What she did for him was amazing, not just physically but mentally, like she was actually in his head. As the chief looked in her eyes, he saw something he hadn't noticed before. Her eyes not only gleamed, but he saw what he could only explain as a slight glint of evil behind those eyes. Where had he seen that look before? Almost as the thought went through the chief's mind, it was replaced by a more seductive thought.

"You will do what I need done when I need it, and you will be rewarded with pleasure."

At that point, the chief passed out, a grin on his face.

The woman got up and looked at the satisfied man and smiled as she thought, *It's always good to be prepared!*

* * * * *

With the police chief's go-ahead, Bob and Peter proceeded to contact the mayor and the media about a news conference that was going to be given at six o'clock in the evening the next day. It would concern the serial killing of local prostitutes, related murders, and what was being done about it to bring the public up to speed. Bob and Peter had decided to put the news conference in the central area that encompassed where the last murders occurred, the hotel where they had encountered Newel in the alley, and the store that sold the specialized first-aid kits for electrical burns. The special squad had noticed a small three-city block area down near the waterfront that seemed centrally located within the specifications they had outlined.

When the media got wind of the conference, it plastered it all over the television as Peter and Bob hoped they would. They wanted to be sure Newel and Victoria would see it. Unknown to the special squad, Newel and his sister received the news at the same time, and they both smiled sadistically.

"If the chief is going to be there, then the special squad will be present, at least those who are still uninjured," Newel said.

"That would give us a perfect chance to teach the so-called special squad a lesson for messing with us, and maybe a bit of revenge," Victoria said to Newel. They both laughed out loud.

Peter and Bob assembled on the steps where the conference was to be held. When they talked to the chief, he looked calm, but as they shook hands, both Bob and Peter noticed his palms were wet with nervous sweat. But Peter picked up on something else as he shook the chief's hand. He saw Victoria's face in the chief's mind, as if it were waiting for something to happen. Peter was usually able to figure these impressions out but not this one; it was too abstract.

"Bob, when I shook the chief's hand, I got the strangest impression of Victoria's face in his head," Peter said.

"Could it be from looking at the artist's sketch?" Bob asked.

"I don't think so. It was just sort of present, like a post-hypnotic suggestion might be to a hypnotized person," Peter said.

Bob looked very suspicious. "We should watch our chief and be prepared for anything when this goes down, Peter," he suggested.

As the chief made his speech and took questions from the media and concerned public, Peter and Bob slowly slipped off the stage and moved out of public view. Peter started looking for Newel's and his sister's minds and was surprised to find them within a few blocks of the conference.

"Bob, they're close. Get ready," Peter said.

Peter suddenly started to project his mind and expand it like he had practiced, and it was working. As the news conference ended, Bob was looking for any sign of the pair when he noticed a couple just standing on the nearest corner to the news conference area. They seemed confused, and then the woman turned, and Bob saw her face. It was Victoria, and that had to be Newel with her. Peter picked up on Bob's thoughts, looked up, and pushed Bob out of the way as a dagger buried itself into the wall behind them.

That pissed Bob off, and Peter heard his thoughts. "Not this time, you bitch." And with that, he pushed the first piece of metal on the ground with that angry thought. It was a heavy nut and bolt that had fallen from a construction truck. *This is for Amy!* Bob thought. His face was feverish and intense, his muscles and nerves jumping.

Although the item wasn't big, the force—aided by Bob's anger—made it strike a blow that knocked Victoria off her feet as it struck her just below her right breast. She screamed out loud for her brother. Newel turned toward Bob and saw his sister writhing in pain on the ground.

He was going to unleash his full fury when Peter dropped the mind shield, and Newel felt Peter's mind invading his. Before Newel could do anything to Bob, Peter slammed Newel into the corner of Portland's Justice Center, thinking that was kind of fitting. Newel staggered and faced Peter, their minds locked in a mutual struggle to destroy the other's mind. It was a mental stalemate of sorts, except for the slow trickle of blood from Peter's nose and from Newel's tear ducts.

Suddenly, from out of nowhere, a giant water spout appeared and engulfed Newel, distracting him enough to break his concentration. Bob had his veins popping out on his forehead as he worked to control the tower of water he had borrowed from the Willamette River.

"I can't hold this much longer. Can you take him, Peter?" Bob yelled.

"Collapse the water column over by the base of the bridge!" Peter yelled back.

As the water column collapsed, Newel got up halfway, and Peter pushed his mind to deliver an electric bolt to the wet pavement where Newel was standing. The effect was instant as Newel jumped up, yelled, and cursed Bob and Peter to hell until he passed out. Peter and Bob were catching their breath when they looked around for Victoria. Peter checked with his mind and found nothing.

"It looks like she slithered off, Bob," Peter said breathlessly.

"Fuck!" Bob exclaimed.

"Hey, at least we have this bastard, Bob. But we need to make sure he stays here until we can transport him for medical and holding," Peter said.

"I think I can help with that, Peter. Can you pin Newel to the bridge for a moment?" Bob asked with a smile.

"Sure," Peter said.

Then Bob, using his newfound ability to bend metal, wrapped Newel in one of the steel bridge beams to keep him secure. After the police came to take reports and the ambulance arrived, both Peter and Bob rode in the ambulance with Newel, who was breathing but not a whole lot more. Peter and Bob waited until the doctors came out and let them know what kind of condition Newel was in.

"Gentlemen, the person you call Newel is in serious condition. We have treated his burns, but there is a serious problem still," the doctor said.

"What's the problem, Doc? When can we question him?" Bob asked.

"Maybe never, Detective. He is in a coma," the doctor announced.

Peter and Bob looked at each other, not believing what they had been told. They had hoped to find out the last name of Newel's family to track the other killers.

"Bob, I have an idea on how we still might use Newel, even if he is in a coma," Peter said. "Doctor, can I see Newel for a few minutes?"

"As long as you don't disturb him, a few minutes won't hurt," the doctor said, looking skeptical.

"Bob, come with me. Bring a notepad and write down everything I say."

The two men went into the room, and it was shocking to see this serial killer subdued in this fashion, hooked to machines and comatose. Peter went over to Newel and took hold of his arm. As he did, he noticed a tattoo on Newel's forearm that was very unusual. His hand over the tattoo, Peter tried to contact Newel's mind.

"Hello, Newel. That is an interesting tattoo on your arm," Peter said.

"Fuck you and your special squad!" Newel screamed at Peter.

"I think all of us in the special squad should get a tattoo like this to celebrate capturing you, Newel," Peter said, trying to provoke a response.

"You can't, because only members of my family can wear the sign of the jackal!" Newel shouted mentally. Newel then became very quiet. He realized that in his state of emotional rage and his massive sense of pride for his family, he had revealed a fact that could identify his family members. He may have just revealed them all to the authorities.

Peter then pushed with his mind, concentrating on the image of the tattoo. He started seeing first names, which he said out loud for Bob to write down. When no more names came to

Peter, he smiled at Newel. "Thank you, Newel. You have been very, very helpful. Now we can look for your other relatives."

Newel started to have a seizure as a reaction to what Peter said, and the doctor was called to medicate him.

"Peter, how did you get the idea to try communicating with Newel that way?" Bob asked.

"People in comas can often react to voices and other things around them, so I thought if I could reach his mind, we might have a chance," Peter said

Peter told Bob about the tattoo and how it related to Newel's family. As they left to return to the police station, they passed the two police officers posted outside Newel's room. Later that evening, a well-dressed man approached Newel's room and spoke to the officers outside. They seemed to snap to as they saw who it was. After a short discussion, they left their post.

When all was clear, a woman with long hair came with a wheelchair and entered the room. She was walking favoring her right side. Soon, she left with Newel in the wheelchair, and as the police officers returned to their post, the well-dressed man left. As he passed the nurse's station, the light glinted off the well-dressed man's face. It was the chief of police. As Victoria put her brother into the van, she got in and smiled toward the hospital and located the chief's mind.

"Here is the pleasure I promised you." She then pushed hard with her mind, and the chief's heart collapsed flat in his chest, causing him to fall a few feet from the nurse's station.

One Month Later

The police were devastated by the chief's involvement in Newel's escape and his untimely death. Peter and Bob figured out why Victoria's face was in the chief's mind. It was for control as a backup plan. But it wasn't the right time to think about that.

Peter and Amy were getting married. After the ceremony, as they looked over the gifts from well-wishers, Amy noticed one that had no name, just a card. She handed it to Peter, and he saw the symbol of the jackal on the card, just like Newel's tattoo. When he took it away and opened it, he found two chocolate candies in the shape of hearts and the words: "Remembering you both!"

The candies were laced with poison. When they were checked, Peter apologized for messing up their wedding day.

"Peter, don't worry. If that bitch ever comes back, I'm going to make her left side feel like her right side!" Amy said.

London

Victoria and her brother had managed to get through customs, despite the alerts at the airports. She had shortened and colored her hair, which helped. Newel was responding well to Victoria's mental treatments. His mind was becoming more and more reactive with each treatment. When they arrived at the family home, they were greeted like heroes. Later, their parents were talking with Victoria as she shared the latest events.

"What are your plans now, Victoria?" her mother asked.

"I will keep giving Newel his treatments until he is well, and then I am going to visit my other relatives. When I'm done with that, I have some unfinished business to take care of in Portland, Oregon," she said with a smile.

When the whole family learned of her plans, they agreed with them wholeheartedly!

The Future

Peter and Amy had a great start to their marriage with the send-off by their friends and a surprise honeymoon in Hawaii. The fact that Amy was expecting their first child was the icing on the cake. Peter and Amy had a long talk after the case with Newel and Victoria was over. Peter was concerned about the safety of his new family if he kept on doing the same type of work.

"Amy, I don't want our family in danger because of some criminal I'm after. Look what happened to you and my dad with this last case," Peter said, obviously worried.

"Peter, haven't I proven to you that I am tough and able to stand up to whatever happens? I'm also no dummy, and I know how to handle myself. Our family is stronger as we stick together, and I know you love working on the special squad with your friends. So why not keep doing what you enjoy?"

"Okay, Amy, I will," Peter said, smiling and thinking how lucky he was to have Amy.

"Now, mister, why don't you come with me, and I will show you something that I enjoy doing with you." Amy led Peter away, smiling as they walked arm in arm.

* * * * *

Bob and Miranda were living together, and they were loving every minute of it. Bob's control over water had grown even greater, and his ability to read minds was stronger than before, so much that he surprised Miranda a couple of times. When she was feeling amorous and thinking of how she would like to be making love to Bob, at that instant, Bob would come up behind her nude and put his arms around her.

For the most part, Bob's work was normal police work with the occasional case for the special squad. Those cases enabled Peter and Bob to work together again. Otherwise, Peter and Bob tried to get together outside of work for family activities.

* * * * *

As the wheels of the jet touched down, Detective Marsh was rudely awakened. *Home at last,* he said to himself. As he unbuckled his seatbelt, he noticed the red check mark scar on his hand had almost faded clean away. Marsh was eager to get home to see his family, especially his daughter, who Peter had said would come through the operation just fine.

* * * * *

There was a good deal of celebrating on the part of the members of the special squad who worked on the case of Newel and Victoria.

The same couldn't be said for Newel's family and his bride-to-be, Liz. It was a bittersweet joy to have Newel back, even if he was in a coma. Victoria was giving Newel treatments that involved opening new pathways in Newel's mind to overcome the physical and mental trauma he had endured.

So far, Newel had shown only small signs of any type of awakening, but with every treatment, Victoria gained a little ground into reaching into her brother's mind. It was like she was extending her mind into Newel's, massaging, testing, and exploring her brother's mind and finding out which pathways yielded the easiest route to Newel. Victoria found that sometimes the pathways she had to take to reach Newel's mind were very dark and sinister, holding past images of murders he had committed and what he would like to do in future murders. Some of these images Victoria found to be violently beautiful, and she relished them.

One day after a session with Newel, Victoria was sitting in the den with a glass of brandy. She was coming back to reality, as she referred to it, after being deep in Newel's mind. When Liz walked in, she sat across from Victoria and was quiet for a moment.

"Victoria, do you think Newel will come back totally from the coma? I mean, will he be like he was when I first met him?" Liz asked.

"Liz, I'm sure he will. It will just take a bit of time."

"It's just that I miss him so much emotionally and physically," Liz said as she smiled.

"I understand that. As a matter of fact, I think when Newel comes out of the coma, the first thing he will want is to go and lock himself away with you for a few days to catch up on what he has been missing, so be prepared."

Both of the ladies started laughing together. Later that night, with the whole family at the dinner table, Victoria gave an update on Newel's condition and anything new she had encountered. After dinner, Victoria and Newel's parents were sitting in the den relaxing before going to bed when suddenly Victoria got up and almost lost her balance.

"Victoria, are you all right?" her father asked as he sat Victoria up.

"Yes, I think so. I suddenly felt strange and lost my balance."

Without warning, the antique knife used by Newel's great-great-grandfather shot across the room and buried itself into the wall at an angle that made the knife blade edge gleam in the light.

"I think this is the first sign that Newel is coming back to us," Victoria said out loud.

"How much longer do you think Newel will need your treatments?" her father asked.

"I'm not sure, but this shows me that what I've been doing with Newel and my methods of treating him are working," Victoria said with confidence.

Newel felt as if he were in a deep, black abyss filled with a blackness that was thick and stifling. It was frustrating for Newel to be confined like this. The blackness didn't seem to have any substance to it, but there was a binding quality that he could not break through without help from his sister. The only thing more frustrating was dealing with the fact that Peter and the special squad had beat him.

Newel was raging within himself, with only revenge on his mind. The only bright spot in this black hell he was in now was his sister, who was reaching out to him to raise his mind back to full consciousness. Every time Victoria helped him, Newel could feel the bands that bound his mind loosen a bit more. After the last session with his sister, the energy Newel felt in his mind was much greater. He decided to try to show his family that he was beginning to awaken by making the antique knife of his great-great-grandfather shoot across the den all by itself.

Victoria was very excited at the progress Newel was making with each treatment. She could not wait till Newel was back again fully so they could start killing together again.

* * * * *

Peter and Bob sat quietly in their unmarked police car, staking out a suspect in a case of gruesome murders involving torture and dismemberment that had started just recently.

"Peter, how did you know it was the right time to ask Amy to marry you?" Bob asked quietly.

"Well, I felt it in my heart and in my gut, but we had talked about it too." Peter stared at his friend for a while, not saying anything. "Are you thinking about asking Miranda to marry you?" he finally asked slowly.

"Yes, Peter. We have joked around about it, but we seem to get along so well, and we love each other."

"Have you considered the dangers of your jobs?" Peter asked.

"Yes, we did that when we moved in together."

"Well, you just need to figure out how and where you want to ask your special lady to spend the rest of her life with a slob like you," Peter said, and suddenly, they were both laughing.

* * * * *

Victoria was sitting alone in the den when her father came in. "How are you this evening, Victoria?" he asked.

"I'm just so-so. I feel a bit out of it since my days have been full of treating Newel," Victoria said.

"You need to do something that you would enjoy and that would get you lively again. Maybe you might like to borrow the car and go into London to sample the living fodder that roams our streets in the red-light district," her father said, smiling.

Victoria smiled widely, showing all her white teeth, just like a hungry shark before it attacks. Victoria could barely contain herself. The excitement of killing another whore was amazing, and it made her mouth water. Victoria hadn't killed anyone since leaving America. Now she could get into something that would get her into much higher spirits, while at the same time furthering the family mission.

Victoria gathered the items she would need for that night, including some of her special candies. Victoria dressed the part, looking classy but slutty at the same time, a high-priced whore if ever there was one.

"Well, Father, do you think I will get some attention tonight?" Victoria asked.

"Oh yes, from the ladies and the gents," he said, smiling.

As she left, her father gave her a map of the area where she should go to find the prostitutes she was looking for. When she arrived in the area, things were very quiet. Because there had been no murders in quite a while, the police had eased up on their presence in the area, which made Victoria's night out prowling much less stressful. The night was damp and chilly, and Victoria decided to stop into a local pub for a drink before looking for just the right lady to entertain.

As she sat sipping her drink, she noticed her jackal tattoo and was rubbing it, her family's signature. Suddenly, goose flesh raised all along the lines of the tattoo. Victoria couldn't believe it, but she took it to be a further sign that Newel was becoming more aware. Victoria smiled and tried to send a mental message to her brother that tonight's victim was in his honor. Just then, a woman walked in who was scantily dressed but clean. She came over, sat by Victoria, and smiled.

"Hi, hon. Are you in the business?" she asked Victoria.

"Why, yes, sweetie. You too?" Victoria responded. Victoria thought to herself, *Sweetie, you are the one I will do for my brother Newel, and I'll send him the mental images of your death to bring him joy and to help him out of his coma!*

"Do you like candy?" Victoria asked the woman.

"Why, yes I do. As a matter of fact, I would enjoy a bit of candy now if I had one."

"Well, sweetie, I have some. Why don't you try one of mine?" Victoria said as she passed one of her special candies to the fellow pub crawler.

"Why don't we go back to my place and settle down together for the night and maybe have some fun. What do you say?" the whore said to Victoria.

"That sounds fine. By the way, I'm Victoria."

"I'm Camille, sweetie."

They walked a short distance to Camille's apartment, and after warming up a bit, they relaxed.

"So, Victoria, what do you like ..." Camille's speech was becoming slurred because of the drugged candies. Then her speech was stopped midsentence by two scalpel-sharp blades, one in each lung so she couldn't speak. She had the strangest look on her face as she questioned why she couldn't talk, and then horror covered her face as she saw the streams of bright-red blood leaking from her body.

"I'm sorry, Camille, but I can't play with you tonight like you want. But what I will do is help you to die in a very special way, which will accomplish several things. It will help me get rid of scum like you from this earth, it will help my brother to see how you die, and finally, it will cheer me up greatly."

As Camille stared at Victoria, she wondered how her death could be seen by Victoria's brother. This thought left her mind as she saw knives like those used to skin fish start to travel over her body, held by invisible hands. As she screamed in silence, Camille saw through terrified eyes. Victoria was watching and mentally recording the images for Newel and smiling.

Victoria cleaned up a bit and drove home. Upon her arrival, she was greeted by her parents, who wanted to hear all about her visit to London. When Victoria gave them a short version of her night's events, they could barely contain themselves at Victoria's sense of originality. Victoria thought she would save this for the following day to share with Newel.

The next day the police found Camille after a friend of hers stopped by to see her and found her remains. The police who remembered the murders in the past were suddenly reminded of the grisliness of them. Most just held back their urge to vomit. Those officers who had not worked those murders lost their lunches not only because of the sight of the remains but also because of the smell.

One of the officers who was assigned the case was checking around and found an envelope on the table. It had a lock of Camille's hair laid over it. The officer had Detective Marsh, who was fresh back from a vile case in America, take a look. Marsh was starting to recognize traits in this murder that reminded him of his last case. He worried that the case with Newel was coming back to haunt him. Marsh opened the envelope and read the letter.

> This tart made poor use of her skin for men; so at a whim I relieved her of her skin!
>
> The Poet

Marsh's hand shook a bit for just a moment as he realized that this meant one of the serial killers they had been after in America was in the London area. Then he thought, *What if the whole family that Newel and Victoria were part of is from this area?*

But if Newel was active and in the immediate area, his scar would have alerted him to the fact, wouldn't it? Marsh wondered if the scar wasn't active anymore because it had faded so much. One thing was for sure, Marsh had to contact his friends so they were warned. He also needed to bring Interpol up to speed.

The phone rang at Bob's desk.

"Hello, Bob. How have you been?" Marsh said.

"Marsh, I'll be dammed! What the heck are you calling for? Are you in town?" Bob asked.

"No. Actually, Bob, I have some scary news. I just caught a murder case that was nasty. And, Bob, a note was left at the murder scene of a local prostitute. It was signed by the Poet," Marsh said gravely.

This news was met with a long silence from Bob.

"Bob, I think that Newel's family is from one of the towns around the London area," Marsh added.

"Oh Christ, Marsh, are you and your family all right?" Bob asked.

"Yes, but I wanted to warn you so you could let the rest of the special squad know before I contacted Interpol."

"Marsh, if you need our help, call us right away. I'll make our authorities aware of the situation also," Bob said.

"Will do, Bob, and tell everyone I said hi," Marsh said before he hung up the phone and made the call to Interpol.

When Bob had finished contacting the members of the special squad, Peter, Amy, Bob, and Miranda sat down for a more in-depth talk about what this could mean and the impact on any future plans any of them had.

"Unless Marsh contacts us for help, I think we need to just be aware of our surroundings like we have been doing," Bob said.

Peter and Amy were in full agreement, but they were looking at Bob and Miranda. Peter had quietly told Amy about Bob's plan to ask Miranda to marry him.

"Some other plans may have to be put on hold for a while till we see how this plays out," Bob said as he looked into Miranda's eyes.

"Oh, no you don't, Bob. You're not getting out of this that easy. You asked me to marry you, and I said yes, for better or worse, serial killers and their families notwithstanding," Miranda said as she punched Bob in the arm.

For a moment, Peter and Amy were shocked, and then they were laughing at the look on Bob's face.

"Bob, we are partners in life, as well as on the job. I'm with you all the way!" Miranda said as she kissed Bob.

After that was settled, Peter and Amy were eager to find out where Bob had proposed and how. They found out that Bob had taken Miranda up to the rose gardens, and among the roses, he proposed to her. Bob and Peter started talking more seriously about notifying their family members about the situation. It was a hell of a deal, just when they thought they were done with this mess.

* * * * *

Victoria got up the morning after the killing of Camille. She was energetic and eager to share the sights of Camille's death with Newel. On the way to Newel's bedroom, Liz stopped Victoria and asked her for a favor.

"Victoria, would it be possible for me to sit in with you as you give Newel his treatment today?"

Victoria thought a moment and considered what would happen when Newel saw the images of Camille's death. "I think that would be a good idea considering how Newel might respond when I mentally connect with him, but you must do what I say without question," Victoria told her.

As they seated themselves next to Newel with the door closed, Victoria started reaching into Newel's mind, down some pathways she recognized and a few that she didn't. All at once, Victoria reached Newel's mind. It was a whirling black cauldron of evil, and she smiled as Newel's mind recognized her.

She started to feed Newel images of Camille's death, starting with her own excitement and then picking out just the right lady to honor her brother with. Newel's mind reacted positively, especially when he saw through Victoria's mind how she took Camille's life. For Newel, it came to him in slow motion, which created even more excitement. Liz noticed something that Victoria had not expected. Newel was so excited he was reacting as if he had done the killing himself. He was sexually charged, as was evident by the erection he had.

"Victoria, what should we do?" Liz asked.

"What would you do if Newel were awake?" Victoria said, smiling.

Liz smiled back and proceeded to do anything she could imagine to pleasure her future husband in his present condition. Victoria sensed Newel's pleasure and satisfaction and relayed how he felt back to Liz, who was smiling and thanking Victoria. After the session with Newel, both Liz and Victoria went to rest for a while. The sessions always tired Victoria out. Liz was just happy to have some type of intimacy with Newel, but she was emotionally worn out.

As Liz was sleeping, she started to dream. A figure appeared out of the fog of her dream. It was Newel. He was smiling and thanked her for the pleasure she had given him. He also let her know that soon he would be with her as a whole person.

* * * * *

Marsh was just finishing up his work for the day. He had requested all the materials from the Poet case from Austin, Texas, and he planned to cross-reference it with what he knew about this latest murder and his experience in Portland, Oregon.

Possibly, this could yield some added insight that would help catch these murderers.

Without warning, Marsh's hand cramped up, and intense pain shot down his arm. Marsh wondered if he were having a heart attack when all at once the pain going down his arm stopped and was replaced by a new pain. The check mark scar on his hand was bright red and felt hot, like it was burning his skin. Marsh blacked out for a moment as he lay his head on his desk. As the pain subsided, he heard a familiar voice.

"Did you miss me, old friend?" Newel said mentally in a voice full of evil.

Friends came over to Marsh to make sure he was all right. He was obviously shaken up, but he assured his friends he was fine. When Marsh calmed down, he had to face the fact that there was only one explanation for this to start happening again. By some means, Newel was being revived from his coma, and Marsh was betting that his murderous sister Victoria had something to do with it.

Marsh made a very hard decision and talked to his wife about it, telling her all about the case with Newel and Victoria and their special abilities. After making his wife aware of how dangerous the situation was, he asked her to take the kids and leave until the case was solved. He insisted she didn't tell him where she was going, so if his mind was probed by Newel or Victoria, they couldn't find his family. She was very stubborn and wanted to stand with her husband no matter what the danger, but he finally persuaded her to take the family to a place of safety without telling him where.

The last thing Marsh did after kissing her good-bye was to give her a slip of paper with names and telephone numbers for Peter, Bob, and Miranda in case of emergencies. Marsh did not know if he would see his family again; for some reason, Newel liked inflicting pain on him, maybe because he was the first to find one of his locations, which led to their first time confronting Newel.

Marsh arrived the next day at the station with all the information he had requested be expressed overnight and sitting on his desk. The next thing he needed to do was to send a telegram. He had tried to contact Peter and Bob, but they weren't at the station or home. The telegram would have to do. It had only one sentence: "The scar is active! Marsh."

There was a very good reason that Bob and Peter could not be reached when Marsh tried to call. At that moment, they were on the way to the hospital with Amy, who was going into labor with her and Peter's first child. The labor took a few hours, and by that evening, Peter and Amy had a new member of their family, a healthy baby girl named Courtney.

When the telegram came in to the Portland Police Headquarters, one of the members of the special squad called Bob on his cell phone. Bob told the officer to read it for him. When Bob heard the words, his face went dark, and Peter noticed immediately.

"Bob, who was that, and why the change in your mood?" Peter asked.

By then, Miranda had joined them, and she felt the change in the mood in the room as well, which concerned her.

"Peter, a telegram came in from Marsh with only one sentence; it said the scar is active. We all know what that means," Bob said.

The room was silent for a moment, and then Amy spoke up.

"This is a special day for our first child. Let's not ruin it just yet. Okay?"

Everyone agreed, and the mood started to lighten up, but Bob and Peter knew that tomorrow they would be in touch with Marsh. They had to be!

* * * * *

Newel felt unusually strong after his last treatment with his sister and Liz. All those feelings and images seemed to be just what Newel had needed to loosen the bonds on his mind. He was almost to the point where he felt he was within reach of returning to his normal self with all his abilities, maybe even a bit stronger. He had a sense of revenge, but he was definitely his evil self!

The day was dark and stormy even though no storm had been forecast. It seemed like Mother Nature had plans of her own, or was it some other force rather than nature at work today? The force of pure evil waking to everyone's horror perhaps?

Victoria decided that she would try to bring Newel all the way back out of his coma that day. This would take all her strength and mental abilities, because, like her, her brother was not only in a deep coma despite her treatments, but he was very stubborn. Victoria would have to make Newel want to wake up by luring his mind to do so. Victoria had thought about what would be most attractive to Newel. It would have to be more than his family or marrying Liz. Then Victoria smiled a knowing, evil smile, because she had found the perfect thing to lure Newel to the conscious world.

As Victoria sealed herself in Newel's room, she started. Once she reached Newel's mind, she reminded him of all his family who was waiting for him and then of his bride-to-be and their future. Newel's mind was whirling like a storm was brewing, and his body was twitching. Finally, Victoria added the evil topping on this concoction that she had devised. She started to show Newel and suggest all sorts of ways that every member of the special squad could be killed.

Newel started to react violently. Objects started being thrown against the walls of the room as Newel struggled to awaken. Suddenly, out of the boiling blackness that was Newel's mind, an image appeared to explode right at Victoria with such force she fell off the bed where she sat. It was the image of a dragon on fire. As it roared, it said: "Thank you, Sister. Your brother is back!"

With that, Victoria sat to watch Newel to make sure he was back. As she watched Newel's eyes open slowly, Victoria smiled. She then realized something was different. Newel's eyes had changed from blue to bottomless pits of black.

Edwards Brothers Malloy
Oxnard, CA USA
June 30, 2015